The Wives of Marty Winters

by Alec Clayton

Cover photograph by Michael Christopher
digitally altered by Alec and Gabi Clayton

first edition
copyright © 2007 by Alec Clayton

ISBN 978-0-9800322-0-8
printed in the USA

DISCLAIMER
This is a work of fiction. All characters are the product of the
author's imagination. Resemblance to any person, living or dead,
is entirely coincidental.

Acknowledgments

Thanks to Larry Johnson, a great poet and writer who read the manuscript in numerous incarnations, and to my good friend Linda Delayen for her helpful editorial comments. To my wife, Gabi, and Margaret Ward for reading and critiquing parts of the manuscript, and to Thomas F. Burk, M.D., who read through the hospital scenes and offered valuable advice. Thanks also to Michael Christopher for his great photo, and to Heather Lenox for throwing one hell'uva summer New Year's Eve party.

Finally, a special thank you to Carolyn Wagner, her son William and the Wagner family for their inspiration.

Also by Alec Clayton

Fiction
Until the Dawn
Imprudent Zeal

Non-fiction
As If Art Matters

Books by Alec Clayton available online at

www.alecclayton.com
www.claytonworks.com/publishing
www.amazon.com

ClaytonWorks Publishing

Pride

There was always the chance, however slim, that some nutcase in the crowd would pull out a gun and blast somebody away. Marty and Chloe knew it, so they kept their eyes peeled. They might have felt a little silly about being so cautious; after all, nobody'd ever shot a Pride Day speaker, but they weren't taking any chances. Marty stayed on his feet, keeping one eye on Selena and one eye on the crowd. Chloe did the same. The crowd was happy and boisterous. Most of the people were seated in the grass, a lot of them with heads resting in lovers' laps, some in outrageous costumes and more than a few practically naked. So much exposed skin was distracting to Marty, but not to Chloe. A top Secret Service agent couldn't have been more single-minded. Both Chloe and Marty would later say that alarms went off at the sight of a man wearing a red baseball cap and a camouflage T-shirt.

Marty's wife, Selena, was slated to speak to the crowd in Volunteer Park. She was a fifty-year old mother of two grown children and grandmother to a set of twin boys. A small woman, proud of her still-girlish figure and resplendent in her simple red cocktail dress, Selena was Grand Marshall of the Pride parade.

The crowd shouted hurrahs, applauded and whistled as a punk band called Muthuh Effer finished its set. A minute passed as band members and their fans who had been crowding the stage left the performance area. The Mistress of Ceremonies, a well known Seattle drag performer named Mother May Belle, took microphone in hand and said, "Thank you, Muthuhs. Now, let's hear from a real mother, our Grand Marshal Selena Winters."

Mother May Belle's introductory spiel was filled with glowing references to Selena's work as a civil rights activist. She finished with, "Let's give this little lady a great big welcome." Marty applauded along with the rest of the crowd. He watched the big drag queen step to the edge of the stage to take Selena's arm and help her up the three rickety steps onto the stage.

He was proud of his wife. He thought she looked as beautiful as ever she had, more beautiful even than she had been at seventeen. Of course he was seeing her through a veil of memory. He knew that. He wasn't blind. Objectively, he knew that age was catching up with her. Just in the past few months she had begun to look like a worn and fragile version of the lost little girl he had first met thirty-four years earlier in a Nashville bus station. He couldn't help but notice how frail she seemed as she leaned into Mother May Belle while walking to the microphone. Still, there was an inner beauty, a strength of character, that shone through; and he had no doubt it was just as clear to everyone else in the crowd as it was to him. Besides, fifty wasn't very old at all. It was just that in his mind's eye she was still nineteen years old, and he was always somewhat shocked in those moments in which she clearly looked fifty.

Marty kept moving, aware that he might be blocking someone's view, but unwilling to sit down. He thought: If I was sitting in the grass trying to watch and some asshole kept walking around in front, I'd be pissed. Too bad. Chloe also kept moving, her brilliant cape and rainbow wig like flags flying over the hundreds of people seated on the grass in the park. The two of them were Selena's self-appointed guardians, even though only one of them — and not the one you might think — was in any way capable of reacting decisively in an emergency.

Marty could tell that Selena was nervous. Despite years of public speaking, she never got over the terror that gripped her every time she had to speak in front of a crowd. He could see that the smile on her lips was forced. Scanning the crowd in the area right in front of the stage, he caught a glimpse of their son, William. Then, focusing back on the stage, he tried to catch Selena's eye and flash her a reassuring glance. That was when he saw a blur of motion in front of the stage.

Whatever it was that moved so suddenly was unclear to Marty, distracted as he was by other bits of motion: small clouds moving quickly overhead in a mostly blue sky, bits of paper flying in the wind, people moving about, semaphore flashes of bright sunlight across the assembled crowd. For just a moment Marty had begun to let the flashing light lull him into a reverie, remembering a sparkling disco ball and a beautiful young girl at a high school dance — not Selena, but Maria, his first wife. All day he had been haunted by memories from long ago. Where they had come from, he had no idea. This one came and went as quickly as the flash of a strobe.

Then he saw that other more immediate and dangerous flash of light. For a glimmer of time less than a full second it was a meaningless flash of light, and then he realized that it was light reflected off the barrel a gun. He shouted "Gun!" and rushed toward the stage. At the same instant, he saw Chloe go flying like some kind of circus performer, her ridiculous but beautiful rainbow wig and fiery cape streaming behind her, trying with all her might to put her own body between Selena and the gunman, willing, if she only could, to take the bullet for her friend.

But she was too late.

Selena clutched at her head and crumbled to the boards. It was almost as if she melted there. Rivulets of red between her fingers. Marty reached the stage in seconds. He clambered up the steps and fell to his knees in front of Selena. He lifted her head and cradled it in his lap. Their son, William, also rushed to the stage. He leaned over his mother's body and wailed in a loud keening voice like the call of some huge bird. Blood gushed from Selena's head wound, soaked into Marty's shirt and dribbled down her limp arm where it drooped to the hardwood stage.

In the crowd, Chloe's dive through the air had landed her in the middle of a group of people. Frantically she tried to extricate herself from a tangle of arms and legs. People scrambling out of her way. She pushed to her feet and scanned the crowd for the gunman, but there was so much chaotic movement it was impossible to spot him. She then turned toward the stage and attempted to push herself to where Marty and William hovered over Selena. By then policemen had taken up position in front of the stage and would not let anyone approach. "But I'm family," Chloe said. "Marty, tell them. Tell them I'm family."

There was an ambulance nearby. At major events such as the Pride celebration, there was always an emergency vehicle posted in the parking lot in front of the art museum, that hulking old art deco building that sat just across the open field from the outdoor stage. The ambulance made its way across the grass and through the parting crowd. Uniformed medics hopped out, leapt to the stage, lifted Selena to a gurney, hooked oxygen to her nose, and carried her into the ambulance. They were swift and efficient, not a word or a motion wasted. Marty stood up, his hands hanging helplessly by his side. William put his arm around his father's shoulder.

"I'll go with them," William said.

"Are you a relative?" a medic asked.

"Yes. Her son."

Marty asked, "What hospital are you taking her to?"

"Harborview."

He told William he'd get Chloe and meet them at the hospital. Quickly he scanned the crowd for Chloe. "Chloe, where are you?" he shouted.

"I'm right here. Let's go." She was standing at the edge of the crowd. They ran out of the park. At the sidewalk they panicked momentarily, unable to remember where they had parked. "This way," Chloe said, and they ran the four blocks to Marty's car. Harborview was no more than ten minutes away, depending on traffic. On the way, Marty said, "Why were you standing back in the crowd?"

"The cops wouldn't let me near. Didn't you hear me? I was yelling, 'Tell them I'm family, Marty.'"

"I'm sorry. No, I didn't hear you. I don't know. It's hard to think straight right after seeing the love of your life get shot."

(Much later Marty would recall that a strange memory had come to mind right in the middle of the most chaotic moments following the shooting. He suddenly recalled a scene from Alan Rudolph's great cult film *Trouble in Mind*. In the film, there was a shooting melee in the gangster's mansion, guns going off all around while the hero walked calmly away, completely unnoticed. The hero in the film was Kris Kristofferson. The gangster, played by the great transvestite Devine, was named Hilly Blue. Marty remembered that scene and thought Selena getting shot was like a parody of the scene. Her assailant must have escaped by walking through the milling crowd in the same calm manner. And here comes the irony: that scene in the movie was shot in the same location. The art museum in the park served as Hilly Blue's mansion in the film.)

#

Marty parked at the emergency room entrance. They ran into the hospital. At the ER desk, he said, "I'm Marty Winters. They just brought my wife in. Selena Winters. She was shot."

"We have a Jane Doe gunshot to the head," the nurse said. "She didn't have any identification."

No, of course not. Her ID would have been in her purse, left behind in the staging area. Hopefully Mother May Belle or someone in charge would hold on to it. He couldn't be bothered with worrying about her fucking purse. A nurse took Marty in to see Selena, who was hooked up to tubes and looked dead already, a bandage at her temple. Questions came at him from all sides: from a policeman who wanted to know what he had seen in the park, from some woman with paperwork, from a doctor wearing Hawaiian print scrubs who didn't look old enough to be out of high school. He was overwhelmed with a frantic need to pee. He was relieved when a nurse led him to the family room, and on the way he spotted a restroom.

Soon the whole family was gathered in the family room waiting while the ridiculously young looking doctor removed a blood clot from Selena's brain. He had said the operation would be her only chance for survival. He had also said she might never again be functional. There was a chance she could survive, but in a vegetative state from which she could never recover. Marty would rather she died.

#

William called his sister, Marianne, and she drove up from Portland with the twins, Jackson and Chick. They arrived at the hospital in a little over two hours. "We went a hundred miles a hour," Jackson said, and Chick added, "Momma drove like crazy."

Marianne asked about her mother.

"We won't know for a while," Marty said. "She's still in the operating room, but she should be out soon. But even then it may be a long wait before we know if she's going to make it."

"All right. I guess we just wait then. I'm going to take the boys to the cafeteria. Anybody want to come?" Her tone was clipped and business-like, her demeanor calm. Marianne had always been the one to take charge and remain calm in a crisis.

Chloe said, "I could use a cup of coffee, but I'd rather wait here. Can you bring me a cup? With lots of sugar?" She was pacing, crumpling her wig in nervous hands, her scarlet cape tossed over the back of a chair.

"I could use a cigarette," Marty said.

William said, "I thought you quit."

"I did. But if I could get my hands on a cigarette right now I'd start back."

One of the policemen who had questioned Marty earlier came back into the room. He asked the room at large, "Did anyone see what happened?"

"I did," Marty said. "I saw the shooter."

"Can you describe him?"

"Yeah, a little. I think. He was wearing a camouflage shirt and a red cap. He had a tattoo of a heart on his cheek. I've seen him before. I recognized that tattoo. I saw him pull the gun and shoot, and then he was gone. Just vanished in the crowd."

Chloe interrupted. She said, "I saw him too. I recognized the bastard. He's the same Nazi creep that beat up William. He had that same heart tattoo."

"And who are you, m'am? And who is William?" the cop asked.

Marty said, "She's Chloe, our housemate. William's my son." He pointed at William, who was seated nearby.

They all turned to William, asking if he could identify the shooter. "I'm sorry," he said, "I didn't see a thing. I heard the shot and I saw Mama fall. I saw that horrible splatter of blood. But I didn't see the shooter." His hands were still shaking, and there was a tremor in his voice. William had been more visibly shaken than any of them.

The policeman left, and shortly after the doctor came to the room to let them know he had successfully removed the clot from Selena's brain. "The good news is there doesn't seem to be any damage to her heart or her lungs. But the bleeding in her brain was extensive. We'll have to wait to see if she comes out of it." He suggested that if they had some place to stay the night they should go. "There's no reason to hang around here. She won't wake up tonight. If there is any change we'll let you know."

They went to the house on Capitol Hill that William and his partner, Jake, shared with two other men. Serendipitously, their housemates were out of town at the time, so there was room for everyone. It was decided that Marty could sleep in the guest room and Chloe could share the other couple's bedroom with Marianne — a situation Marty thought was pretty funny, since he knew Chloe and Marianne had never gotten along very well. The twins would have to sleep on the couch.

William and Jake had been together for years. They were married in a beautiful ceremony on the deck overlooking Puget Sound at the family home in Olympia. Their wedding may not have been recognized by the state, but they were married in the eyes of their family and friends, and — as Jake put it, "in the eyes of God, whoever the old queen might be."

Shortly after their wedding Jake got a job as a chef at Bistro Pagliacci, a small Italian restaurant near his home in Seattle. William, a writer of young adult novels, was free to move to Seattle to be with him since — thanks to the success of his second novel, *Rainbow Club* — he had been able to quit his teaching job and write full time. Or, to be more accurate, to spend three-fourths of his time promoting his book while working weekends and nights on his next one. When not cooking at Pagliacci's Jake acted as William's unofficial public relations manager, setting up book signings and lectures, and writing press releases — doing all the things William's publisher or agent should have done but didn't.

William and Jake ran out to a neighborhood pizza parlor and brought back pizza for everyone. Nobody ate much. After dinner they served coffee for the adults and hot chocolate for the twins. Marty sat stiffly on one of two easy chairs near the fireplace, his coffee balanced on his knees. Marianne lounged comfortably in the other easy chair looking bedraggled yet lovelier than she had in a long time, her braided hair like strings of black diamonds, her long legs encased in black silk pants and crossed at the knee. (Marty often quipped, "I can't imagine who she inherited those gorgeous gams from," adding that they probably came from some great grandparent on Selena's side of the family.) The boys sat nearby on an ancient beanbag chair pouring through an old photo album and pestering everyone with questions such as "Who's this?" and "Why is he wearing that funny hat?" and "is Grandma singing in this one?" referring to a picture of Selena standing before a microphone.

"No," Marianne replied, "She was giving a speech in the park."

"Oh, she's always doing that," Chick said.

"But she did sing later that day," William said.

"Did she do the Y.M.C.A. song?" Jackson asked. The twins had been at a rally in Sylvester Park in Olympia where everyone sang the Village People classic.

Marianne said, "No, it was a different song, but one you ought to learn. I'll teach it to you later."

Chloe broke in. She said, "I'll never forget that speech. I bawled my eyes out." She was leaning with one arm on the mantle like the imperial lady of the manor. If anything, she was even more regal than Marianne. Taller too, but not so beautiful. She was more of a Katherine Hepburn type, whereas Marianne was cast in the Ingrid Bergman mold. Of course there was a vast difference in their ages, and it showed. Chloe was in her sixties, Marty's age, and she had put up with a lot of stress and heartbreak in her life. It was written on her face. She was not related to the Winters family, but they all thought of her as a member of the family. She and Marty had been inseparable friends throughout most of their childhood but went their separate ways for a few years after they got out of school, and later renewed their friendship when they both ended up back in Washington when William and Marianne were in high school.

Jake said, "You're not the only one that bawled your eyes out. I was just a blubbering mess. But William didn't shed a tear. He can be such a cold-hearted man."

"Hey, stow it, Miss Compassion. I was just as proud and just as moved as you, and you know it. The only reason I held it in was because I knew if I let myself lose it I would have been such a basket case you'd have had to scrape me off the grass."

"I know, honey. I'm just teasing you."

The speech they were talking about was one Selena had given a few years earlier. She had been asked to speak at a rally in support of anti hate-crime legislation that was pending before the state legislature. The rally had taken place shortly after yet another gay kid had been beaten up on the streets. In the park that day, Selena told the story of a young man named Billy who found the world too much to bear.

Billy was the one who got away. He had e-mailed Selena with a message that said, "Help me. I want to kill myself." Counseling suicidal youth was nothing new to her. There's no telling how many lives she may have saved simply by listening or responding to e-mails. But nothing she said to Billy seemed to register.

He was sixteen years old. Six boys ganged up on him in the locker room at school. They took turns raping him. He was too scared to fight back or scream for help. When they were done with him, the leader of the gang said, "From now on, queer boy, any time one of my boys decides he wants a piece of ass, you'd better drop your pants."

"They guaranteed I was gonna be their whore from now on and I better be prepared to put out whenever they wanted it," he told Selena in an e-mail. They never spoke face to face.

She consoled him and offered him emotional support, and tried to persuade him that things would not always look so bleak. She sent him contact information for a gay youth support group and referrals to therapists. But nothing she said dissuaded him from his notion that for as long as he lived bigger and stronger boys would be beating him and raping him. He would have killed himself immediately, but it took him a month to build up a big enough stash of pills.

When Selena gave her speech at the rally in the park, she recalled Billy's story and posed the question: "Why did those boys have to attack him? Was it for sex? No. It was out of hate. They wanted to punish him for being different. And where did that hate come from? Were they born with hate in their hearts?"

"There's a song," she said, "from the musical *South Pacific*. Many of you remember it." Selena was not a good singer. She couldn't carry a tune in a barrel. But she had never let that stop her from joining in on sing-a-longs whenever she had the chance. On that day she sang acapella with her birdlike voice in front of hundreds of people. She sang verses from the Rodgers and Hammerstein song "You've Got to Be Carefully Taught":

You've got to be taught to hate and fear, You've got to be taught from year to year, it's got to be drummed in your dear little ear. You've got to be carefully taught.

You've got to be taught before it's too late, before you are six or seven or eight, to hate all the people your relatives hate.

Her voice grew as quiet as the chirp of a faraway bird, and then she just stopped in the middle of the next verse. There was a stunned silence when she quit singing, and for a long time Selena stood behind the microphone as if unable to move. Chloe stepped up onto the stage and took her by the elbow and guided her back to her place in the crowd as if she were a frail old woman. (She was forty-six at the time). Only after they stepped down from the stage did the throng burst into applause.

#

Jake was cooking dinner and William was reading the latest issue of *The Advocate*. Marianne and the boys were playing Scrabble on the living room floor. It was late afternoon. It had been more than twenty-four hours since Selena was shot, and everyone's nerves were on edge. They had spent most of the day in the hospital. Selena was still in a coma, with no signs that she would ever come out of it. Marty was nodding off in his chair but didn't want to admit he was sleepy. Marianne noticed and said, "You look beat, Daddy. Why don't you go upstairs and take a nap?"

"No, I'm all right," he muttered, blinking his eyes open and sitting up straighter. But she ignored his protests. She said, "Would you like for me to help you up the stairs?"

"Do I look crippled to you?" he snapped. William laughed at his father's petulant retort. "You better watch out, Sis. Start treating the old man like an invalid, he's liable to put you over his knee and spank you."

"Yeah, him and whose army? He never spanked me when I was growing up. What makes you think he'd start now?"

"'Cause he's gotten ornery as an alley cat in his old age."

It was getting to the point where they couldn't tell who was kidding and who was truly irritated. Barbed exchanges had always been the family's way of showing affection, and they had always walked that line, but this time the tone was getting dangerously bitter. Chloe, sensing an oncoming argument she wanted no part of, excused herself and went into the kitchen to see if Jake needed any help. When Chloe was safely out of hearing range, Marianne said, "Why does *she* have to be here all the time? She's not family."

"Yes she is," Marty said. "She's been part of this family since long before you were even born." That was not literally true, and everybody knew it. Chloe had moved in with them when Marianne was in high school. There had always been an edginess between the two of them.

The twins, unaware of the tension in the house, started running around the living room and tossing a ball back and forth. Marty snapped at their mother, "Can't you control your kids!"

She corralled them and headed them out the door with instructions to play outside until dinner was ready. Closing the door behind them, she said, "I'm sorry. They're just a little wound up."

"I'm sorry, too. They're just being boys, and I was over-reacting."

Chloe came back in from the kitchen with a stack of dishes to set the table. Jake brought in dinner: a salad with fruit and toasted nuts, planked salmon, baked sweet potatoes and asparagus swimming in a buttery sauce. It was quite a feast. Jake figured after what everyone had been through, they needed something special. Plus, he loved showing off his culinary skills.

During dinner Marty and Chloe started reminiscing about good times shared with Selena and the kids. "Remember the shopping trip to the factory outlets in Centralia?" Chloe asked.

William said, "How could we ever forget? You smothered me with packages on the back seat. I couldn't even see out the window."

Marty whispered to Jake, "He's always been given to exaggeration."

Chloe said, "And that sales clerk. Remember her? What a dimwit."

Marianne said, "Remember my graduation? It was raining cats and dogs, and Mama stepped in a pile of dog doo getting out of the car."

"She was wearing new shoes and it was like slick with the rain, and her feet went out from under her and the shoe hit Randy Smith in the back," William said.

William said, "He turned around and scowled at Mama, and she said 'Would you kindly hand me my shoe, please?' Then he spun back around and walked into the school all huffy-like with that big brown smear on his back."

Marty said, "And your mother was the soul of dignity."

After dinner, and after most of the old stories had been repeated, Marianne curled up on the beanbag with a paperback novel, Toni Morrison's *Beloved*; Jake turned on the television and plopped down on the couch next to William to watch the news. Chloe sat next to them. There was a brief item on the news about Selena. The anchorman said she had been shot while giving a speech at the Pride event, and that her condition was stable.

"What the hell does that mean? Stable! She's in a goddamn coma," Marty said.

William turned the TV off. Marianne said, "Daddy, you hardly ever talk about the years before we were born. What was Mama like back when you were dating?"

"She was like a bird with a broken wing."

"Really? I can't envision her like that."

"Oh yeah, she was. She was painfully shy, and she was so dependent on me that I felt like I had to kick her out of the nest and make her fly on her own." What he thought, but would never tell them — an inappropriate thought under the circumstances — was that when he first met their mother she was a crazy, manipulative liar. She had tricked him into marrying her, and it took years and years (and a lot of growing up on both their parts) before he learned to love her. He wondered that if even now he had ever truly forgiven her.

"Aw come on," William piped in. "You can't be talking about our mother."

"Yep. One and the same."

"As far back as I can remember she'd always been strong and independent."

"And self-willed," Marianne put in, "a real take-charge kind of woman."

Marty resisted the urge to tell Marianne she was describing herself, or the way she liked to see herself. Instead he said, "That's true. That's what she was like when you guys were teenagers. But she wasn't always like that. Up until you guys were around middle-school age she was pretty much helpless and really unsure of herself."

"Aw, come on," William said.

"Really. I remember once when you got hurt and she just absolutely went into hysterics. She was totally useless. Didn't know what to do."

"Was that when I got the stitches over my eye?"

"Yeah."

"I don't remember much about it."

"Well, you fell off your bike and got a gash over your eye. And you just calmly walked into the house and washed it off and said, 'Mom, I need a Band-Aid,' and she was like 'Oh my, oh, my. What do we do?'"

"Not our mom," Marianne scoffed, and Marty said, "Really, I mean it. She was like Little Eva or something — Minnie Mouse in a panic. So anyway, I called the doctor and we took you to get stitches. And you had a book with you, and the whole time Doctor Porter was stitching you up you just calmly read your book like getting stitches was nothing more than a mild inconvenience."

"*The Lion, the Witch and the Wardrobe*. That's what I was reading."

"The point is you were only ten years old and completely calm and in control, but your mother was a helpless mess. Nothing like the take-charge woman you guys knew later."

"Well, what changed her?" William asked.

"You did. All of you."

Chloe said, "Blame it on William. When he got beat up that time, she was a tiger. You don't mess with a mother's child."

"That was the main thing, yeah," Marty said. "But it was much more than that. It was the whole shebang, just year after year of being a mother, taking care of scrapes and bruises and making sure you did your homework and putting up with the both of you during your rebellious teen years—"

"What rebellious teen years? I was never rebellious," Marianne said.

Ignoring her, Marty finished his sentence: "and consoling you when your hearts were broken."

"And putting up with *your* bullshit," Chloe chimed in, putting the italics in *your* so everyone would know she meant Marty. "That was what really made her so strong and independent: having to survive your orneriness."

Normally Chloe had a knack for diffusing tense situations and a way of making even the most snide remarks in such a loving way as to put everyone at ease, but in this instance her attempt at humor didn't register with Marianne. She said, "Hey, that wasn't nice."

"She's just kidding," Marty said. "Besides, she's probably right."

Marty had never told his kids how he first met their mother. He never told them what a flighty little hippie chick she had been back then. They didn't know anything about his first wife either. Maria. He couldn't recall if he had ever even told them her name or revealed the fact that Marianne had actually been named after her. Marty thought, She'd throw a hissy fit if she ever knew that.

Back in the hospital the next day, Marty sat beside his wife. There were no changes in her condition. The hours dragged long and wearying. A nurse said to Marty, "It might help to talk to her. We don't know if she can hear you or not, but some people who work with comatose patients believe that a familiar voice can help trigger a recovery."

"Is that true?"

"I don't know. But it can't hurt."

Marty was at a loss for what to say. At first, he felt as if anything he might say would seem contrived. He started off with a casual, soft tone. "Everybody's here. Marianne and the kids. We all stayed over with William and Jake last night." There was a long, long pause. Then: "Funny, I just thought about cabbage and beans. Remember cabbage and beans from Nashville? And that good Owlsley acid. Wow! Remember that. Of course everybody back then claimed their acid was genuine Owlsley. God-a-mighty, it's a wonder we have any brains left at all."

He rambled on throughout most of the day, rehashing their whole life together: the wild and carefree hippie days back in Nashville that hadn't been so carefree after all now that he thought about it, their child-rearing years, every cut and bruise that had to be tended to, every play and concert they had gone to together as part of his job as an arts reporter (a lifetime together as a series of "dates" thanks to his job), the panic when he lost his job and the heartbreak due to abuse suffered by William and Chloe (hurt to them as painful as hurt to themselves). He talked about all of that and more. The one thing he never said, however, was *I love you*. But anyone who knew Marty would know he did. The one unexpected thing that came out of his mouth, as if unbidden and previously unthought-of — almost as if some third person had entered him and spoken with his mouth – was: I forgive you for not being Maria.

Book One
1960 to 1971

The heart senses a moment of magic. It is the evening of June 10. Elvis has just come home from the Army, and Marty is at the graduation dance at Priest Point Park. A mirrored ball flashes bubbles of light on swirling skirts, red and violet light floating across figures and walls like a laser show on clouds. Never mind that it was long before the days of laser light shows. Couples move together in ways that look more like sex than dancing, Jimmy Collins humping his date like a dog, while on the bandstand The Twilights play Pat Boone's "Love Letters in the Sand." Charlie Sizemore lets loose with a long sax solo, and the singer, Randy White, grips the microphone stand and sways to the beat. The guys in the band are wearing light gray tuxedos with ruffled shirts and pink cummerbunds. The twinkling lights flash across the bandstand and onto the dance floor.

Marty sees Maria Perez among the groups of teen dancers. She is wearing a pink chiffon dress with tiny shoulder straps. A silky white sash accentuates her tiny waist. He makes his way between the dancing couples to where she is dancing with Bobby Carson. He taps Bobby on the shoulder to cut in. Bobby practically bows in his polite acceptance that it is now Marty's turn — a ritual performed with a show of formality — and Marty takes possession of Maria with as much grace as he can possibly muster (visions of Fred Astaire and Ginger Rogers in his head). His left hand clasps her right while his other hand reaches around her waist to rest on the jut of her hipbone. The soft palm gripping his left hand is warm and damp. Sweat glistens on her face. She lays her cheek against his, their faces glued together by strands of hair plastered with sweat and Aqua Net hair spray. They sway with bodies touching and feet hardly moving. Neither of them is a particularly good dancer. He's no better at leading than she is at following, so when he tries to steer her left she goes right. They giggle at their clumsiness and press their bodies even closer. Now the only parts of their bodies that move to the music are their hips. He's got a raging hardon, and he knows good and well she can feel it.

The song comes to an end, and they stand together and smile with liquid eyes, their arms still around one another. The Twilights go into their next song, "Stardust," and Marty and Maria dance again. After that comes a rocking number with growling horns called "Raunchy." They slip off the dance floor and stand together on the periphery, watching the other kids jitterbug. During the rest of the night they dance together on all the slow songs, Maria apologetically declining whenever some other boy attempts to cut in. They sit out the rocking numbers, leaving them to the kids who can really cut a rug. They help themselves to punch and sit at one of the small tables and watch the aurora borealis cast on walls and ceilings by that magical glass ball.

The band takes a break and kids all shift in their various groupings, some crowding around the punch bowl while others jostle for seats at the tables. A lot of the boys head outside, reaching for the whiskey flasks in their inside jacket pockets as soon as they step out. Couples head to parked cars for some heavy backseat smooching or head for the bluff overlooking Puget Sound. Marty and Maria walk out to wander wooded paths. It is beautiful there in the park. The teen center itself, which was stupidly torn down a few years later, is housed in a rustic building patterned on an old Swiss-style chalet surrounded by towering Douglas firs and ancient pines and cedars. There is no moon visible in the night sky. Distant stars sparkle through the dark canopy. They can barely see to follow the path up to the overlook where they look down on the quiet waters of Puget Sound and across the way to the lighted dome of the state capitol. They hear the giggles and groans of other teens making out in the back seats of their cars.

They kiss. It's the first of many kisses.

Heading back into the dance, they pass a group of boys sitting in the bed of Chuck Nagel's battered old pickup, swigging beers and smoking cigarettes. Chuck, as usual, is regaling them with tales of his prowess on the baseball diamond. "Hey Marty," he hails the approaching couple, "you coming to the game tomorrow?"

"Maybe. Don't know yet."

"You better. It's going to be a good one."

Chuck had been catcher and captain of the high school team for three years and had been named most valuable player two years running. Talk going around has it that big league scouts have an eye on him as a future prospect. But unless he goes to college, which he has said he is not so sure about, his baseball career is over. The game he's talking about is just a pickup game with a bunch of local boys.

As they pass on by Chuck says, "You guys look like you were made for each other."

Marty waves at him and drops his hand over Maria's shoulder, and they walk on in to the dance, smiling in mutual recognition that they like the idea of looking like they are made for each other.

Chuck shouts after them, "If you can't make it to the game, I'll see you at the Reserve meeting Monday night." Marty and Chuck are both Seaman Recruits in the Navy Reserve. They had joined not out of a sense of patriotism, but as an alternative to the draft. They have three months in which to decide whether to go ahead and serve their tour of active duty and get it over with or go to college and have future service in the Navy hanging over their heads for the next four years. They've vowed to make it a mutual decision. "Together all the way." Marty and Chuck have done everything together for pretty much as long as they can remember. Marty is leaning toward going in the Navy because he has had enough of school. Besides, he knows that his Aunt Lily can't afford to send him to college. She has already taken a lot of money out of her savings account just to help support him through high school, and that was money meant for her retirement. She had taken him in three years earlier when his parents died. They had been coming back home from a Huskies' game when some drunk ran off the freeway, crossed the median, and hit them head-on. So Aunt Lily took Marty in. She never talked about how taking Marty in had changed her life, but he knew she had been planning on selling her beauty salon and moving in with her sister in Seattle. That's what she really wanted to do, but she was determined to hang on as long as necessary — even if it took drawing down her savings to practically nothing — in order to get him through college. Aunt Lily was determined that at least one person in the family would have a college education. So yeah, Marty thinks, it might be a good thing to just go ahead and do his two years in Uncle Sam's Navy and then get a job and a life of his own, and let Aunt Lily have her life back.

#

Ah, those magic moments from high school days. We remember them forever. Watching Chuck hit a line drive between the third base and shortstop, skinny dipping at Ocean Shores, making out with Barbara King on the backseat of Aunt Lily's Plymouth Fury — a stunning red convertible with its distinctive white stripe leading to those massive tailfins. The fashions, the mischief, the heroes we looked up to (Marty's hero had always been Chuck, his best friend since grade school and a star athlete who moved on the field of action with the grace of a ballet dancer). Moments Marty could never forget included falling crazy in love with one girl after another; the regular Friday night makeout tussles at the drive-in on the road to Shelton, trying as hard as he could to unclasp Betty Brown's bra or reach his hand up between Mary Robert's thighs while she kept grabbing his hand and moving it away — crushingly kissing him all the while (some of the near-misses in the game of love being as memorable as his one conquest in the summer of fifty-nine); sweating math exams, writing a book report on *Uncle Tom's Cabin* from a *Classics Illustrated* comic book; watching Jimmy Collins get fall-down drunk on a six-pack of Bud. But more than anything, it's the music that defines the times — silly love songs played on those little 45rpm record players with the big holes in the center. Marty and Chuck and all their friends pretty much formed all their ideas about love from the hit songs of the day. And what passed for love in those songs usually boiled down to either terminal cuteness or to a profound longing that could never be fulfilled, neither of which, of course, had a damn thing to do with the reality of love.

If you ever heard it, how could you ever forget Johnnie Ray's heart rending "Cry" or Julie London's "Cry Me A River," the yearning in Elvis's voice when he pleaded with a lover, "Don't say don't" or the silliness of lines like: "I fell in love with you first time I looked into (pause) them there eyes" or "How can I tell them this is not a puppy love?" or "I love you a bushel and a peck, a bushel and a peck and a hug around the neck"?

Some of those songs were remnants from an earlier era, but radio station KLOY kept playing them anyway. Can you imagine singing lines like those to the love of your life? With a straight face? But that's exactly what countless love-starved teens did back then. Marty and Maria, in the days shortly after their graduation dance, used to sing that bushel-and-a-peck song to each other while walking on the sidewalk by the Capitol Theatre or out by Big Bob's Burgers, where they'd buy burgers and eat them in the park and wipe the juices off one another's chins. Singing that song loudly and off key, they'd stop to kiss on the "pecks" and hug on the "hug-around-the-necks," and then laugh with the shared joy of their own cleverness.

#

Maria was the last of a long string of girls Marty fell madly in love with that year. He had known her long before that night at the graduation dance, but they had never been close friends. Until the spring of their senior year, they had hardly exchanged half a dozen words. Freshman year, Maria Perez was but one of many girls seen around school from time to time who never registered with him as anything more than a passing figure in the hallways. Junior year, nasty rumors about Maria began to spread around the school. By senior year, all the boys at Oly High noticed her whenever they saw her. Marty was no exception. But he never dated her and seldom even spoke to her. They didn't run with the same crowd. Popularity was all-important to Marty. He hung out with the cool kids, dated the Homecoming Queen, edited the school paper and yearbook, and would not be caught dead with a trashy girl like Maria Perez. Maria was a slut. Everybody said so. Not just a slut, but a slut of gigantic magnitude. She wore short skirts and low-cut blouses, heavy eye shadow and bright red lipstick. There was a rumor going around school that she took on five guys at once — Billy Boone and his buddies, boys that Marty and his friends never had anything to do with. The funny thing was, Marty didn't believe any of it. He knew that most of the tales going around about kids at school were highly exaggerated, if not outright lies. He had been taught to always think the best of everyone, and never put stock in gossip. He never believed half of what the other boys said about Maria, but he never accused them of lying, either. He wasn't about to go so far as to stand up and defend her, and he certainly didn't want to be seen socializing with her, which would really hurt his reputation.

Little by little Marty began to take notice of Maria, beginning when he happened to notice her in the cafeteria one day in the spring of his senior year. He was slouching with his feet stretched out in the aisle between tables. Trying to pass by with her lunch tray, she playfully kicked at his feet and said, "Move 'em, Mister."

"Sorry." He pulled his feet out of her path and flashed her an apologetic look. He saw that she was wearing a sleeveless blouse that rode tightly across the swell of her breasts. Her dark hair had a shine to it like polished metal. He thought: She's kind of cute. I never noticed.

After that, it seemed that she was always showing up wherever he was. She came to pep rallies. He was sure she had never done that before. In English class she moved from a seat near the back to a front-row seat right in front and one aisle over from him. In the library, she seemed to always browse the same shelves. Her low-cut blouses and short skirts barely covered one of the sexiest bodies at Olympia High School. He would have had to be blind not to notice. Had she always dressed so provocatively? Surely he would have noticed long before senior year.

One day in English class she leaned forward in her seat in such a way that her breast was completely exposed to him. She wasn't even wearing a bra. When class let out he couldn't wait to find Chuck by the lockers and tell him all about it. "She flashed her tit at me, man. She did it on purpose, I swear to God. Right in Mrs. Robinson's English class. She was wearing this skimpy little shirt with nothing at all underneath. I went ape shit, man. Liked to've creamed in my pants."

After that, he could not get her out of his mind. And when, a few months later, he saw her under the romantic lighting of their graduation dance, he was blinded by her beauty. The entire arc of his young life took a new direction the moment he decided to dance with her to The Twilight's version of "Love Letters in the Sand."

He had been looking forward to a summer of hanging out with his buddies, cruising out to Long Lake in the afternoons to swim and sunbathe, and maybe make out with some of the girls on the beach. He had a list in his head of every girl in school he had wanted to date and hadn't, and every girl he had almost made it all the way with and hadn't (but thought maybe he still had a chance with). He just knew that before the summer was over he was going to have some exciting times in the back seat of Aunt Lily's Plymouth while parked by the lake or at the drive-in movies or by the overlook in the park, or maybe even — God bless the luck — in his own bedroom at home when Aunt Lily went to Vancouver for two weeks' vacation.

But there were no more fantasies about other girls after the graduation ball. From that night on he thought only of her. Maria and Marty were together almost every waking moment. They took turns burying each other in the sand at Long Lake, and poked their noses in every shop in Pike Place Market in Seattle, an easy hour's drive. Afternoons when they didn't have anything else to do they would wander around town, sometimes on foot and sometimes in the Fury, when Aunt Lily would let him use it. They'd pull in to Big Bob's for a burger at lunch or a mid-afternoon soda sipped from a single straw at the Woolworth's lunch counter where a waitress caught them necking in a window booth and told them to leave and not come back until they learned to behave themselves.

They went to the drive-in two or three nights a week, and there in the Fury they groped and clutched and moaned their desire, but stopped short of going all the way; while on the screen Doris Day broke out in hives at the mere thought of having sex with Cary Grant in *That Touch of Mink* and while Richard Breymer risked his life for love of Natalie Wood in *West Side Story*.

Actually, they didn't make out at all during *West Side Story*. They watched every moment, from that marvelous opening scene with the camera zooming in from outer space, right down to the tragic ending. The story was so compelling they couldn't take their eyes off the screen. When Tony sang "Maria, I just met a girl named Maria," Marty knew there was no way he could not be in love with his own girl named Maria. He took that song as an omen that they were fated to be together. He wanted so much to sing it to her, even if he did have the worst singing voice in the state of Washington. More than that, he wanted to *be* her Tony, almost up to the moment when he dies for love of her. If he could have found a way to die for her without, you know, really dying, he would have done it. He wanted that passion.

The funny thing about watching *West Side Story* with Maria was that Marty never got the connections, there being vast areas of inexplicable unconsciousness in his eighteen-year-old brain. He knew that in the movie there was a war going on between the Puerto Rican Sharks and the barely American Jets, and he was able to grasp the lessons about prejudice on some level. He also sort of got it that Maria — his Maria — was Puerto Rican, but he never thought of her as such and never imagined that they would ever face the kinds of conflicts that tore Tony and Maria apart. The future newspaperman and book lover never even recognized that *West Side Story* was a modern version of *Romeo and Juliet*.

The truth was he knew next to nothing about Maria Perez. He knew nothing about her family. If someone asked him, "Did you even know she has three brothers and that all three of them are kind of half-ass criminals — one of 'em's even in jail for god's sake?" he probably would have said, "Well yeah, I think I kinda knew that, but not really." He'd never been in her house and didn't know anything at all about her mother or her crazy Aunt Alize up in Seattle, the woman who had been Maria's role model since early childhood; and he was completely in the dark about her interests or her hopes for the future, other than her often stated hope that that future would be shared with him. He hadn't the slightest idea what she did with her life when he was not around. All he knew about her was that he loved her desperately.

Their dates took place all over town and up and down Interstate Five, but never inside her house. They usually met downtown, and on the few occasions when he did pick her up at home she'd be waiting for him at the curb. When he brought her home at the end of the night, they would kiss goodbye without getting out of the car, and she would run up the sidewalk to her porch while he watched until she got safely inside before pulling away from the curb. There was always a single light burning in a side window, probably the bedroom where her mother waited for her. Sometimes Marty could see a flutter of curtain that reminded him of his Aunt Lily's old slips hanging on the line. He did bring her home to meet Aunt Lily once, and she ate supper with them, but she never invited him in to her house to meet her mother. If he thought about it at all, he would have known why, or at least he would have been able to make a pretty good guess about the (at least) more superficial reason that she never invited him into her home. It was because she was poor, and she was ashamed of it. She would be embarrassed for him to see the worn furniture and cheap tablecloths and the laundry that was draped over chair backs to dry. She would be embarrassed for him to see her mother's choices in interior decoration — religious icons and paintings of bullfighters on black velvet.

#

Maria Delgato, formerly Maria Winters, maiden name Perez. Her mama told her she was born bad. That's the way she liked to put it. Born bad. Bad to the bone.

Six years old, first grade, first day of school. The teacher is calling the role. She calls out, "Mary Louise Perez" — getting the name wrong; it's *Maria* Louise, not *Mary* Louise. And she hates her middle name. Maria refuses to answer. The teacher calls her name again. Again Maria fails to respond. "Young lady," the teacher spits, approaching her desk and getting right in her face. "Are you Mary Louise Perez? Answer me, young lady." And again she refuses to respond. For two days Maria sits silently in her desk, refusing to respond to the teacher in any way. The teacher drags her to the principal's office; the principal calls Maria's mother. Mrs. Perez comes to the school and meets with the teacher and principal. When they explain to her what has happened, Mrs. Perez defends her daughter, saying, "Naturally she does not speak. If you would bother to learn her name, maybe then she would speak."

But back at home she berates her child, saying, "You bad, bad girl. You're going to grow up no count just like your Aunt Alize'"

Aunt Alize was the black sheep of the family. Her bad taste in men was notorious. She had lived with three of them. The first one beat her, and the family suspected the others had as well. All of them had abandoned her. After the last guy left, she took off for parts unknown (with rumors surfacing now and again that she was living with a drug dealer or a pimp or a lesbian lover in Seattle or Vancouver or Portland). Her man troubles aside, Alize was a loveable woman who loved to sing and dance, and who lavished attention on her nieces and nephews — especially Maria. The threat of growing up just like her Aunt Alize was no threat at all to Maria.

Neither Alize, when she was still around, nor any of Maria's brothers, Jimmy or José or Pico, nor Mrs. Perez's on-again off-again boyfriend, Roger Wilson, knew why Mrs. Perez was so convinced that Maria was destined for a life of sin. But convinced of it she was. Maybe it was because Maria, with her soft black hair and eyes that could set charcoal on fire, was a carbon copy of Mrs. Perez, who had no illusions about her own worth. Maybe it was because as a very young child Maria beat the crap out of José, the littlest of her older brothers. Maybe it was because she regularly stole toys belonging to her brothers and either broke them or hid them or threw them away out of pure spite. (She once filled her Radio Flyer wagon with toys belonging to her brothers, hauled them downtown to the bridge crossing Budd Inlet, and dumped them all into Puget Sound.) Or maybe it was because she liked to run around naked, or because when she was eight years old Mrs. Perez caught her playing doctor with her older brothers — stretched out buck naked on her bed while Pico "examined" her body and the other boys watched.

Maria was a spirited child who learned early on how to get her way with her big brothers and how to survive life with her often erratic mother. The brothers adored her, and even though they sometimes fought like alley cats, they would do anything she asked. Mrs. Perez's parenting skills were bad in every way, but the worst of it was her extreme inconsistency, which left Maria never knowing what was expected of her. One moment Mrs. Perez would dote on her daughter and call her pet names like "My Heart" and "My Angel," and in the next moment she would scream at her and call her "Satan's spawn" and threaten to kick her out of the house or "whip the devil out of her" — lapsing into streams of Spanish curses, absolutely none of which Maria could understand.

When Maria grew older and started showing interest in boys, her mother was downright puritanical in insisting that she remain a virgin, while berating her as a *puta*, a slut; yet when Billy Boone started sleeping over with Maria, Mrs. Perez welcomed him like a prized son-in-law. Such were the infuriating contradictions Maria had to live with.

The determining factor in whether Mrs. Perez loved or hated her child at any given moment often depended on how drunk she was. It was always a matter of degree, since Mrs. Perez was never not drunk (and believe you me, if I exaggerate, it's not by much).

From the time she learned to walk, up until she was old enough to go to school, Maria loved to run around naked. And she persisted in doing it even though she knew she would get spanked for it. "Don't you ever, ever step foot outside this house bare ass naked again. Do you hear me?" Mrs. Perez would demand.

And poor little Maria, naked and shivering, would stammer, "But, Mama, I—"

"Don't you 'but Mama' me, young lady. You march yourself outside right now and break me a switch off the willow tree."

What could she do? She couldn't go out to get the switch, because she was naked, but if she tried to go into her room to get dressed first, her mother would think she was trying to run away from her, or at least trying to delay her punishment, which just made her mother even madder. Besides which, Maria could be unreasonably obstinate. So she learned to stand her ground and say, "I won't do it, and you can't make me."

Infuriated beyond all sense, Mrs. Perez would grab her child by her arm and spank her with her bare hand until both her hand and Maria's butt were blistered. The more it hurt her hand, the madder she would get, and the harder she would hit, screaming, "Don't you defy me, you little bitch! *Puta! Pendejo!*" The harder she hit and the louder she cursed, the more stubborn Maria would get, stoically refusing to cry — which, naturally, made her mother even madder. Finally her mother would break through the circle of pain and anger and defiance and break down in abject regret with great howls and tears, and she would hug her daughter and beg her forgiveness, and then she would go to the bathroom to grab a tube of soothing ointment to rub on Maria's blistered buttocks.

The closest thing to a daddy Maria ever knew was Roger Wilson, the sometimes boyfriend who tended to show up late at night and sleep until mid-day, when he would leave and not show up again for weeks or even months. Usually, the only adult in the house was her mama, whom she described as "just a mess and not ever *really* there" — of whom she said, "I can't hardly ever remember her not being drunk or hung over, one or the other."

José and Pico and Jimmy took care of Maria more than her mother and her boyfriend did. They did the grocery shopping and cooking, and did the laundry while their mother got drunk. When Maria was an infant, and then a toddler, they bathed her and dressed her and put Band-Aids on her cuts and scrapes.

The only family outing Maria could remember took place when she was eight or nine years old. It was one of the rare occasions when Mrs. Perez wasn't drinking. She packed a picnic lunch in a wicker basket and drove Maria and the boys to Priest Point Park on a morning when the sky was so blue it looked like somebody had pasted it above the trees. Alize went along, too. This was before she had babies, back when she was living with her sister and working at the aluminum plant. Alize wore a bathing suit with shorts thrown on top, even though the water where they were going was not safe to swim in. Maria wore white shorts and a shirt with pictures of big yellow daisies, and rubber flip-flops with daisies to match the shirt. Mrs. Perez told her she should wear tennis shoes because the flip-flops would be too hard to walk in, but Maria paid her no mind.

In the picnic basket were bologna sandwiches and pickles and potato salad, and watermelon already sliced into wedges and individually wrapped in plastic. José carried an ice chest with bottles of Nehi orange and grape soda and Cokes all sloshing around in the icy water. They also brought empty buckets for the clams they planned on digging up in the mud flats at low tide.

The park was so close to home that the kids often walked there by themselves. It was, in fact, situated on the shores of Budd Inlet, at the tip of Puget Sound, no more than half a mile from where Maria had dumped her brothers' toys in the sound. Near or far, on that particular day the excursion in their 'forty-four Studebaker seemed like a trip to the far side of the world for Maria.

Back then a bunch of peacocks and peahens roamed freely in the park, and the first thing the Perez family did when they got there was toss bread to them. Pico let one old peahen come up and take a slice right out of his hand. Maria tried to do it, too, but when the big bird got close, she panicked and tossed her bread away. José called her scardy cat.

"I'm not neither scared!" she protested. To prove how brave she was, she grabbed the bread back from right under the bird's beak, and then held it out and let the bird eat from her hand.

The grownups and José and Maria followed the winding trail down to the beach. Jimmy and Pico took the shortcut, which was a fast tumble down a steep hill where it was a wonder they didn't break their necks. José would have taken the downhill plunge, too, but he had to carry the ice chest. Maria followed behind Mama and José with tentative steps on the scary trail. The path was little more than a foot wide, and there was a sheer drop off on the water side. Pebbles moved underfoot and slippery spots in deep shade left from a recent rain were slick as oil. Once or twice she thought she was going to crash into a ravine. Tumbling downhill with Jimmy and Pico might have been safer, she thought, and the treacherous footing convinced her that for once in her life she should have listened to her mama and not worn those flip-flops.

The beach was a wide swath of dirt littered with rocks and broken shells and driftwood. The driftwood was worn smooth by wind and water, bleached a dull brown on top and almost black in places where the sun never hit. If you moved hunks of driftwood, you'd find clear pools underneath occupied by tiny water creatures. Here and there were fallen trees that looked like they were made of shale. The tide had receded, leaving a mucky mess of wet sand and gravel and sticks and algae and bi-valve shells. They plodded through wide stretches of mud to reach the water's edge, where they dug for shellfish, Mrs. Perez wearing rubber boots, but the kids all sloshing barefoot through the muck, having deposited their shoes on higher ground. Alize remained far back from the water's edge, watching from a shady perch under a bluff. Farther out, the gently rippled water flashed like millions of mirrors. Distant boats were silhouetted against the farther shore, and behind the tree line loomed the huge dome of the state capitol. In the opposite direction stood the jagged and snow-capped ridges of the Olympic Mountains.

The boys found clams and mussels, and caught scurrying crabs, and Maria picked up anything that looked pretty. After they filled their buckets and washed their feet in a runoff stream, they sat in the shade of a fallen tree to eat lunch. Then, after lunch, Mrs. Perez asked if anyone wanted to take a walk. The boys said they wanted to clam some more, and Alize said she was going to read, but Maria said she'd like to go.

They followed a path that was barely wide enough for one person. Long stems on bushes with pointy green leaves brushed their legs as they walked. The trees were so tall and so close together that they couldn't see the sky. Deep in the woods it was cool, almost like going into an air-conditioned room. Maria spotted a rotted-out tree trunk that looked like a gnarled old man with fat legs and five or six skinny arms. The old trunk was almost as tall as a house, and a new baby tree was growing out of the top of it. There was a cave in the bottom part and moss all on one side. It reminded her of pictures in the storybook *Sleepy Hollow*. With a delicious shudder, she imagined the headless horseman crashing through the brush.

She heard the sound of birds chirping and the caw of crows, but when she looked for the birds she couldn't see any. She began to think about ghost birds and imagined flocks of them hiding in the treetops. Any minute now they would dive-bomb her and tear her flesh with their beaks. She told herself to cut it out. They were just harmless crows, but it was weird that she could hear so many and not see them.

Looking down, she saw a banana slug on the ground. It was shiny and wet like green snot. She reached down to feel it. It didn't feel as slimy as she thought it would. When she tried to pick it up, it held on to the ground. She stood up and glanced ahead, and she could not see her mama. "Mama," she called, "where are you?" But there was no answer from her mother.

She reasoned that her mother couldn't have gotten far. She kept going, trying to walk a little faster so she could catch up. But a big log across the path slowed her down. When she tried to climb over it, one of her flip-flops fell off. So she had to stop and pick it up, and she managed to lose one flip-flop on each side of the log. So she sat on the log and swung her bare feet from one side to the other, tearing her shorts in the process, and finally slipped the shoes back on and pushed up to continue her walk, now even farther behind.

She didn't worry about catching up with her mama, because she knew if she just stayed on the path she'd find her sooner or later. She remembered that Jimmy and Pico had told her you couldn't get lost in the woods because all of the paths led back to the water.

She saw some mushrooms growing on the side of the path and stopped to pick them, breaking the stems near the ground, thinking that José would be able to tell her if they were the kind you can eat. After awhile she came to a place where the path split off in two directions, and she decided to go to the left. Pretty soon it split off again, and again she went to the left. The path got thinner and thinner, and before long she couldn't see it anymore. That's when she started getting scared. And just about then the cawing crows started getting louder and louder. There seemed to be hundreds of them all around, and now she was sure they were getting ready to attack her. They were mean, nasty birds that hated little girls, and they were going to surround her and swoop down and peck her to death. Then she was really scared. She started screaming, "Mama! Mama! Where are you? Help me, Mama." But Mama was too far away to hear.

Maria didn't know how long it took her to find a path out of the woods, but it seemed like hours. At last she spotted a little trickle of a stream and followed it to where it came to the beach, and there she saw her mother and her brothers in the distance. Her mother was flicking a long switch against her leg while she waited for her to approach. She knew she was going to get a whipping, but she didn't care. What was one more whipping to her? Her mama made her drop her shorts, and she put stripes on her butt with the switch. Maria pulled her shorts back up, and her mother said, "You had me scared to death, girl. If you ever do anything like that again I'm going to tear your hiney up" — as if that wasn't what she had just done.

Maria wouldn't let any of the others see her cry, but when she got a chance to be alone with her Aunt Alize, she let it out while Alize held her and rubbed her back.

#

One night when Marty drove Maria home after they had spent the day swimming at Long Lake he opened the car door for her at the curb the way he always did, and she said, "Hey, why don't you come up on the porch with me and let's sit on the swing?"

"Sure," he said. "That'd be nice."

It was after ten o'clock and the late-setting sun had finally gone down, and there was a chill in the air. They walked up to the porch and sat on the swing and spoke in whispers while the swing chain creaked its singsong rhythm. They had thrown on long sleeve shirts but still wore bathing suits underneath. Both of them had chill bumps on their exposed legs. Maria darted inside the house and right back out, bringing a blanket, which they threw over their shoulders and wrapped around their legs. Snuggling, shivering, giggling, porch swing creaking. They had not been there more than a few minutes when the front door was thrown open with a succession of crashes as first the screen door and then the solid door banged against the side of the house, and Maria's mother burst out shouting, "You, boy, get away from here. You leave my Maria alone. My Maria is a good girl."

"Mama, it's OK," Maria said. "He's a good boy. It's OK."

She was a stout woman with a mop of coarse black hair streaked with gray. She wore a floral print dress and fuzzy slippers. She grabbed the edge of the porch swing and almost lifted it with both of them on it, making them have to clutch the edge and hang on, and she shouted, "You go now. You go away and leave my girl alone."

"But Mrs. Perez, I love your daughter."

"Love! *Muchacho estúpido.* What do you know about love?"

"Mama."

"You go away from here."

"But I do love her. I want to marry her."

"We'll see about that," she said turning to storm back into the house. He knew good and well she wasn't calling it quits that easily. Hell, he wouldn't even have been surprised to find out she was going for a gun. But Maria seemed unfazed by her mother's actions. She turned to Marty and whispered incredulously, "You do? You really want to marry me?"

Wow, he thought, did I say that? Yeah, I did. And he said, "Yes, I do. Will you?

"Yes. Yes I will."

She threw her arms around him and kissed him. And just as they kissed there was a sudden crashing sound and an immediate sharp pain shot through his head as a broom handle wielded by Maria's mother connected with the side of his head. She hadn't gone for a gun, but she hadn't just calmly turned to go back into the house and gone to bed, either. No, she had rushed inside in search of a weapon, and she had come back out to the porch wielding a broom just in time to see the brash young man kissing her only daughter. Suddenly the daughter she had called bad to the bone was an innocent child in need of protection. She was probably off-balance when she took her mighty swing at Marty's head, so she connected only with a glancing blow. But it was enough to make his head ring and send him stumbling down the steps. Luckily for Marty, there were only three steps, so his fall wasn't fatal. But it sure as hell felt like it for a moment or two. He was stunned. One moment he had been kissing the love of his life, and the next moment he was on his hands and knees in the dirt clutching his throbbing head. He dropped his hands to look for blood but there wasn't any.

Maria leapt off the porch and grabbed his arms in an attempt to help balance him as he pulled himself unsteadily to his feet.

"Are you all right?" she asked.

"Yeah. I think I'll be fine."

By then her mother had made her way down the steps, her fuzzy slippers slapping the back of her heels as she walked. She swung the broom in a circular motion over her head like a batter waiting to belt a homer out of the park. Marty scurried back out of her reach.

"Mama, quit it, now," Maria said.

Mama said, "I don't want to hear no more talk about getting married. You're too young for that." Focusing her fiery gaze on Marty, she said, "*Tu, zorrero. Ahua!* You go on away now before I put another knot upside your head."

"Mama, don't you dare," Maria said. And then she added, "We are too old enough. We're older than you were when you got married."

"I was a idiot. Me being a idiot don't give you the right to be one too."

"That's right," Maria shot back at her mother, "you must have been an idiot because none of your marriages lasted past the honeymoon. My God, you're the last person on earth to tell me about love and marriage."

Then she turned back to Marty and said, "Maybe you'd better go for now. She'll calm down later and we can talk."

As he drove away Mama shouted, "And don't you come back."

First Woolworth's and then her front porch. It seemed like every place they kissed they got evicted.

When Mrs. Perez finally dragged herself out of bed shortly after eleven the next morning, Maria served her a hot cup of coffee and pastries from the bakery around the corner. She said, "Mama, we've got to talk about last night. About Marty. About me getting married."

She begged and cajoled and sweet talked her mother, and finally Mrs. Perez gave in, at least to the point of saying, "OK, you bring that boy around tonight and we'll talk."

Marty felt as if he were a soldier sneaking into an enemy camp when he walked into the fortress of the formidable Mrs. Perez (he didn't think of it as Maria's house, because he could not visualize her living there; up until the night before he had simply thought of it as the place where he dropped her off). As soon as Maria opened the door for him and he stepped in, a cat darted in a flash to the shelter of some hiding place in the back of the house. The chair he sat on was covered with cat fur. It was upholstered with a floral pattern, and the arms and back were covered with multi-colored, knit doilies. Instead of the bad-taste art he expected to see on the walls, there were pictures cut out of magazines and tacked to the walls with thumb tacks. On the mantle was a picture of a boy he recognized. Billy Boone. Seeing that was a shock.

Maria's mother sat in a straight back chair facing Marty and Maria and said, "Now you tell me why you have to get married. You're not pregnant, are you?"

"No, no. We haven't even done anything."

They talked and they talked, and finally Mrs. Perez begrudgingly consented that if they had truly made up their minds to get married there wasn't much she could do to stop it. But, by God, she had no intention of being happy about it. "And what about Billy Boone?" she asked Maria. "What do you propose to do about that poor boy? Just leave him hanging like a rag on the line?"

"Mama, hush now. I don't want to hear anything about Billy Boone." In a sudden panic, she looked up and screeched, "Oh my god, you've still got his picture up there."

Marty hated Billy Boone. Just hearing his name come out of her mouth made him so mad that if he had shown up right then, Marty might have very well picked up a two-by-four or a baseball bat or anything else he could get his hands on and smashed his face in. At least that's what he fantasized that he might do. In truth, Billy was bigger and stronger, and would probably be much more ruthless in a fight; Marty would not stand a chance against him. He never had liked him or any of his buddies. They were a nasty bunch, Billy and Roy and Chico. They hung out together and terrified the smaller kids and the bookworms and the Asians, and anyone that didn't have a bunch of strong friends to stand up for them. Besides, Marty thought, they were like hillbillies from the Deep South somehow misplaced way out in the Pacific Northwest. They had a little band and played country music. Sweet Jesus Christ! Nobody played country music.

#

It was the youngest of Maria's big brothers who first introduced her to Billy Boone, which was no surprise considering it was those brothers of hers who were her portal to anyone and anything dangerous or risky. It was also José and Jimmy and Pico who taught her to shoplift way back in elementary school. She soon got so good at it that by the time she reached puberty she could walk out of a department store with a radio hidden under her coat and flirt with the sales clerk on her way out. Thirteen years old and able to make college dropouts salivate with the sparkle of her big brown eyes — flirting to the point of devastation being yet another skill she had learned from her rascally brothers and perfected at an early age. Practically from the cradle, she had played childish sex games with José and Jimmy and Pico and their friends. By the time she reached high school, she could work a boy's desire as skillfully as a circus shill works a crowd. That is not to say she was promiscuous, at least not that early on, but she was far from frigid. She reveled in being bad. As she loved to say with a mischievous twinkle in her eye, "My mama said I was born bad, and by God she was right." It was a proud boast. Another way she sometimes liked to put it was: "I'm good at being bad. Really good." — trilling the R in *Really* with a rumble her Puerto-Rican mother would be proud of. It was to Billy Boone and his friends that she boasted like that, never to Marty.

Her body matured early. She had prominent breasts before most of the other girls her age, and she quickly learned that they could be an asset. Anything she might want from one of the boys she could get with the merest hint that she might let him see them. Jimmy's friend Chico was a prime example. "I'll do anything you want if you just let me get a little peek," he said, "Anything at all. I swear." And she shot back, "I'll bare 'em for you if you snitch me a watch from Woolworths." When Jimmy Cunningham, the smartest boy in the eighth grade, pestered her to let him touch her breasts, she parlayed that into a month's worth of algebra homework. But her teasing sex play never went beyond a touch or a fleeting glimpse of those beautifully budding breasts. If the boys wanted to go further than that, they were too shy or bumbling to know how to ask for it (at least most of them were). Still, Maria found it much to her advantage to create the impression that they *could* go further if only they had the courage to ask. The unfortunate downside of all that — which she swore never bothered her in the least — was that she became known as the town whore.

The one boy who seemed unaffected by her allure was Billy Boone, and that drove her crazy. She was twelve years old the first time she saw him. It was summertime. Late afternoon. She was in the kitchen at home frying hamburgers on the stove top. She looked out the window and saw her brother José tossing a baseball with a boy she'd never before seen. He was slightly taller than José, and very muscular, the sleeve of his T-shirt rolled up to reveal a sinewy shoulder and bicep. His eyes were deep set and, from her vantage point in the kitchen, looked as black as the old tire swing that hung from an oak limb in the yard. He was wearing his hair in the new style: short and flat on top, with longish sides brushed back into a ducktail. She didn't try to get to know him then, nor the next time José brought him over. For the first time ever, she was scared of meeting a boy.

When she finally did get to know him and began to hang out with him, it was Billy who called the shots, a new and unexpectedly tantalizing experience for her. She never made the first move. While she had been able to manipulate other boys at will, Billy turned the tables on her. In high school, she cajoled other boys into cheating and stealing for her and spending their money on her. But Maria did Billy's bidding. She did his algebra homework for a whole year. Not that she actually solved the problems herself. She copied Jimmy Cunningham's homework for both herself and Billy, making a few changes in each so the teacher wouldn't suspect.

She loved Billy Boone from the moment she met him, and would do anything he asked. He was the handsomest boy she had ever known, especially after he let that silly flattop grow into a thick wave of black hair that swept back from his forehead like an ocean swell. He was six feet tall with broad shoulders and a cute little butt that filled his jeans quite nicely (Maria hated the caved-in look of buttless boys). He wore a black leather jacket over a T-shirt no matter the weather. He always had a cigarette stuffed under the earpiece of the sun glasses he wore day and night. He was a wild and fearless boy who would do anything on a dare.

Billy's father was a mechanic. He had easy access to other people's cars, which he let Billy drive, starting even before he was old enough for a license. And Billy's way of driving was like target practice with immovable objects. He loved to swerve off the road to sideswipe children's toys left on sidewalks, sending wagons and tricycles flying. No corner lawn was safe from him, as he loved to cut across corners leaving deep ruts in the ground. He taught Maria to drive, and one night he got her to drive for him while he leaned out the window with a baseball bat and knocked mailboxes off their stands. Then he gave her a turn at bat while he drove, but the first time she hit a mailbox the bat flew out of her hand and smashed against the side of the car leaving a dent that Billy's dad had to repair.

Billy worked with his dad in the garage. The owner of the garage was a man named Gabe Hatfield, the rebel heir to a manufacturing fortune who dabbled in the auto repair business because of his love of fast cars. Gabe owned a vacation home on the beach in Baja, Mexico, and, locally, a large home west of town that was hidden in a forested area well off the nearest road and protected by a high fence with a locked gate — where word around town had it wild parties were held, with wealthy people, even movie stars, flying in from all over the country for the festivities. "They're orgies," Billy claimed. "Everybody goes swimming naked, and they all swap partners."

During a sweltering summer weekend, when Gabe and his wife were staying at their beach house in Baja, Billy and Maria, and Billy's friends Chico and Roy broke into Gabe's house and went skinny dipping. It was their scaled-back version of the wild orgies they imagined took place there.

The driveway to the Hatfield estate was a winding road canopied by oak trees on either side. Behind the oaks stood a row of towering Lombardy poplars that completely hid the property. They drove to where the road was blocked by a six-foot-tall stone fence with an ornamental aluminum gate. They pulled off the road and parked under cover of a tree. The boys climbed the fence and helped Maria up and over. Billy knew his way around the house because he sometimes cut the Hatfield's grass, so everyone followed him. They followed a path through the garden to the back of the house and the swimming pool, which was lighted by underwater spotlights. The boys immediately kicked off their shoes and pulled off their pants and shirts, and dove into the pool. "Christ! It's colder'n a witch's tit!" Chico shouted.

"It's cold enough to shrivel your dick," Billy taunted, "'Cept you ain't got one to shrivel."

All three boys treaded water, their bodies as white as corpses and surreally distorted by the wave action of the artificially blue water. They all looked to Maria who stood fully dressed by the diving board. "You're chicken if you don't come in," Billy said.

"Oh yeah?" She pulled her shirt over her head and stepped out of her shoes and shorts, and walked slowly toward the steps at the shallow end of the pool.

"No chickening out and going in your underwear," Billy said. "You got to go all the way naked like us."

"Yeah, all the way," the other boys challenged.

Without bothering to answer, she shucked her bra and stepped out of her panties, and eased into the water until it was up to her neck. And then she dog paddled out to the middle of the deeper end where the three boys were. As soon as she got close enough for them to touch her, Roy and Chico started grabbing for tits and ass. She kicked and slapped them away, not in anger or fear, but playfully, laughing all the while.

Soon they climbed out of the pool and got partially dressed, slipping into their underwear but leaving pants, shirts and shoes where they lay. Billy found an unlocked window, climbed in and opened the patio doors for the others. They dripped their way across the cold terra cotta floor of the den and down a hallway where they left squishy footprints in the carpet, and made their way to a bathroom where they found towels to dry themselves. They scampered back to the den, where they found a fully-stocked bar and generously helped themselves to drinks. A wooden box on top of the bar was filled with cigars that Chico and Roy lighted and puffed on, coughing and crushing them out on the floor. In a sliding drawer underneath the bar, they found a Polaroid camera and a stack of photographs. They were doing all this rummaging about by the meager light that filtered in from the patio and ankle-level night lights throughout the house. Billy scooped up the stack of Polaroids and switched on a lamp to better see them. "Jesus fucking Christ!" he shouted. "Get a load of these."

They were pictures of men and women wearing very little or no clothing, in groups of two, three and more — not candid sex shots, but posed pictures of people in titillating but somewhat coy positions. Billy recognized Gabe and Melissa Hatfield in some of the pictures, so he knew these were not purchased pictures of models. They were snapshots of real people taken right there in the Hatfield's house. "This proves it," Billy said. "The rumors about orgies are true."

Chico pulled out the camera. "Hey, hey! Let's add to their collection," he said.

"Are you out of your mind?" Maria shot back. "I'm not about to let anybody take pictures like that of me."

"Just pretend," Chico said. "You and Billy."

"Nuh uh."

"Chicken."

Knowing she could never resist a dare, they teased her until she gave in. Chico snapped pictures of Billy and Maria making out in their underwear. It took awhile, because they had to wait after each picture for it to process, gathering around in a crush of flesh to watch images appear.

After a few shots, Billy said, "Let's get Roy in the picture." So Roy and Billy posed with Maria while Chico photographed them, and then Billy took the camera and she posed with Roy and Chico. After they had taken about a dozen photos, they found scissors and cut their faces out of the pictures, so nobody could identify them, and they spread them out on Gabe and Melissa's bed before they left, chuckling about the imagined prospects of the Hatfields finding photos of an orgy taking place in their bed while they were gone. But one photograph didn't make it into the collage on the bed. Chico palmed it and tucked it under his Jockey shorts before they snipped all the faces out of the other pictures. They rushed back out to the pool to get dressed and they scampered back to the car. Billy stole the camera.

Chico kept the photograph and eventually showed it to one or two friends, but only after making them swear they'd never tell anybody. The picture showed Billy lying on top of Maria with her arm across Chico.

#

Like everyone else at school, Marty heard the rumor that Maria Perez had been photographed in an orgy with Chico Demint and Billy Boone, and that Roy Martin was in on it, too. At first he attributed it to wishful thinking on Chico's part. But after graduation, after he fell in love with Maria, he thought about it a lot. He pictured it in his mind and it drove him crazy, the mental image of them all naked and sweaty and laughing, and her just taking it and taking it, knowing in his mind that if it really happened they must have somehow forced her into it because she would never willingly do anything so depraved. Never mind that Maria denied the whole thing. He still couldn't shut it out of his mind. She had gone with Billy for a long time. There was no denying that. And when Marty asked her about Billy, all she would say was, "That's over now. It's been over so long it's ridiculous. There's no sense in talking about it."

But there was a picture of Billy Boone on her mantle at home.

#

The principal of the school was Mister Madison, a sweet little man who was constantly mystified at the malicious stunts pulled by his rowdier students. Why anyone would want to put a dead fish in the science teacher's car or hang underwear from the school flagpole was beyond his comprehension. "Poor Mister Madison," Maria said. "He's so goddamn clueless, sweet little *pendejo.*"

Across town from the school, in a new housing development off Mud Bay Road, was a childcare center operated by a single mother whose first name, coincidentally, was the same as the principal's last name. Madison. Madison Willingham. The plywood sign in front of the beige shingled house read: *Madison's Day Nursery*. It was printed in raised red letters on a yellow background. Pictured under the lettering was a mother duck leading a waddle of baby ducklings. With Maria in the driver's seat of a pickup truck borrowed from Gabe's garage, Billy Boone backed up to the *Madison's Day Nursery* sign, unbolted it from the posts it was attached to, and threw it in the back of the pickup — all while Madison Willingham and her son were eating dinner inside the house. Back in the driver's seat after loading the sign, Billy gunned the engine and dug satisfactory ruts in the Willingham yard taking off, and laid down equally satisfying rubber on the pavement. His squealing tires startled Madison, who rushed outside in time to watch Billy's tail lights vanish in the distance.

They sped back across town to the school and parked behind the cafeteria, where Billy used ropes attached to the sign to pull it up to the roof. Maria stood in the bed of the truck and watched until the sign was on top of the building, unnecessarily directing him with mighty waves of her arms. Billy, of course, just dragged the sign straight up the side of the building. No maneuvering needed. He couldn't even see her gestures in the dark. She, on the other hand, could clearly see him silhouetted against a moonlit sky. When she saw him haul the sign over the parapet, she jumped down from the truck and ran to the front of the building to watch Billy drag the sign to where he could prop it against the parapet above the main entrance to the building. There the colorful sign proudly proclaimed the school to be *Madison's Day Nursery*.

Billy then entered the school by way of a rooftop doorway and went downstairs to let Maria in. They skipped down the hallway to Mrs. Robinson's English class, rifled through her desk drawers and ripped to shreds her tests on sentence diagrams. Maria pulled a box of Kotex sanitary napkins from a drawer, and they tossed them around the classroom. Billy threw the roll book in a trash can and set it on fire with his Zippo. With the roll book still smoldering in the trash, they left Mrs. Robinson's room and snuck into the teachers' lounge. There, in the teachers' restroom that was shared by men and women, Billy planted a magazine he had brought just for the purpose, a sex magazine for gay men called *Boys in Touch*. He bookmarked it with a business card stolen from his Algebra teacher, Mister Bullock. On the bookmarked page he had underlined an ad that read: *School teacher wants to meet young men, preferably college educated, for fun and games. Must be discrete.*

"Where in the world did you get that?" Maria asked.

"Never mind where I got it. Can't you just imagine what's going to happen when they find that?"

"Well, I imagine they're going to figure out it was some student that planted it. And guess what student's going to be their number one suspect."

"Maybe, and maybe not. But I bet you some of the teachers are going to start whispering about it, and pretty soon the whole damn school's going to think Bullock's queer."

"That could get him fired."

"No shit, Sherlock. Tough titty's what I say. Tough titty and sour milk."

They ran up and down the halls. They went into the girls' restroom, stoppered the sinks and turned all the spigots on high. Then they went into the room where the yearbook staff was putting together the annual *Bears' Den*. Partially completed pages were spread out on desktops. Piles of pictures scattered on tables. "Here's our chance to screw with the socialites," Billy laughed.

"Yeah. The snotty bitches."

Maria found an eight-by-ten glossy of Brenda McKnight wearing a sleek, off-the-shoulder cocktail dress. The lettering under her pictures said: *Most Beautiful* and *Homecoming Court.* She found a marking pen and gave Brenda a black eye and a Hitler moustache, and drew snot coming out of her nose.

Billy snatched up a picture of Richard Robbins and ripped it into little pieces. "Oops, there goes Richie Rich," he said. They attributed vast wealth to all the kids they considered high society snots, even though most of them came from middle class families.

Maria blacked out the face of Barbara King.

Chuck Nagel in his baseball uniform went fluttering into the garbage can, ripped in half. "Tough guy," Billy said.

"Hey, I like Chuck. He's nice."

"Yeah, you're probably banging him."

"Am not."

"Bet you'd like to."

He fished Chuck's photo out and sloppily taped the two halves together. "There, all fixed. I got to admit, he *is* pretty damn tough. He's strong as an ox. I remember seeing him in gym once doing push-ups with Joel Carpenter sitting on his back. Pushing up his own weight plus Joel's."

"Yeah, but I also remember how he used to be a real sissy boy."

"That's right, he was. Something how he changed, huh?"

Maria picked up a page with Marty Winters' picture. The caption read: *Most Likely to Succeed.* "Most likely to suck up," Billy said.

But Maria defended Marty. "You got to give him credit. He's smart, and he's hard working. And he's no rich socialite either. His folks are dead and the aunt he lives with is just a regular person."

She became very pensive for a moment. She said, "You know, if a guy like that can be Most Likely to Succeed, then there ain't no reason you and me can't make something of ourselves."

"Who says we ain't going to? I'm going to be a big country star. What about you? What are you going to do?"

"Well shit, what can I do? I'm a girl. I guess the best I can do is marry some guy that's got a chance of making something of himself."

"Like me, huh?"

That conversation killed their merry mood. Soon they headed out of the building. Before leaving, Maria grabbed Marty Winters' picture and stuffed it under her shirt. On the way out, they stopped at the girls' room and turned off the running spigots. Water was standing a good quarter inch deep on the floor and had seeped out into the hallway and all the way to the teachers' lounge. They thought that was quite enough. They didn't want to do any real damage.

#

Marty and Maria went shopping for an engagement ring and wedding band. She tried on a dozen or more. Most of them were far too expensive. They finally found a set for less than two hundred dollars, and the jeweler agreed to let them pay it off in three monthly installments.

The next question was when were they going to get married and where. If he went to college they could not afford to get married right away, but if he went ahead and completed his active duty in the Navy, they would be able to afford it, barely. At least the Navy would provide a living wage of sorts. That was one more item in Marty's growing list in favor of active duty. Maria could get a job — he assumed she would be willing — and he could save up so he could finish college or do whatever he might want to do after his two-year hitch was up. So they agreed that he would go ahead and sign up, and as soon as he got settled in a permanent duty station she would catch a bus or a train to wherever he was, and they'd get married. Being on the West Coast, he assumed he'd end up being stationed in San Diego, or maybe even as close as Bremerton or Whidbey Island. It never entered his mind that the Navy could send him all the way cross-country to Norfolk, Virginia.

Marty's Aunt Lily never took that vacation to Vancouver. She just couldn't afford it. But she did drive up to Seattle to spend one night with her sister, and Marty and Maria spent that night together in bed in Aunt Lily's house. They started out on Aunt Lily's couch, sitting up, arms wrapped around one another, kissing so long and hard that their lips were soon swollen. And then they slipped down to lie together, and he crushed her breasts with his hands and reached a hand up her skirt until she grabbed his wrist and clamped her thighs together, preventing him from going any further. Breathlessly and almost in tears she said, "I want you so much. Oh my god you can't imagine how bad a want you. But we have to wait. We have to wait until we're married."

"But why?" he moaned. He rolled off of her, relieved to take a deep breath and work the kinks out of the hand that had been trapped between her legs. "What's so special about it being after we're married? I'll still love you just the same."

"But the first time is special, and I want it to still be special on our wedding night."

"Oh, it will, it will," he said. "It will be special every time from now until we grow old and die."

She had brought with her a brown paper bag, which she had dropped on the floor next to the couch. She said, "I've got a nightgown in the bag. I'd like to put it on, and I'd like for us to sleep together. Just sleep. Just hold each other. Can we do that?"

He said, "I guess so. Yeah. That'd be better than nothing. But can I watch you get undressed? I just want to see your body."

But again she said, "No." She said, "That's special, too. When you see me naked for the first time, I want it to be on our wedding night."

"Oh, that's so romantic. Yeah, I can do it. I can wait. But it won't be easy."

"Not for me either."

She carried her brown paper bag into the bathroom and, a few minutes later, came out wearing baby doll pajamas and a gauzy pink nightgown. The body he so much wanted to see naked was clearly visible through the translucent cloth. He had already stripped down to boxer shorts and crawled under the sheets. She climbed in the bed next to him and snuggled close. Throughout the rest of the night they kissed and rubbed their bodies together, periodically falling asleep but waking up whenever one or the other moved.

#

Before putting in for active duty, Marty went over to Chuck's house to tell him his plans and remind him that they had vowed to go together, to hold him to their promise.

Marty had first befriended Chuck when they were in the seventh grade, back when nobody else would, back when Chuck was gangly and clumsy, and so shy he couldn't even bring himself to saunter up to the counter at Dairy Delight and order an ice cream, back when bigger and stronger boys called him sissy and his only response was to cry, long before he grew into the self-assured and fun loving athlete all the other kids looked up to. It was Marty who first talked Chuck into trying out for the baseball team, and it was Marty who set up Chuck's first date with a girl — a double date, Marty with Barbara King and Chuck with Brenda McKnight. Whenever he thought wise-cracking Chuck was getting a little too big for his britches, Marty would remind him of his "humble beginnings." He'd say something like, "Just don't forget how I stuck with you back when you weren't such a hot shit athlete."

Of course it went the other way as well. Chuck had stuck with Marty, too. He'd gotten him out of no telling how many scraps. Marty had a horrible temper that boiled over many times in the first years after his parents were killed. He'd get mad over silly things. He'd throw things and punch the walls. He got in so many fights it was a wonder he had a single friend left in the world. He surely would have alienated all of his friends if he did not have, when he was not angry, such a winning personality. He truly wanted to be liked by everyone and would go to great lengths to please others. He had no problem agreeing with both sides of an argument. Everybody was right. Nobody was at fault. Until something unforeseen and usually trivial triggered that violent temper. And Chuck was always there to break up the fights before they got good and started. He would calm everyone down and get them to shake hands and make up.

It was Chuck who talked Marty into joining the Navy Reserve. "They're going to get you, man. One way or the other. When you turn eighteen, they're going to draft your ass, yours and mine both. I'm talking about the Army, marching through mud and slime, combat boots, heavy backpacks, assholes shooting at you."

"They won't get me if I go to college. I can get a deferment."

"Yeah, but a deferment, man, that's just putting it off. Sooner or later we're going to end up in the Army. But the Navy Reserve, that's just two years active duty. No big deal. And we'll be on a ship. We can go to places like Paris and Rome and make out with foreign chicks."

Marty parked Aunt Lily's Fury in front of Chuck's house, one wheel up on the curb. He hesitated to get out, embarrassed to face Chuck after abandoning him for a girl, thinking about that silly song "Wedding Bells are Breaking up That Old Gang of Mine." Purple shadows cast by the huge oak tree in Chuck's front yard lay like swathes of cloth across the sidewalk. On his broad front porch a big hammock swung between a post and an eyehook screwed into the wall by the door. It looked so inviting that for just a moment Marty wanted to lie down and stay there for the duration of the summer.

But he didn't lie down. He knocked on the door, and Chuck opened the door with a snide, "Well look who's here. If it ain't Don Juan himself. Man, show a guy a nice pair of tits and he forgets he has friends." He said it with a mischievous smile on his lips — lips that had always looked strangely soft and downright pretty for such a big, strong guy. Marty was relieved to see the welcoming grin on his friend's face.

"What can I say?" Marty said. "I'm thoroughly pussywhipped."

"You wish. I bet she ain't even puttin' out."

"Not yet," he conceded, "but the time's coming soon. We're going to get married."

"When?"

"Soon. I'm signing up for active duty. I hope you'll come with me. As soon as we get stationed somewhere permanent, I'll send for her. You can be my best man."

Chuck's reaction was breezy and matter-of-fact: "Sure. Might as well. Can't dance. There's nothing else I want to do for the next two years."

#

Maria kissed him goodbye at the railway station. They boarded the train and secured their gear in the compartment, and then headed for the club car where they got into a poker game with two other sailors traveling from Naval Base Whidbey to Norfolk. These were older men, first class petty officers with grizzled faces making them look much older than their thirty-some years. They drank beer and played poker all the way across the country. The rocking of the train made the beer go to Marty's head faster than usual. He felt a little queasy but tried not to let it show in front of the older men. He also suspected they were cheating them, but he couldn't catch them at it. By the time the train arrived in Norfolk, Marty was flat broke. Thankfully, Chuck was not as broke. He had hidden away what his mother always called mad money, and that was all the two of them had to keep them going until payday. There wasn't much of anything on base to spend money on, anyway — cigarettes and beer at the EM Club, and postcards to send home to Maria. Marty didn't even smoke, although Chuck did take it up.

They put in for radio school. Thirty guys in their Navy whites sitting in front of typewriters with headphones to their ears six hours a day learning Morse code. "Forget about dots and dashes," the instructor said — a grumpy petty officer with a pot belly. "Alls you got to do is train your fingers to hit a certain key when you hear a certain sound. Dit-dot, you hit the *A* key. Dit-dit-dit the *S*. And like that there. We start slow and build it up."

Pretty soon the more advanced students were sending each other dirty jokes in code.

Six weeks after Chuck and Marty entered radio school, Maria arrived on the bus from Olympia, rumpled and bedraggled from the long trip, but looking fabulous to Marty.

He had rented an apartment in anticipation of her arrival. The rent was thirty-five dollars a month — dirt cheap even then and even in that neighborhood. He bought fresh linens for the bed and towels for the bathroom, and cooking utensils. He wanted everything to be perfect before she arrived, but he'd never before furnished an apartment, so he left out a lot of essential items such as forks to eat with and soap for washing up.

He met Maria at the bus station, and they walked to the marriage office with him carrying her bags. The ceremony was conducted by a government man with a title something like Norfolk Marriage Officer. There were so many sailors in Norfolk wanting to get married in a hurry that they had to have a special guy whose only duty was to perform marriages. Marty thought that was neat. The ceremony lasted no longer than fifteen minutes. When it was done, they caught a city bus to the apartment. Their wedding apartment. Upstairs to their wedding bed with its fresh new linens. The ceremonial altar he had prepared for the moment when, at long last, he would see her naked body, touch her, enter her. He wanted to carry her over the threshold, but she didn't give him a chance. As soon as he got the door open, she rushed in and plopped down on the bed, giving it a bounce or two. Marty followed lugging her two suitcases and dropping them just inside the door.

"This is it, huh?" she said.

"Yep. Our own apartment." He pulled the door shut but remained standing just inside as if stupefied to be there.

"Married at last. I'm Mrs. Marty Winters."

"Yeah. I love the sound of that. Now we can — I mean, can we — I mean, should we wait until — "

"Oh no, I want you right now. I've been waiting a long time for this."

She immediately sat up on the bed and pulled her blouse over her head and tossed it on top of the suitcase. She kicked her legs up in the air and scissored them to wiggle out of her pants and throw them in the general direction of where she had thrown her blouse. She unsnapped her bra and slipped out of her panties. He stood in a dumb stupor gawking at her. She said, "Undress. Hurry up."

He started undressing as fast as he could, fumbling with buttons (God damn the Navy and their thirteen-button pants.)

Naked at last, he lay down beside her. She tossed a leg across his body and straddled him. After they made love and she brought him to a climax once inside of her and a second time with her mouth, and afterwards when they were lying satiated on top of the rumpled sheets in pools of sweat, he said, "Wow! I never expected anything like that. Where in the world did you learn to do those things?"

"Nowhere," she said, sounding somewhat taken aback. "I mean, I-I've never done this before. You know that." And after a big blow of wind to catch her breath she added, "I just did what felt natural."

His only response was another breathless "Wow!" He counted himself extremely lucky.

#

The apartment was on Ocean View Boulevard, a street that ran straight from the base to the beach. It was about ten blocks from the gate to the apartment, and another four or five to the beach. There was a dinky little amusement park at the beach, with a clanky little roller coaster and a few other carnival rides and tawdry games of chance. It was open only in the summer. At the road side of the beach stood a clump of gnarly trees that leaned severely away from the ocean, tilted that way from years of standing up against winds off the sea. On summer afternoons the beach was crowded with families and young adults, nearly all Navy families.

Between their apartment and the beach there was a grocery store and a coin laundry. That little nexus of beach, home, grocery and laundry was their whole world, not counting Seaman Apprentice Winters' duty on base, first at radio school and later aboard the U.S.S. Taconic. Their main form of entertainment was people watching at the beach. They would watch young families with their children cavorting in the sand or lovers strolling along the water's edge, and make up stories about them. At night they listened to music on Marty's portable stereo (they didn't have a TV), and they talked, and they made love. Rarely, they went to a movie at the little movie house on the corner. But the movie house showed mostly old war movies, which neither of them liked. There was the occasional backyard barbeque with Chuck or their across-the-hall neighbors. The only time they ever splurged on an evening out was on Marty's birthday, when they went night clubbing in Virginia Beach.

Their apartment was one of many in an old gingerbread house. At the very top of the house, in what had obviously once been an attic, two apartments were separated by the landing at the top of the stairs, a space measuring three-by-five feet with three doors and an open stairway. One door opened onto an outdoor metal staircase that looked a lot like a fire escape and gave access to the back yard where seven military couples and three young children shared a small patio and barbeque grill. The inside stairway led down to the second and first floors where there were more, and larger, apartments occupied by petty officers and their wives and children. The top floor apartments were so close that if the doors were opened at the same time, they would knock together. Sammy and Melissa Greenwood rented one of these attic apartments; Marty and Maria lived in the other. It was a single ten-by-twelve-foot room with a six-by-eight-foot kitchen jutting out on one end and a bathroom just large enough for a shower stall, sink and toilet. They didn't need much space. Marty had his stereo and his Royal typewriter. Those and his books, all paperback novels, were the only things he owned and the only things he had any interest in. (Years later he would become a news junkie, but back then he had no interest in what was going on outside their own little world). So far as he knew, Maria just hung around the apartment all day when he was on base. The idea of her getting a job, which they had talked about before getting married, seemed to have been forgotten; and for reasons he could not explain he hesitated to talk to her about it — put it off for so long, in fact, that the passage of time itself became a reason for not bringing it up. The only things in their apartment that spoke of her existence were her clothing and makeup. She didn't *do* anything. Oh yeah, sure, she cooked — her limited repertoire of meat balls and mashed potatoes, hamburgers and cheese omelets — and she cleaned the apartment, which took all of ten minutes; but she didn't do anything for relaxation or entertainment. She didn't read or play board games or collect anything. The only thing she did do was exercise to keep her body in shape. And never was there a body more perfectly in shape. She knew it, too. Her figure was her greatest source of pride. She loved to show it off. Sometimes she exercised in the nude, doing deep knee bends and stretching exercises, and down on her back bicycling her legs in the air. It drove Marty crazy watching her do that, and of course she dearly loved driving him crazy that way. Remember the way female figures were described back then? By the number: measurements in inches of bust, waist and hip. *Playboy* always listed the Playmates' measurements, as if pictures of them in the altogether weren't enough proof that they had lovely bodies. Well, Maria's measurements were 34-24-35, just about perfect by Hugh Heffner standards, but not perfect enough to satisfy her. She believed the top and bottom numbers should match on the ideal figure, and she refused to accept that that 35 was right. "Aw, come on, you must have made a mistake," she said when Marty ran the tape around her hips at her request. "Do it again." So he measured again. The number was undeniable.

"See," he said, holding the tape up with his thumb marking the spot. It's 35 inches."

"Try it again. It's supposed to be 34."

Finally catching on that she would never be satisfied until she heard the number she wanted to hear, he measured again and said, "You were right. I must have read it wrong before. It's 34-24-34." That made her happy.

As Chuck had pointed out, much to their delight, they were a perfect match physically. She wasn't the only one with a beautiful body. Even though Marty wouldn't have been caught dead using such a feminine term as *beautiful* in relation to his own body, it was something to behold —

not as massively muscular as Chuck's body, which he greatly admired, but sleek like a statue of a Greek boy, with muscular calves and biceps, and a belly that was tight as a drumhead. He was just as vain as Maria, too. He was adept at striking provocative poses without making it look as if he were posing. It was a skill he had developed in high school during gym classes when the girls shared half the gym, a skill he had further perfected out at Long Lake during the summer when he wanted the girls to take note. His fantasy had been that once a girl saw his perfect body in nothing but bathing trunks she should throw herself at his feet. Of course it never worked quite like that with most of the girls back home. But it sometimes seemed to work that way with Maria. They had a kind of mutual but unspoken voyeur pact.

He would always put his book down to watch her perform her naked calisthenics. One time he decided to strip down and join her in her exercises, with unexpected results. When he tried to do jumping jacks and push-ups with his penis hanging loose, he became acutely aware of the heft of it bouncing about, and it started to grow like Pinocchio's nose. It got as hard as a fence post. It took on a life of its own, convulsing like a runaway fire hose. Maria went into hysterics laughing at it. Her laughter infected him. They both started rolling around in fits of laughter, and she grabbed him and shouted, "Put that horse in the barn before it stampedes!" — and they forgot all about doing calisthenics. After that, naked jumping jacks became a regular prelude to sex. But that, of course, is redundant; everything they did was a prelude to sex.

#

Maria made friends with Jennifer Greenwood, their across-the-hall neighbor. They spent a lot of time together while their husbands were on base. They fixed each other's hair and compared notes on eye shadow and blush and mascara. Jennifer, who was close to the same size and build as Maria, only thinner (32-24-34), and who — like Maria — was obsessed with her looks, had drawers full of sexy lingerie that they took turns trying on and modeling for one another. One day Maria met Marty in the hallway just as she was coming home from Jennifer's and he was coming home from the base. She had a sly sparkle in her eye and a thick paper catalog in her hand. Pictured on the cover was a sexy model in black lace underwear. It was a Fredericks of Hollywood catalog, specialists in sexy clothing. She had borrowed it from Jennifer. "How'd you like to see me in some of these?" she teased.

"I'd much rather see you *out* of them," he retorted, matching her teasing tone.

They looked through the catalog together. It was filled with pictures of models in sexy lingerie. Lots of lace and lots of cleavage, most in virginal wedding white or S&M black, some in fiery reds, and all catering to the popular notion of women as either whores or angels, or, more enticing to the men, angels who become whores just for them. "I don't know," Marty said. "Why would I want to see you in stuff like this when I get to see you all the way naked?"

"But I thought men liked that sort of thing."

Actually he did, but he thought she would be more impressed with him if he was above such clichéd male obsessions. He said, "Well, yeah, but — I don't know. Maybe."

Continuing to leaf through the catalog, they came to a section featuring swimsuits, and Marty said, "Now here's something I'd really like to see you in," pointing to a tiny, butter colored bikini.

"Oh God, I couldn't wear that."

"Why not? You sounded more than willing to wear see-through underpants."

"Yeah, but that would be just for you. A bikini, that's in public. Look at how little that thing is. I'd be mortified."

"Aw, come on," he challenged her, "I know you'd get a kick out of it. All the other girls would be jealous, and all the guys would be thinking how lucky I am."

She did order the bikini, and she did wear it to the beach. They spread beach towels on the sand and plopped down in the sun, she on her stomach with Marty sitting beside her. They had brought along bath towels for drying off after they plunged into the surf, and they had packed suntan lotion and snacks and Marty's Polaroid camera in her large tote bag. Maria rolled a towel into a ball to use for a pillow. "Grease me up," she said, "before I burn."

He poured generous globs of Coppertone suntan lotion into his palms and rubbed it on her shoulders and down her back, and covered her legs and feet. "Turn over now so I can get the front."

She turned onto her back. He slathered the lotion across her shoulders and collarbone, and over the soft swell at the top of her breasts. Sneakily he let a hand slip under the top of her suit and circled her nipples with his fingers. "Stop that, now, you silly man. People are looking." She slapped his hand away.

"I need to get some pictures of you," he said.

"OK," she said. As she pushed herself to her feet she looked around to see who might be watching. There was a heavy woman off to the left who was busy digging in the sand with her two young children. To their right were two young men, probably sailors judging from their short hair and tattooed arms, reclining on folding chairs with an ice chest between them and cans of beer in their hands. Marty got out the camera and she struck a series of provocative poses, typical pinup poses with jutted hips and hands clasped behind her head, and leaning forward to accentuate the roundness of her breasts. She looked at the beer drinkers and saw that they had their eyes on her. When she saw another couple walking toward them, she said, "That's enough," and she lay back down on the towel.

A few minutes later the two men stood up, folded their chairs and picked up their cooler, and walked past Marty and Maria, stopping not five feet away and staring at her. They didn't sit down or say anything. They just stood there staring at her with the most blatant lust in their eyes either Marty or Maria had ever seen. If she had been a stripper in a club and they had been drunks sitting right up against the stage slipping dollar bills under her G-string, they couldn't have been any more obvious.

Maria jerked to a sudden sitting position and covered herself with her bath towel. The two men sauntered on down the beach. Marty heard one of them say to the other as they were walking away, "It was a good show while it lasted."

Maria waited until they got about twenty yards away, and then she stuffed everything back into their tote, pushed herself up and headed toward home, kicking sand with every step. Marty had to run to catch up with her.

"Did you see the way those men looked at me?" she asked, once they were back in their apartment and had changed out of their bathing suits. They had not said a word all the way home, but had walked as fast as they could and had burst into the apartment gasping for breath.

"Yeah, I saw. God, I've never seen anything like that. I thought it might be kinda cool to see other guys look at you in your bikini and be envious of me, but Jesus Christ I've never seen such pure naked lust."

"It was creepy."

A few days later they went back to the beach. This time she wore her old one-piece bathing suit. It was late afternoon, the coolest part of the day, but in Norfolk in the summertime there were no cool parts to any day. The sun was white hot. They had to wear sandals or else suffer sand scorching their feet, something they had painfully learned on their first outing to the beach. The combination of rolling waves licking the beach and heat waves hovering above the sand created the optical illusion that the world was shifting. Their bodies were wet with sweat, and at one point while walking through the sand Maria faltered and grabbed Marty's arm for support. "Let's find some shade," she said.

They headed away from the shore, their feet making mouse squeaks in the sand, and found a shady spot underneath one of those gnarled up trees near the street. Maria complained about the heat and begged him to get her a cold drink. There was a little store about a block away, so he walked to the store and bought two ice cold Cokes from one of those wonderful old coolers where you reach down into the icy water and swirl your hand around to find the drink you want.

When he came back, he saw that Maria was in trouble. The same two men who had stared at her with such naked lust were there with her again, and it looked like they were attacking her. One of them was holding her by both elbows from behind, and the other one had what looked like a beer bottle in his hand, and he was holding it against her upper chest. Marty ran to them as fast as he could, and without stopping or slowing down in the least, he ran smack into the man in front, swinging the Coke bottle gripped in his right hand. He felt the jar of bodies colliding when he ran into the men. It was as if he had dashed blindly into the side of a wall. Maria was knocked to the side, and he did not even see her fall. He felt blood in his eyes and on his hands. His vision blurred and everything was tinted crimson. The man fell backward and Maria screamed, and the other man grabbed Marty around his chest, but he somehow shook free of him and pounced on top of the first man, hitting him over and over while the other one tried to pull them apart, and for a while he could not see or hear or feel anything but was lost to all consciousness in a bloody red rage.

Then he felt other arms wrap around him, and he couldn't break free, and there were sounds of men shouting, but he could not understand the words. Gradually he calmed down and came to his senses. He realized that the men holding him were the cops who regularly patrolled the beach. The cops asked questions that he could not at first understand. A babble of words that sounded like garbled chatter on a radio station with bad reception. Then, as if someone were fiddling with the knobs to tune it better, the words began to become clear. "How'd this get started?" the policeman asked.

"These guys were attacking my wife. One of 'em was holding her and the other one looked like he was trying to hit her with a beer bottle."

"I was just holding the beer," one of the guys said.

The other one said, "I was rubbing suntan lotion on her. She asked me to."

"I did not! I just had the lotion in my hand, and I asked you what you were looking at."

"We're sorry. It was just a misunderstanding. And this guy, hell, he was just trying to defend his lady. I'd a probably hit me too if I'd been him." He had an ugly red whelp on his cheek where Marty had hit him.

Maria said, "Maybe it was just a misunderstanding. I don't know. I don't want anyone to get in trouble."

"Ya'll better git far away from each other," one of the cops said. "And stay the hell away from each other. If I catch a one of ya'll fighting again you're gonna go straight to jail."

"Yes sir," the men said, and they turned and walked away. Marty also said "Yes sir," and added a thank you.

It was only later at home that he realized just how berserk he'd gone. "I liked to've shit in my pants," he told Maria. He had gone into such a murderous rage that if the police had not broken them up, he might have killed the guys. To be overtaken by such rage was something he knew he could never let happen again. But how could he stop it when he never saw it coming and never knew what he was doing while he was caught up in it?

He thought about it constantly over the next few days. He talked about it so incessantly that Maria finally said, "Just shut up and leave it the hell alone."

He began to think that maybe he should see a psychiatrist about his anger, because he knew there was something scary inside of him that he could not control. But he didn't seek help. He let it simmer until it cooled, and then he pushed it out of his mind, just as he had pushed it out of his mind the many times back in high school when Chuck had kept him from starting some stupid fight.

The first time his temper had blown out of control like that was when he was in the ninth grade. He had never before been in a fight, and he was sure he never would. If it came to that, he thought, he would simply walk away. His parents, his aunt, coaches and teachers had all impressed upon him the idea that it was more courageous to walk away than to fight, even if your friends called you queer or sissy. But he said it was Chuck who really convinced him. He thought of Chuck as the biggest, baddest boy in Olympia High School. Chuck wasn't scared of anybody, but he'd never let anyone goad him into fighting. The object lesson to Marty was that if a guy like Chuck could walk away from a fight and not care who called him sissy, anybody could.

Perhaps he would have backed down anyway. With or without Chuck's Gandhi-like example, Marty had simply never been the kind of person who would get in a fight. He might get mad enough to scream at his friends or maybe even hit a wall or throw something, but he would not intentionally hurt another person. Not until after his parents were killed and his emotions were raw and jangled, not until once at a high school dance when he snapped for no good reason. At the time, his arm was in a cast. He had taken a hard fall while playing baseball and suffered a small fracture. He was rather proud of his cast, signed by all his teammates. It was like a badge of courage, a war wound. He was dancing with Barbara King, holding onto her with one hand only, the glaring white of the cast held out like a shield near her face. Barbara was wearing a wide skirt that flared out like a tent. One nasty little trick the boys at school liked to pull on the girls was to sneak up behind girls wearing those big skirts and flip them up, exposing layer after layer of petticoats. They all did it. Sometimes they'd gang up and a couple of the boys would hold the girl while a third slowly, and with great fanfare, lifted her petticoats one after another, counting out loud. It was just one of the many rituals in the sex games they all played. The boys never went far enough to expose more than was acceptable, and the girls trusted that they wouldn't. It was a teasing game. The girls usually played along and laughed with the boys, even if they didn't think it was funny. Marty, however, suspected that deep down the girls were scared to death and madder than they ever let on. This time, while he was swirling Barbara on the dance floor, some kid he hardly even knew reached out and flipped her skirt up from behind, not even exposing anything but a brief flash of white silk. And Marty lost his temper. He attacked the guy in a fury, trying to bludgeon him with his cast. The guy backed off the dance floor and picked up a chair and held it up to ward off the blow. He was like a lion tamer with a whip and a chair. Marty swung at him with his cast. He slammed it against the chair and cracked it open. Searing pain shot up his arm, and everything went black. He later said he couldn't remember anything between seeing the guy reach for Barbara's swirling skirt and Chuck and two other guys holding him off. That was the first time Marty could recall such a murderous rage.

#

When Marty came home on the day of his twentieth birthday, Maria met him at the door with a lump of collapsed chocolate cake held out in her hands like a sacrificial offering, tears streaming down her cheeks. "I can't do anything right," she wailed. "I'm such a bad wife."

"Aw, honey, it's all right. You tried. That's all that matters." He fought off the urge to laugh at the sad looking cake.

"Do you still love me?" she asked.

"Of course I do, more than ever. I love that you cared enough to bake a cake and that you care enough to cry when you messed it up."

With that, she let loose a whole new flood of tears.

"I'll tell you what," he said, "Let's go to the Cavalier Club and have a real celebration."

"We can't afford the Cavalier Club. That place is really expensive."

He said, "To hell with the expense. Let's do it anyway."

The Cavalier Club was a swanky club. Everything was red: red lights, red candles on round tables covered with red tablecloths, seats cushioned with scarlet. The band played show tunes and old standards from the big band era. Marty asked the bandleader if they could play "True Love," a lush, romantic tune from some movie they'd seen, which they had decided was their song. The bandleader laughed at them as if he thought they were just the cutest couple he'd ever seen, as if they were little kids playing at being grownup and in love. They were a little bit embarrassed and a little bit peeved, but dancing to that song in that romantic setting was one of the most wonderfully grownup things they had ever done.

#

After finishing radio school, Radioman Third Class Winters was stationed on the *U.S.S. Taconic*, a lumbering old ship homeported in Norfolk and designated for communications between other ships in their group. Chuck also stayed in Norfolk, but not on a ship. He was assigned as an instructor in the school they had just graduated. That winter Marty got word that his ship was going to embark on a six-month Mediterranean cruise. "I know it seems like a long time," he said when he told Maria.

She asked, "What am I supposed to do in a one-room apartment when you're overseas?"

"Chuck will check on you, and you have friends across the hall and downstairs."

She said, "I don't want Chuck checking in on me. He's your friend, not mine."

That surprised him, but he didn't pursue it. He asked her what she wanted to do, and she said, "I think I want to go home to Olympia and stay with Mama until you get back."

The night before he was to leave she said, "I'm not going to cry. I'm not, I'm not." She cooked meatloaf and mashed potatoes for supper that night, and they ate in silence. She blinked back tears, and he saw her bite her lower lip a few times to keep from crying, but she had sworn not to cry and she didn't. They promised to write every day. They went to bed, made love, drifted off to sleep, woke up and made love again.

He cooked the breakfast the next morning and had it ready to eat before she crawled out of bed — scrambled eggs, toast and grits with sausage links and two cups of coffee. He told her again that he'd write every day. She said, "Me, too." Neither of them could think of anything else to say. He got dressed. He hefted his duffle bag to his shoulder and kissed her goodbye, and he walked out and slowly descended the stairs. At the front door he heard her cry, the cry she had been holding back since the night before, the loudest, longest cry he had ever heard, like the cry of an abandoned child, like the cries of Third World women seen on television newscasts of a flood or hurricane in which their loved ones are swept away. It was all he could do not to turn around and rush back up those stairs and cradle her in his arms and swear, "I won't leave, I won't ever leave." But he walked out the door and to the sidewalk, turned left, and walked the ten blocks to the Naval Station. There he caught a bus to the piers where he headed up the gangplank of his ship, her cry ringing in his ears all the way. He heard that agonized cry reverberate off bulkheads and rattle over steel gray decks, he heard it in the twisted twang of ropes and in the slap of water against the ship's hull as the *Taconic* crept across the wide Atlantic. He replayed it in his mind every day for two weeks of plowing across open water, until they finally reached their first port of call, the Rock of Gibraltar.

He stood in line at mail call and waited while they passed letters out to what seemed to be everyone else on the ship. There was nothing from Maria, not even so much as a postcard. After mail call there was a pep talk of sorts from the deck officer who told the men to enjoy the sights on the rock and warned them not to pet the monkeys. Gibraltar, they were warned, was overrun with wild monkeys. The officer warned that although the monkeys might seem playful and harmless, they could do a lot of damage with their teeth.

Nobody got bit by a monkey. There were no predatory monkeys in any of the other ports they visited. After Gibraltar, the only thing they were warned about was venereal disease. They cruised to Valencia, Spain, where they wandered narrow streets and toured ancient cathedrals. Next they went to Barcelona, where Marty visited a replica of Christopher Columbus's ship the *Santa Maria*. It was much smaller than he would have imagined. Then for two weeks they played war games, circling a little island called Cabrera while a Marine contingent practiced beach landings. During these exercises, the radio shack was on constant alert, even though nothing real was happening. They worked eight-on and eight-off. Barely able to sleep during the off hours, most of the guys played poker. Marty played some, but mostly he spent his time reading or just wandering the decks looking out over endless gray ocean. It was during that time that he took up smoking. There wasn't much else to do.

Their next port was Naples, where the guys from the radio shack went on tours to Rome and Pompeii. In all of those ports, the sailors toured the sights in the afternoon (liberty call began at sixteen hundred hours) and then hit the bars as soon as night fell. And the bars they went to, no matter what port they were in, catered almost exclusively to American sailors. In every bar there were three or more whores for every sailor, and few sailors resisted the temptation. Among the few who resisted were Johnny Craybill, a third class petty officer from some little town in Texas, who was engaged to a girl from his hometown and said he couldn't cheat on her, and a boatswain's mate named Abe who was reputed to be gay. And there was a guy named Rossing who avoided the bars and the whores for religious reasons. And there was Marty. It wasn't that he wasn't tempted, and it wasn't that he was any more virtuous than his shipmates. But he was afraid of what might happen if he went with some whore and Maria found out, or if he got some kind of disease and went back home and gave it to her.

As it had been at Gibralter, there was no letter from Maria in Valencia, and there was no letter in Barcelona, nor in Naples. It wasn't until they anchored in the harbor at Cannes that he finally got her letter. He carried it down to their compartment and sat on the edge of his bunk to open it. He read it, dropped it on the deck, and picked it up and read it again. Could this be some horrible mix-up? Someone's letter sent to the wrong person? Some other Maria? Some other Marty? She said she wanted a divorce. She had come to realize that she didn't really love him and he didn't love her. They had been children playing the game of love, she said, and now that he was gone she had had time to become fully awake to reality.

He was stunned. There had been not even the slightest hint of a warning. If someone had asked Marty then, he would have said their marriage was perfect. They never fought. They made love voraciously. How could she possibly claim they had never loved each other? He wrote back, pleading with her to reconsider, offering every proof of their love he could think of. She answered the first of his letters but none of the many that followed. Then his letters started coming back marked *Moved, no return address*. He called her mother. She said she hadn't heard from Maria. He thought about calling their friends back in Washington, but when he tried to recall who their mutual friends were he realized there were none. Throughout the remainder of the Mediterranean cruise, he kept trying to contact her, but it was like shouting into a canyon and not even hearing an echo.

While anchored near Naples, he got a letter from a lawyer in Nashville, Tennessee, with divorce papers and a waiver for him to sign. "Fuck it!" he said out loud. "I'm not signing this shit. If she wants a divorce, she's going to have to meet me face to face in a courtroom." But he eventually came to accept the futility of his situation. By the time he finally signed his name to the waiver and put it in the mail some three weeks after receiving it, it had been folded and unfolded so many times it was almost in tatters.

Unlike dropping a letter into a post box back home in the states, dropping it into the mail slot onboard the *Taconic* was not an irretrievable act. But symbolically it was an act of utmost finality. He dropped the letter then caught the next liberty boat to the pier in Naples, and he went into a bar and quickly downed a whiskey sour and ordered another, and when a whore came up to him and said, "Hey Joe, fucky fucky?" he said, "You goddamn better believe it, Babe."

Yet he couldn't help but hold out hope that he was caught up in some strange nightmare he would eventually wake up from. Maybe at the last minute she would realize her mistake and change her mind and rush back to Norfolk to be waiting on the pier when his ship pulled in.

#

From their last port of call it took fourteen days to cross the Atlantic. When they finally pulled into the harbor at Norfolk he stood waiting at the rail in his dress whites, standing at attention with hundreds of other sailors as the boatswain's mates cast out the lines to secure the ship to the pier, straining to see all of the faces in the waiting crowd. The boatswain blew his whistle and sailors ran down the gangplank to sweep up wives and children and girlfriends in their arms. Still he stood scanning the faces, wondering if there was the slightest possibility that she was standing on the pier but had changed so much he could not recognize her, knowing, of course, that that was impossible. He stood in place until there was no one left on the pier except for sailors on work detail, and then he went below decks to their sleeping compartment and changed out of his dress uniform and lay on his bunk in his skivvies and listened to the creaking of the ship.

Nothing but gray soup outside. Then white light flashing off the wing. A wing tip sliced through a cloud obscuring the summit of Mount Rainier, and Marty felt at home. He had never before appreciated the beauty of home. Growing up where clouds banked under the mountain, he had assumed that everyone had a mountain in their back yard that reached almost three miles into the sky, that 400-foot waterfalls and 200-foot trees lurk around every bend. Going away and coming back, he fell in love with his homeland — discovered it as if for the first time. He could hardly wait to haunt the stalls at Pike Place Market again, or eat a juicy burger at Big Bob's in Olympia.

His plan was to stay with Aunt Lily while attending classes at the University of Washington. At least for the first quarter. Once he got settled in, he would find a part time job and maybe get an apartment. Maybe find a couple of buddies to split the cost.

Aunt Lily picked him up at the airport shortly after noon and treated him to a late lunch at a restaurant near the site of the recently held World's Fair. The restaurant was way out of her price range, but she wanted something special to welcome him home. They faced each other across a small table. He found himself staring at her because she looked so much like his mother. He wondered if they'd always looked alike and he simply hadn't noticed or if the family resemblance was increasing with age. "I know you'll need a way to get around," she said. "You can use my car any time. I hardly ever drive it. Since I had my eye operation, I don't see well enough to drive safely. Oh, I guess you didn't know about that, did you? Yes, I had a cataract operation."

"I'm sorry. No, I didn't know."

"So I tell you what, I propose an exchange. You take me to my doctor's appointments and my Friday evening bridge club, and shop for me once a week, and the rest of the time the car is yours."

"That sounds like a good deal to me," he said. "Would it be OK if I ran down to Olympia tomorrow? There are some old friends down there I'd love to see."

"Sure. You go right ahead. I'm sure you must miss your friends."

After lunch they walked around the site of the fair. Aunt Lily proudly pointed out the Space Needle and the monorail. "It's like living in the twenty-first century," she said. "Can't you just picture what it will be like when you're my age — people zipping around in little one and two person jets, moving sidewalks? They say cars will drive themselves and nobody will ever have a wreck." But he was thinking about a run-down twentieth-century amusement park on the beach in Norfolk, and walking hand-in-hand with

Maria on a sidewalk that moved not from some futuristic mechanics, but from the giddiness of their love.

Early the next morning he headed to Olympia. It was a nasty day, like God had poured dirty water over the whole damn world. Driving through Tacoma he heard what he thought was the dull rumble of thunder, a dire omen, he thought, since thunder is so rare in the Pacific Northwest. But then he realized it wasn't thunder at all, it was the damn soldiers at Fort Lewis shooting off their big guns. He'd forgotten about their incessantly booming ordnance.

Aunt Lily had not taken good care of the Fury during the few years Marty had been away in the Navy. It was badly in need of a tune-up. It shook whenever it got over sixty. The worn-to-the-bone windshield wipers smeared more than they cleaned, and made a squeaking noise as if they were dragging a pebble across the glass. Despite the smeary wipers and the thunderous boom of guns, and a gray sky, he was excited about going home. He kept running various scenarios through his head, in all of which Maria welcomed him back with open arms, in all of which they kissed and hugged with passion such as he could barely remember. He also imagined beating Billy Boone to a pulp. Over and over he pictured a right cross to the jaw and Billy flying backward to the ground. So engrossed was he with his silly reveries that he almost missed his turnoff in Olympia. He swerved at the last minute and nearly sideswiped another car. The driver sat on his horn. Marty made a futile attempt to signal his apologies with flying hands. His heart was racing so he had to pull to the curb and drop his head to the steering wheel and take a few deep breaths. He tapped a Marlboro from his pack and fired it up, the flame from his Zippo dancing from the shaking of his hands. The cigarette tasted like crap, so he tossed it out after a few puffs, vowing for perhaps the twentieth time in the past six months that he was going to quit. He cranked up his car again and drove more slowly along the waterfront on East Bay Drive. He looked for the Olympic peaks in the distance, but they were hidden behind a wash of gray. He drove up the steep and winding hill on San Francisco Street and right on Puget to Maria's mother's house, circling the block twice, finally deciding he needed to freshen up before confronting her. So he drove to a nearby convenience store and bought a toothbrush and paste and a comb, and used the men's room to wash up and comb his hair. Finally he drove back to her house, parked and walked up to the porch. He noticed that in the few years he had been gone her house had deteriorated considerably. Paint was peeling and dandelions in the front yard were a solid expanse of yellow. The front porch swing he had sat on with Maria was hanging by a broken chain with one corner of the seat touching the floor. He felt like King Arthur when everything in England was dying — go away a couple of years and everything falls apart, well, if not everything at least Aunt Lily's Plymouth Fury and Mrs. Perez's crummy little house.

He knocked on the door. Mrs. Perez opened the door but stood behind the unopened and locked screen. She slumped to one side with a ratty old robe hanging loose off one shoulder, a bottle of beer in her hand. "She not here," she said.

"Oh. Uh —" He didn't know how to respond.

"She not live here no more."

"Oh. Well, uh, Mrs. Perez, do you know where I could find her?"

"I don't know where she's at. I not seen her since you took her away" — followed by some mumbled Spanish he couldn't understand.

Marty didn't believe her. He said, "Please, Mrs. Perez. I just want to talk to her. I just need to find out what happened. If she still doesn't want anything to do with me, I'll go away and never bother either of you again." He clung to the hope there had been some ghastly mistake. There had to have been, some crazy misunderstanding that he could clear up if only he could talk to her. It just didn't make any sense that she would up and leave him with no reason, that she would suddenly decide she no longer loved him or, as she indicate in her letter, that she never had — not when she had been so obviously in love with him right up until the night before he left for the Med cruise. He remembered walking away from her for the last time, that horrible cry as he descended the stairs and walked away from the house. No woman who could cry like that at the prospect of separation would then want to extend that separation to forever. He thought someone must have gotten to her somehow and forced her to leave him — and if that someone wasn't that goddamn redneck Billy Asswipe Boone, then it had to be that self-centered mother of hers.

But she sounded pretty sincere when she said, "I'm not lying to you, son. If I knew where she was I'd tell you. She wrote to me back when she left you, and she told me not to worry 'cause she was fine. But that's all. Not a word about where she was going or anything. *Nada.* I not hear from her since. I been worried sick."

"Well if you do hear from her, please call me."

"I don't have your number."

"Oh. Right. I don't have it either, right now. I'm staying with my aunt in Seattle. I'll get the number to you as soon as I can."

He didn't know what to do afterwards. He didn't want to drive back up to Seattle until he was absolutely sure Maria wasn't in Olympia. But other than finding her — which was beginning to look futile — there was nothing in particular he wanted to do in Olympia, no old friends he wanted to visit, despite what he had told Aunt Lily. He drove downtown and had a cup of coffee at the Spar. He sat in a booth near the front window and watched people passing by on the sidewalks. Some scruffy guy was strumming a guitar right outside the window. Every once in a while passersby would stop and listen for a few minutes and drop a few coins into his open guitar case. Marty recognized one of the tunes he played, "Michelle" by the Beatles. It made him want to cry.

He went to a few auto repair shops and asked if anyone knew Billy Boone, figuring that he had probably worked at some of the local garages. At the third garage the owner said, "Yeah, I know that bastard. He left here owing me over two hundred dollars."

"Do you know where he went?"

"Nah. But if you find that sumbitch tell him I want my fucking money."

"I'll tell you what," he said, "If I find him I'll beat the two hundred out of him and gladly give it to you." That made him feel better. He asked the mechanic if he knew anyone else who might know where he could find Billy Boone.

"There's a guy named Chico. Bartender at No Cover. He might know sumpin." He remembered Chico. He'd been one of Billy Boone's buddies in high school.

Back downtown he located No Cover, a nondescript concrete block building with beer advertisements on the window. Through the smeared glass he could barely see the dark interior. A sign on the door indicated they opened at six o'clock. He drove back past Mrs. Perez's house and parked half a block away, and kept an eye on the house until about six. Then he went back to the Spar and grabbed a bite to eat and walked from there to No Cover. He asked for Chico. "He comes in at eight," the bartender said. He looked at his watch. Seven fifteen. He ordered a beer and found a seat in a corner where a lounge area had been set up with a few chairs and a chess set and some magazines — outdated *Playboy* and *Esquire* and *Sports Illustrated* and *Rolling Stone.*

The walls were painted the dull and brittle black of old roofing material. Psychedelic posters were plastered on the wall behind the bar, unreadable in the dim light. Other than a lamp in the reading section, the only lights were small spots on the empty bandstand and lighted beer signs in the windows and behind the bar. He skimmed through the magazines and waited for Chico. When he walked in, he recognized him immediately — the squinty eyes and oily black hair, now grown shoulder length, his arrogant way of rolling his shoulders when he walked. He was wearing an Army jacket. Marty recognized a shoulder patch indicating service in Vietnam. He gave him a little time to take over from the afternoon barkeep. Then he approached the bar. He was still the only customer in the place.

"Hey, Chico. I'm Marty Winters. I went to school with you. Remember me?"

"Yeah, I remember you, but I didn't figure you knew me." His head twitched when he spoke, like he was dodging phantom punches.

"Sure, I remember you."

Chico had played drums in Billy Boone's band and also, for a brief time, in the high school marching band. "You were a hell of a drummer, Man. You had hands like lightning. Do you still play?"

"Some. I sit in sometimes with some of the groups that play here."

"I see you were in 'Nam. That must have been rough."

"Yeah. Tough enough. What about you? Were you in country?"

"No, not me. I did my tour on a ship in the Med. My buddy Chuck was over there, though. Chuck Nagel. Remember him?"

"The baseball player. Sure."

They swapped do-you-remembers and whatever-happened-to-so-and-sos for a minute or two, which gave Marty the opening to ask, "Whatever happened to Billy Boone?"

"Ol' Billy took off for the East Coast a while back, chasing after some little piece of tail."

"Really?"

"Yeah. He couldn't keep his hands off that bitch. Same little slut he dated all through school. You probably remember her. Maria Perez. Good looking bitch. Not bad in bed either."

Marty gripped the barstool as tight as he could and tried not to let his rising anger show.

Chico said, "That chick, man. She was one hot tomato. There was this one time, man, me and Billy and Roy Martin all had her. I shit you not. Oh man! One after another with the other'uns watch—" He cut it off with dead suddenness when he recognized the expression on Marty's face. He could see that Marty wasn't tickled. In fact, he looked as he was seething inside. Chico cleared his throat and then said, "To tell the truth, I — uh, well, I ain't so goddamn proud a what we done." He started up with the head twitching again. Marty could tell that he was conflicted, ashamed of what he was saying and wanting to back away from it, but at the same time wanting to uphold his manly pride. He said, "Ya see, the thing is I don't think she wanted it. She done it just to please Billy. She'd do anything he asked. I don't know why. Maybe he had something on her, or maybe she was just that crazy in love with him."

In the thirty seconds or so it took Chico to blurt that out, Marty felt first a flood of anger and then complete defeat and resignation. All the old rumors about Maria were true after all, and he was the biggest cuckold of all time. The Maria he thought he loved was a fiction. Hadn't she admitted as much herself in her letter, and hadn't he been stupidly denying it all along?

He finished his beer and tossed a dollar on the bar, saying, "Thanks, man. I got to go now. Nice talking to you." Then he walked out and to his car and drove back to Seattle. He told himself he simply had to forget her and get on with his life. He made up his mind to quit torturing himself about Maria. But it took him a long, long time to get her out of his mind. For years after that he did double takes and stopped in his tracks every time he saw someone who looked the least bit like her. He got a job in a frame shop and went to school part time. It took him six years to get his journalism degree. He continued living with Aunt Lily and seldom went anywhere other than work and school. During those years he seldom dated. He wanted to. He thought it would really be nice to have a girlfriend, but he never felt that kind of attraction for any of the girls he met at school or work. There was a girl named Amy, an English major, that he dated off and on during his senior year. They went to an occasional movie together, and sometimes she would lend him books that he would read and then discuss with her. She loved Richard Brautigan's *Trout Fishing in America*, which he did not like at all, but they both admired Kurt Vonnegut. Amy was a good friend, but they were never romantic.

His college years were a time of upheaval and great social changes, or so the television and newspapers told him. Protests over the war heated up. There was something called the Summer of Love, and later a historical music festival in Woodstock, New York that Marty didn't hear about until after it was over, and later still another historic music festival at the Altamont race track near San Francisco that brought the era to a tragic end. But between work and school, Marty hardly noticed any of those things. He sort of halfway kept up with the news, but hardly kept up with popular culture at all. He heard names such as Leon Russell and Joe Cocker and the Byrds that meant nothing to him, although he could tell from context that they were popular musicians. On the other hand, he knew all about Squeeky Frome and Bobby Seale and Eugene McCarthy.

After getting his journalism degree, he thought newspapers would come begging him to write for them, but it didn't work that way. He sent resumes to all the newspapers in Western Washington and as far south as Eugene, Oregon. Many of them didn't even reply, and the few that did sent polite notes saying there were no openings at the present time. He decided things might be better in another part of the country. Impulsively, and with no plans beyond the next move, he bought a Greyhound bus ticket to Nashville, Tennessee. The last letter he had received from Maria had been postmarked Nashville.

It was a comfortable seventy degrees with a refreshing breeze when he boarded the bus in Olympia. When he crawled off in Nashville three days and four transfers later, it was pushing a hundred, with humidity to match. He peeled the sweaty shirt away from his back, hefted his duffle bag and headed straight for the men's room, where he sponged himself with damp paper towels and put on a fresh T-shirt. Then he carried his bag out into the waiting room and took a seat on a hardwood bench. For the longest time he sat on that bench with his feet resting on his duffle bag, reading the knifed inscription, "Berny loves Ber" on the back of the seat in front, wondering what the unfinished name could be (Bernice, Bernadette, Bernadine?) and imagining some kid carving his name on the seat and running away when some authority figure approached — scared to ever come back and finish the name.

He listened for a while to music coming from a portable radio held by a guy on the other end of the bench. It was Bob Dylan singing "Blowin' in the Wind." Even Marty knew who Dylan was. He recognized his nasal tone, but he'd never paid close attention to his music before. The voice grated on his nerves at first, but after listening to a few bars, it started to grow on him. He was singing about how many years can some people exist before they're allowed to be free, and Marty thought he must have meant black people in the South, and here he was in the heart of Dixie feeling as out of place as a black man at a Citizens Council meeting in Philadelphia, Mississippi, where the three civil rights workers were murdered. (He had been on a ship in Norfolk when they were killed, and some of the Southerners on the ship joked about it, saying, "It was just a bunch a ol' boys out coon hunting.")

He thought the guy with the radio looked like a bum. Unwashed. Hair like broom straw. Untrimmed chin whiskers a shade lighter than his hair. He watched the guy push himself off the bench, pick up his radio, sling a tattered pack over his shoulder and walk away. The tune from his radio kept playing in Marty's mind long after he had pushed through the door into the bright sunshine and turned a corner out of sight. It was such a strange and haunting sound. The lyrics wouldn't let go. Singing about freedom. He had never given much thought to freedom except as a kind of rah-rah, All-American platitude with little concrete meaning. Supposedly he had spent two years in the Navy in order to protect freedom, although all they did was sail from port to port, get drunk and get laid. And now he was in a strange city where he knew no one and no one knew him, as free as he had ever been.

Maybe it was the heat that started him reminiscing about the Navy. Summers in Norfolk had been so unbearably hot, and below deck on the

Taconic had been an oven. Right before he got out of the Navy he had talked to Chuck about what they might do, still entertaining fantasies of two lifelong buddies facing life together. It was another of those oppressively hot days in Norfolk. Chuck was alone in his barracks, wearing skivvies and a T-shirt, sitting in front of an oscillating fan and an open window, curling twenty-pound dumbbells. The smell of his sweat was strong. The whole time they talked he kept curling those damn dumbbells, machine-like. "I'm not planning on getting out," he announced.

"Are you crazy?"

"Maybe I am, maybe I'm not. I'm putting in for underwater demolition training, the SEALS."

There was nothing more dangerous in the Navy. "Now I know you're crazy," Marty said, "but that's you all over again — always got to prove what a man you are." Chuck sat the weights down and flashed him a culpable look, but picked them up again without owning up to it.

Starting along about the time he entered puberty, Chuck had become one of those guys who have to prove they're manlier than anyone else — not a bully (in fact he had been the target of bullies and had great sympathy for kids who got picked on) — but definitely a guy obsessed with strength and courage. In the eighth grade, he could lift more weight and run farther than any other boy in his class, and later, in high school, he could chug-a-lug the most beer in the least amount of time and make out with the prettiest girls. But there had been a time, back in elementary school, when he had been so much the opposite of that that his parents and teachers were seriously concerned. He played with dolls. He preferred girl playmates over boys and would play dress-up games with them. He would get into his mother's makeup and paint his face. When he was in the second grade, the teacher asked all the boys and girls to tell what they wanted to be when they grew up and Chuck got up in front of the class with such a proud smile on his face, like he'd been waiting all his young life for this chance to share his wonderful secret, and he said, "I'm going to be a ballerina."

The class howled. The teacher turned red in the face and stammered, "You can't be a ballerina. Only girls can be ballerinas. Wouldn't you rather be a fireman or a policeman?"

"No. I want to be a ballerina."

"But that's for girls. You're not a girl."

"I will be," he said. "When I grow up." He said God meant to make him a girl but made a mistake. "But He's going to fix it before I'm all grown up."

All the kids started chanting, "Girly, girly, girly. Sissy boy."

"Shhh. Quiet now. That's not nice," the teacher reprimanded them.

On the playground that day, one of the bigger boys started a fight with him. Chuck held his hands over his head to ward off the blows, and all the other boys and girls circled them and shouted, "Hit 'em, hit 'em, hit 'em!" until the teacher finally broke them apart.

"You were right there with the rest of the kids shouting for him to hit me," Chuck reminded Marty many years later, but Marty claimed he didn't remember that incident.

Eventually Chuck got fed up with being picked on. He quit playing girly games, to the great relief of his parents. He started to get really good at football and baseball. He started lifting weights. He took boxing and wrestling lessons down at the community center. When he became a star athlete in high school, hardly any of the kids remembered that he'd ever been anything but. After two years in the Navy Reserve, he was still obsessively bent on proving his manhood. And if anyone accused him of over compensating for being a sissy as a young boy, he would adamantly deny it. To Chuck, joining the SEALS was just the logical next step in growing up.

But it was the worst possible time to re-enlist and become a SEAL. The war in Southeast Asia was escalating, and the SEALS were in the forefront of the action, with some of the most dangerous missions in Vietnam.

Marty said, "If you stay in they're going to send your ass to 'Nam."

"I know that," Chuck said. "That's why I want to stay in. I think I have a duty to defend our country."

Marty knew there was nothing he could say to change his mind. "It's your funeral," he said. "Write to me if you live long enough."

He had not heard from him once in the six years since. Seated on a bench in the bus station in Nashville, hardly willing to admit he was there because the divorce papers from Maria's lawyer had come from an office in Nashville, and not having the slightest idea where to go from there, he puffed on a Marlboro and thought maybe he should go out in search of a cheap hotel. A figure passed by in front of the window, wavering like a desert mirage in the sunlight. It was the flower girl he had been watching off and on since getting off the bus. He judged her to be about eighteen or nineteen. She wore a yellow dress of the kind you'd expect to see on a farm wife, cotton worn smooth and frazzled at the sleeves, hanging from her shoulders like wash from the line. He watched her sell the last of her flowers and take a seat across from him. From a shoulder bag appliquéd with daisies she drew out a book and opened it on her lap. The book wore a woven burlap jacket. The girl glanced up from her book and caught Marty's eye, smiled a tight little smile, and crossed her arms over her chest. She looked down at her feet and then briefly glanced up at him again. The corners of her mouth turned up, and then she looked at her feet again. He returned her smile. He couldn't tell for sure, but it seemed like she was flirting.

He hesitated, not too sure of his ability to read such signals, then stepped across to where she sat. "Hi," he said. He saw that her eyes were moist, her skin pale, her face slightly flushed. "I couldn't help but notice your book."

He almost said *boob* instead of *book* because that was what he was noticing at the moment. Her breasts, small but shapely and obviously unfettered by any kind of support beneath the cotton dress, pulsed with rapid breaths. It looked like she was hyperventilating. He said, "I don't think I've ever seen a book cover like that. Did you make it yourself?"

"It's just a cut-up croker sack."

"What's the book?"

"It's the Bible. King James version, the original pure word of God."

"Oh, OK. I just — I don't want to disturb you."

He didn't want to get caught up in any Bible talk. He turned away, but she reached out and grabbed his arm and held tightly. "No, don't go. You're not disturbing me. Sit down."

So he sat down next to her. She took his hand in both of hers and rested their cupped hands in her lap, scissoring her feet against the hardwood floor. She whispered, "Father sent me."

He didn't say anything.

She said, "I prayed for you."

"What do you mean you prayed for me? When? You don't know me." He quickly looked all around the bus station as if searching for someone to save him from this crazy young girl, wishing he'd never approached her in the first place. "You're saying your father sent you here to find me? I don't understand."

"Not my father. Just Father. *The* father. Our father. That's what we call him. He told me it was my time to find a mate and I would know the one when I gave the signal and he came. I gave the signal and you came. You are the one."

"Oh no, I don't think so. I just —"

Suddenly, without warning and with such an innocent expression on her face that you'd have thought it was as natural as sneezing, she farted. She casually hiked her leg and twisted her mouth as if she might have been straining to loosen a bit of food caught between her teeth, and she let out an explosion of gas that would have rattled the windows if there had been windowpanes nearby.

Marty was dumbfounded. First she told him she had come seeking a mate and found him, and then she just cut a big one right there on the bus station bench, and acted like it was nothing out of the ordinary. She didn't even turn red or make excuses or anything. He wondered what could possibly come next. A part of him wanted to get as far away from her as he possibly could, while another part of him was strangely drawn to her. But he couldn't have broken free if he'd wanted to, because she grabbed his arm and held tightly. He also found her very attractive, not just physically but also (he had to admit) in her weirdness and unbelievable audacity, and in her vulnerability and natural beauty. There wasn't anything particularly sexy about her, at least nothing so obvious as luscious lips or sleek and revealing clothes, and yet she stirred sexual need in him, and that had rarely happened since Maria left. He didn't want to admit it, but there it was.

She asked him whether he was waiting to catch a bus or had just got off one.

"I just got here," he said. "I was thinking about looking for a place to stay, maybe find a job and stick around for awhile."

"Are you a guitar picker?"

"No."

"I thought maybe you was a guitar picker. Just about everybody that comes to Nashville is a guitar picker."

"Nope. Not me."

"If you need a place to crash, you can stay with us. We've got a big house and everybody's welcome."

She farted again and said, "Praise the lord." Then she said, "I didn't tell you my name. I'm Marigold. We're all named after flowers. All the girls, that is. Father says we're all flowers in the garden of the lord." (He was tempted to say something sarcastic about farting and fertilizing the garden of the lord, but decided against it.) She said, "The guys are all named for men in the Bible. What's yours?"

"My what?" It took him a second to realize she was asking for his name. She rushed so headlong from one subject to another that he had a hard time keeping up. He told her his name was Marty, and she said, "That'll do for now."

The house where Marigold lived with a ragtag group of young people was in a neighborhood not far from Vanderbilt University. It was a neighborhood of stately old homes with aged brick and faded white siding set on gently rolling lawns shaded by gigantic oaks and magnolias. It was a long walk from the bus station, but they took their time, stopping to rest now and then. Sweat beaded on his brow and his shirt was plastered to his back again. He might as well not have bothered with a sponge bath in the Greyhound station. Marigold offered to carry his bag, but he told her he could handle it. He would have felt funny having a girl carry his bag.

They stopped at a park where there was a large replica of the Parthenon. He told her he had seen the real thing in Greece, and she said, "Far out." Seated on the grass in a ragged circle in front of the Parthenon, a bunch of young people passed a joint around. "We could probably grab a hit if you want," Marigold said, but he said no, he didn't want to.

After walking another five or six blocks through a residential neighborhood, they arrived at the house. It was a two-story house fronted by a large porch with Corinthian columns and whitewashed walls that were peeling and worn through to the bare wood in places. A sloppily painted peace symbol and a Christian fish symbol adorned the front door. Tie-dyed sheets served as front window curtains. Marigold took him in and introduced him to the eight or nine people living there at the time. Their names were Lily, Rose, Petunia, Orchid, Peter and Paul, and of course, the one they called Father. They arrived just in time for dinner, which Rose and Petunia served at a large table with mismatched chairs. Before eating, everyone held hands and Father said a prayer. Someone farted during the prayer, and someone shouted, "Praise the lord!" Dinner was steamed cabbage and pork and beans cooked with maple syrup. Beans and cabbage was a staple of their diet, and it gave everyone gas. Since they figured the beans and cabbage were God's blessed bounty, they habitually said "Praise the lord!" when anyone passed gas.

After dinner Father led everyone in another prayer. "It seems like all they do is pray and fart, and fart and pray," Marty said to himself.

Everyone said "amen." There was a general shuffling, pushing back of chairs, gathering of dishes. Marigold leaned close to Marty and asked, "Do you want to sleep with me tonight?" That threw him for a loop. Right out of nowhere, tossed off between "Amen" and "Grab those glasses, will ya?" He felt like he had to get a handle on this girl, and quickly — this girl who had brazenly blurted out, only moments after they met, that he was ordained for her by the Lord (or maybe by the one they called Father; perhaps in her mind Father and the Lord were one and the same). He felt as if he had waded into a creek and ended up in raging river currents. Was he getting himself into some bizarre religious cult that he wouldn't be able to get out of? Nah, he reassured himself, he was being paranoid. These flower girls and their soft-spoken boy friends were not part of a cult. Even their leader, if that's what he was, seemed harmless. Besides, the house was in the middle of a city; there were neighbors; there were no bars on the windows. There was no way they could possibly hold him against his will.

He hesitated, and her mouth turned down in a pout. They remained uncomfortably quiet for a minute or two. Then she broke the silence by suggesting they go outside away from the others. She took his hand, stood up from the table and led him out to the front porch. The sun had gone down and a milky moon bathed the lawn with light filtered through magnolia leaves. The night air had done little to ease the heat. Two houses down kids were running through the swish of a lawn sprinkler. A mosquito spray truck rumbled up the street trailing its cloud of poison, and the neighbor kids chased after it.

Marty and Marigold sat on the porch steps.

"Don't you think I'm pretty?" she asked.

"Yeah, I think you're pretty."

"But you don't want to sleep with me."

"I didn't say that." He scraped his foot on the edge of a step. He scratched his head. He tried to smile at her, and he shrugged his shoulders. The truth he couldn't quite formulate in his brain was that he desperately wanted to sleep with her, but her casual yet possessive manner scared him. After Maria left him, he assuaged his loneliness with countless whores in every port in the Mediterranean, but then, after returning to the states, there was no sex at all. He might as well have been a monk. But it wasn't by choice. It was because he had lost confidence in how to be with a woman.

Finally he said, "It's not that I'm not attracted to you. I am. Really. Look, if it was just — you know, casual. Well I'd be flattered. God knows I'm really turned on to you. But you said I was *meant* for you. That sounds like you mean for a lifelong mate. I'm not looking for anything permanent."

"Aw pshaw. I don't expect you to marry me. I just want to ball you. You put way too much importance on sex. We're not like that around here. Heck, we're not hung up with all the old fashioned taboos. If you want to know the truth, pretty much everybody here has slept with everybody else at one time or another. It just doesn't mean that much. As for that stuff about you being meant for me, well obviously you're not ready for that. When the time is right it will happen. In the meantime, you're free. No expectations, no jealousy. We love and live for the moment."

Again she took his hands in hers, like she had at the bus station and earlier when she led him out to the porch, but this time more emphatically, as if she were setting a misinformed child down to tell him the facts of life. "We have a belief here that when a new person comes the hospitable thing to do is make sure he has a companion for the night. You're the new person. I'm offering myself. That's all. And it'd be really nice if you accepted."

Like she was the chocolate covered almond in a Godiva assortment. Marty had heard about some native tribes that would offer up their wives for a night. He had heard that it was the custom among Eskimos. Maybe these hippies had adopted that practice as a part of their religion. Marigold said that Father based it on the story of Sodom and Gomorrah. "The strangers came to town and Lot offered up his virgin daughters, but the wicked men of the town didn't want to sleep with his daughters. Instead, they wanted to defile the strangers who came to town, who were messengers from God. God was pleased with Lot for offering his daughters. That's why he saved him but destroyed the rest of the town."

He could think of many reasons to avoid Marigold's bed. For starters, she was nowhere near as beautiful as Maria, and he was not in love with her. And the strangeness of their way of life frightened him. He could picture what it might be like if he gave in to the pressures of the cult and ended up marrying her. There'd be a day and a night of intimacy and maybe a celebration with lots of pot, and then — wham! the very next night watching as she traipsed off to bed with the next hippie to stop in for a night, her turn to play ultimate hostess. He pictured himself ten years down the road selling flowers to travelers at the bus station and carrying all his hard earned pennies back home to Father. Six years of college resulting in him turning into Eliza Doolittle. And speaking of Father, which night of the week would be Marigold's night to fuck Father? Would he get the solace of a romp in the hay with Orchid or Petunia on those nights — a consolation prize as it were? He even thought for a moment that sleeping with Marigold would be a betrayal of Maria. Would he ever let her go?

Finally, embarrassed that he'd made the whole thing into something much more momentous than it was, he told her that yes, he'd love to sleep with her. "I don't know why I hesitated. It's just that — well, I was married, you see, and we got divorced, and I'm not quite over her yet."

"Well if you're divorced, I guess it's about time you let her go," she said.

"That's what I just told myself."

Back in the house everyone had plopped down on couches and chairs or sprawled on quilts in the front room to listen to music. Most of the music was new to Marty, except for an album by the Doors. There was some Indian music, which was dreamy and kind of created in his mind a sensation of floating, and there was a Dylan album. He was proud that he recognized Dylan's voice. The record got stuck and repeated one line over and over — "Everybody must get stoned" — and nobody bothered to fix it for the longest time. Everybody laughed about the endlessly repeating verse, and one of the guys said it was groovy.

Then it hit. The gas. As if it had been lying low since dinnertime just waiting to catch him off guard. It was like a boulder in his stomach cramping his abdominal muscles and roiling downward in spite of his manly efforts to hold it back. Never mind that the whole lot of those flower girls and would-be apostles had been cutting farts left and right, he wasn't going to let one go in front of people he'd just met. But he couldn't stop it. It rolled out like a long note on a tuba, and suddenly all of those people who had been incredibly blasé about their own symphony of gaseous percussion acted like they were horribly offended at his social blunder. One of the Bible boys shouted, "Eeyew!" and another one shouted, "Jesus, man!" The one called Orchid said, "Something must have crawled up in you and died, man!" Marty's face flushed red. He felt the fire. He tried to stammer an apology. That's when they all broke into laughter. Marigold said, "They're just kidding you. We do that to every new person that samples our beans. It's kind of an initiation rite around here."

#

It was getting late. Conversations had quieted to sporadic murmurings. It had been a good half hour since anyone had put a new record on the turntable. For long moments the only sound was the constant whistle of katydids and occasional creaks and groans of the old house. One of the guys wandered into the kitchen and came back with a bowl full of mushrooms. The bowl made the rounds, with people pulling out hands full and popping them into their mouths. Marigold said they were magic mushrooms. "They're hallucinogenic. Don't worry, they won't hurt you. They'll just put you in a real mellow place, and maybe you'll see some nice colors."

The mushrooms were sour tasting and gritty, and whatever magical effect they were supposed to have was slow in coming. For a while Marty didn't think they had any kick at all, but then at one point, when he went to the bathroom and looked at his reflection in the mirror, he thought his face was the funniest thing he'd ever seen, as if he were seeing himself for the first time and realized how silly he looked. His hair looked like a bunch of wires sticking out from his head. He imagined them all sparking like the Frankenstein monster when they shot the juice to him. He stuck his tongue out, looked crosseyed, made monster faces in the mirror. So this is what it's like to be stoned, he thought. He wandered back into the living room laughing hysterically.

He snuggled up to Marigold and cradled his head in her lap. She smelled like summer rain. Colors swirled overhead, and he felt as if he were in an inner tube floating on gentle waves. One of the other girls, Petunia, crawled around the room kissing everybody. When she got to Marty, she planted a long, hard kiss on his lips and filled his mouth with her tongue. Then she kissed Marigold just as long and hard. Such passionate kissing, such freedom from shame and possessiveness, such beautiful colors and otherworldly music, such uncomplicated joy in touching and seeing and hearing — he felt as if he had entered a world where all of the harsh edges had been brushed away, and he wished he could share it all with Maria.

#

When he woke up the next day he could tell from the angle of the sun through the front windows that it was nearing noon. He was on the couch. He vaguely remembered having drifted off to sleep the night before. Marigold had thrown an old blanket over him and kissed him goodnight and gone off to bed, leaving him alone on the couch, still a virgin in Father's house. The house was quiet. He got up and slipped into the bathroom and borrowed someone's toothbrush to brush his teeth, after discovering he had failed to pack one. He told himself it was Petunia's toothbrush. Since she'd had her tongue down his throat the night before, it was too late to worry about getting her germs. Nevertheless, he ran hot water over the bristles for a long time before using it.

He opened his duffle bag and dug out a clean shirt and pants, and quickly dressed and walked out the front door. He halfway expected Father and some zombie-like recruits of his to bar the door and not let him leave, although there had been little other than his feverish imagination to give rise to such suspicions. Nobody saw him leave.

He caught a bus downtown and searched out the law offices of McCain and Neuman, the office that had sent him the divorce papers. It wasn't much of an office, a waiting room with two chairs and a receptionist's desk. Nobody in the straight back chairs to read the year-old copies of *Life* and *Look*. The receptionist looked to be no older than sixteen. Blonde hair fanned out from her face in thick clusters, heavy makeup failed to hide pimples on her nose and chin. She was chewing gum and wearing a lime green mini-dress with a huge bow at the waist. "You got an appointment?" was her greeting to Marty.

"No, I just need some information. I need to know how to get in touch with one of your clients."

"Can't help you there. That's privileged information."

"But she's my wife. You handled the divorce."

"If we handled the divorce, she ain't your wife no more." (He wished people would quit pointing that out.)

"But it's really important," he said. "It's a matter of life and death." (That line always seemed to work in the movies.)

She wouldn't give in and neither would he. He told her he wasn't going to leave until he got what he needed (which also worked in the movies). She pushed a button on an intercom and said, "Mister McCain, can you come out here, please?"

McCain came out, a corpulent man with a too-tight tie and a face like a ruby red balloon. "What's the trouble?" he asked.

Marty told him he needed to find Maria and tried to explain how important it was. He told him that she had filed the divorced papers under duress. Making it up on the spot, he said, "The man she's living with now is abusive. He's practically holding her prisoner, and he'll hurt her if she tries to contact me. I got a message from her mother begging me to find her and get her out before it's too late."

It looked like McCain was softening. His expression said he was beginning to believe Marty's story. Or maybe not. More likely he just figured telling him what he wanted to know was the easiest way to get rid of him. He said, "I can't give you her address or phone number. That would be illegal. But I can tell you this much: She said she was going back home, and I reckon you know where back home is."

Back home? Had she been there all along? Had he come all this way for nothing? He decided to walk back to the house, thinking a slow stroll would give him time to think about whether he should stay in Nashville or head back to the West Coast.

The house was empty when he got there, except for one girl who was washing dishes. "Where is everybody?" he asked.

"They're all at the airport selling flowers. That's how we pay the rent on this place."

"Oh, I see. And it's your turn to stay home and clean house?"

"Smart guy. You figured it out. We share the work and we share the play, and we share the love of the Lord. That's how it works around here. Far out, huh?"

"I forget. Which one are you?"

"Orchid."

"Orchid. Oh yes. Is there anything I can do to help you?"

"No, I'm just finishing up. I was going to go outside and soak up some rays. You want to join me?"

"Sure. Why not?"

She went into the bathroom and came out a few moments later carrying two large towels and a tube of suntan lotion. She was wearing cut-off jeans with patches on her butt cheeks and a bright red halter top. She grabbed a portable radio on the way out. In the front yard she spread the towels on the ground, sat down and tuned the radio to a rock station. And then lay down on her back and threw one arm across her eyes. Marty snatched his shirt over his head and dropped it to the ground, and stretched out next to her on the other towel. She squirmed about a moment trying to assume a comfortable position, sat up, untied her halter, tossed it aside and lay back down, her breasts exposed to sunlight and to Marty, as well as to anyone who might happen by, including two men seated in lawn chairs next door. The neighbors looked to be in their mid-twenties. They were shirtless and wore white cotton pants of a type worn by adventurers in Arabian deserts. One of them was quietly strumming a guitar. They waved at Marty and Orchid. Marty waved back but Orchid didn't. Her eyes were closed. He looked at her naked torso, breasts flattened against protruding ribs, brown skin sparkling in the midday sun. He gathered that nakedness, or near nakedness in front of the neighbors was commonplace.

A large truck turned the corner, music blasting from within. It was the strangest truck he had ever seen. It was an old delivery truck spray painted with swirls of color not unlike those he had seen under the influence of the magic mushrooms. A hole had been cut in the top of the truck bed, and the top part of a 1940s Cadillac had been welded onto it, creating something like a gun turret from a World War II bomber, with windows all around. People were standing in the turret section, and they waved to Marty and Orchid as they drove by. The driver blew his horn. As they drove past and Marty turned his head to watch them recede down the block, he was greeted with an even more startling sight. Another glass turret of sorts had been welded onto the back of the truck, this one a bubble of smoked glass, and projected onto this bubble was a film of wildly dancing figures. Naked men and women with flowing hair, their bodies decorated with war paint.

"That's the truckers," Orchid said, sitting up and putting her halter back on. "At least that's what we call them. They're a bunch of hippies from California. Hey, can you tie this for me?" She turned her back to Marty, holding the two loose ends of her halter. He tied them in a bow. She kept talking. "They live in that truck, all five of them, two couples and a kid. They park next door and the band lets them use their bathroom and stuff. The guys next door are part of a band. They're pretty cool. We sometimes go over and listen to them practice."

He didn't know about the guys in the band, but he sure thought the truckers were cool. He wanted to be one of the truckers.

He wondered why they passed right by if the next door driveway was their current place of residence. He guessed they had passed by for the sole purpose of dazzling them with their music and the crazy film projected on the back of their truck, and that they would circle the block and then park in the band's driveway. He was right. Soon the truckers wheeled around the corner and pulled to a halt next door and piled out of the truck and ambled over. One of them said, "Hey, we're going out to the reservoir. Who wants to come?"

Orchid said, "Nobody's home but me and Marty, but we can go." Turning to Marty she said, "That cool with you, man?"

"Yeah, sure. Why not?"

They all clambered into the truck. Marty saw that it was tricked out like a camper with pull-out beds and a table, and a wood burning stove. On the way out to the reservoir he got to know the truckers. They were Steve and Driver and Mary and Nellie Bly and Nellie's son Free. Steve was one of the most handsome men Marty had ever seen, tall and powerfully built, with eyes like pale azurite and yellow hair that flowed in waves over his shoulders. Marty was shocked to feel what could only be described as a surge of desire when he looked at Steve. If he was a woman or if I was gay— Marty thought, but he quickly dropped it and turned his attention to Driver. Driver was heavy and dark, with a five o'clock shadow that looked like it got started at ten in the morning. When not talking, he constantly hummed to himself, keeping time with hands that drummed on the steering wheel. Mary was a wisp of a girl with dirty brown hair and no discernable figure under her loose dress. Nellie Bly was older. She looked to be in her mid-thirties and could easily have passed for a schoolteacher or librarian if she hadn't been living with a bunch of crazy hippies. Free looked to be about twelve years old. He looked like everybody's picture of Huckleberry Finn.

Steve put Country Joe's "I Feel Like I'm Fixin' to Die Rag" on the turntable, and everybody sang along (Marty learning the lyrics quickly).

> And it's one, two, three,
> What are we fighting for?
> Don't ask me, I don't give a damn,
> Next stop is Vietnam;
> And it's five, six, seven,
> Open up the pearly gates,
> Well there ain't no time to wonder why,
> Whoopee! we're all gonna die.

Marty got swept up in the rebellious spirit of the song, but he wasn't sure what he felt about its message. He was ambivalent about the war. He remembered that Chuck had been anxious to get over there and prove what a man he was, but now, after seeing a barrage of film clips brought back from the jungles, he wondered if he still felt that way. He'd heard horrific tales about innocent villagers being massacred and about American soldiers pushing captured enemy soldiers out of helicopters — stories that war supporters said were made up by the peaceniks. He had heard the chant, "Hey, hey, LBJ, how many babies did you kill today?" And he'd heard about anti-war protestors spitting on returning soldiers. Was there any truth to any of that? Did both sides stretch the truth beyond recognition? He wondered if Chuck still felt the same way he did when he re-enlisted. He wondered if he was still alive or if he still had all his parts. Marty didn't know if he was for the war or against it, but he knew the song had one thing right: Guys got caught up in the patriotic fervor of war just like they got caught up the fever-pitch of a high school football game. They rushed into war without giving it a moment's thought. He knew that some of the men he had known in the Navy did, and so did some of his old high school buddies. Whoopee! they're all gonna die.

Steve said, "We got some killer acid if you want."

"Acid?"

"Yeah. LSD. You never done it?"

"No."

"Well it's a hallucinogen. It'll get you off and make you see heaven."

"We ate magic mushrooms last night. Is it anything like that?"

"Yeah, multiplied by about a million."

The mushroom high had certainly been pleasant, so he decided to give acid a try.

Steve handed him a tiny scrap of paper. "It's blotter acid. The LSD is soaked into the paper. Just put it in your mouth and swallow."

He swallowed it and waited for something to happen. Steve said it might take a long time to notice. "But when you do — oh boy!"

They drove around the reservoir until they found a secluded area with plenty of shade and easy access to the water. It was much cooler there than it had been out on the road. Through the trees they could see another little glade where a similar group of hippies was camped. Driver and Nelly Bly set up a portable grill and immediately started cooking hamburgers. Steve said, "Let's go skinny dipping," and he and Mary and Free shed their clothes and ran into the water. Orchid followed close behind, leaving a trail of clothes. It dawned on Marty that he had seen more naked bodies in the last twenty-four hours than he had in his whole life — not counting the boys locker room in high school or the men's showers in the Navy — and he thought this co-ed nakedness was such a liberating thing. He wanted to live in a perpetual summer with people who never wore clothes. He peeled off his shirt and pants and ran into the water.

He remembered that when he was a kid there had been nothing so enjoyable as swimming, but now, as they splashed around in the tepid water, he began to wonder why he had loved it so much. Really, for adults at least, there wasn't much to do in the water unless you had a raft or a diving board. So they stood in chest-deep water with toes oozing into mucky mud, and after a few minutes they got out and dried off and waited for the hamburgers to finish cooking.

Only Free remained in the water, content to splash around by himself and send a circle of ripples farther out to where the lake was mirror smooth. A single boat was anchored near the far shore. Marty could barely make out the forms of a man and woman with their fishing poles. It brought to mind a time many years ago when his parents were still alive. He was ten years old. They rented a cabin on Lake Quinault in the Olympic Mountains. Everything there was more intense — everything but the heat, that is. The trees were much taller and closer together. The ice capped mountains that defined the horizon stood higher than the hills of Tennessee. The water was a thousand times colder. But the stillness was the same, the feeling of peace that would never end. He had spent almost every waking moment in the water that summer, while his parents went fishing every day. They fished from a small aluminum boat with an outboard motor, and although they could have easily gone for miles, they never got out of sight. At any moment he could look up and see them floating near the far shore, and he knew that every once in a while one of them would glance up to assure themselves that he was still safe.

Free spotted a water bug on the surface and chased it in a circle with his finger. Marty watched Free's mother to see if she kept watch over him as his parents had when he was that age, and sure enough she did. He turned his attention back to the concentric waves flowing outward from Free. He watched them merge with other waves from the boat, which was now moving, and he became mesmerized with the wave action. He sighted a much larger wave coming their way from far out near the horizon, steadily gathering strength and size. It grew, it grew. It lifted above the lake in a sheet that curled back on itself, soaring higher and higher into the clouds. Lavender sparks danced across the top edge of the wave. He realized that the acid was kicking in. "Wow, man, it's fucking far out," he shouted.

"Stupendous!" Steve said.

"Are you seeing what I'm seeing?"

"Who knows? I'm seeing what I'm seeing and it's fucking beautiful."

The sparks that flittered across the top of the wave became dancing figures, little cartoon animals skipping along the crest of a tsunami. Clouds banged together like cymbal crashes. From among the hippies he had spied through the trees there emerged a woman in white. She tiptoed out onto the lake, skimming the surface as if wearing invisible skis on her feet, her diaphanous gown flowing behind her as she crested the wave and joined in the dance of the animated animals. She was the Venus de Milo with arms. She was Mother Mary, mother of Christ. She was — she was Maria.

How silly, he told himself. He was tripping on LSD, after all. For Christ's sake, he was seeing Mickey Mouse surfing a tsunami. He could see anything. It was the drug. Besides, he knew that he was prone to see Maria in any beautiful woman. He had seen her in a shopping center and a movie theater. He had seen her in uniform at the Naval Base, and he had seen her through the window of a passing car. But for all the times he had willed her to appear in the guise of any woman who happened to share the same general body type or walk, he had never before seen anyone who looked quite so much like her as this woman did; although this woman had red hair. All right, he told himself, she could have dyed her hair. But that wouldn't be like her. But then he no longer had any idea what might or might not be like her. He closed his eyes tight, and when he opened them again everything had returned to normal. Free was still splashing in the water. Mary and Steve were lying on towels, Nellie Bly and Driver serving burgers off the grill. Dorothy was home from Oz and Aunty Em had turned back into Orchid — back in the water and floating on her back, her face and breasts and knees like islands, and her hands and feet like water bugs stirring their own little whirlpools. Through the trees he could see the other group of hippies. The woman in the white dress was still dancing, not out over the water as in his acid hallucination but in the confines of their camp area. Her movements did remind him of Maria.

From far off to the south he heard the drone of an airplane, and soon he saw the plane, first just a speck rising over the trees, then growing larger as it approached. It was trailing a banner. It came closer and closer. He almost fell over backwards trying to read the banner as it flew overhead. The words following the airplane were: *You Ain't Seen Nothing Yet.*

The letters flew off the banner, each letter growing larger and larger, one by one, the *Y* and then the *O* and then the *U* filled the sky and pulsed blood red onto his hands and his arms, and he was dripping blood and the blood was flooding in rivulets into great gushing streams that poured into the lake, and he began to scream, "No, no. Stop it!"

"It's the acid, man. Just flow with it," Steve said. "When you start worrying about losing control, you start freaking out. Just relax and go with it. Know it's just the drug and it won't last and it can't hurt you, and it'll be cool."

Steve was right. He had been there before, and he knew. Marty began to calm down and everything became mellow. Soon they had all eaten their burgers and passed around a jug of wine that Driver had pulled from a cooler in the truck. Marty walked off into the trees, drawn by a compulsion to get a closer look at the woman in white who continued dancing in the glade.

In the shade of trees the air was cool and damp. The pungent smoke from their campfire reminded him once again of his summer on the lake with his parents, of how comfortable and safe he had felt there. He felt like a wood sprite playing hide and seek through the trees, always keeping the dancer in sight. He was sure he had seen her before, and the closer he got the more he was convinced that she really was Maria. Sure, he was still tripping on acid, and he was very much aware of that. So God knows what he might have seen. But he knew Maria as nobody else could know her. He knew her every gesture, and this was unmistakably her. He kept saying to himself: Don't be a fool. Don't get your hopes up. Of all the people in Nashville, what could be the likelihood that she and I would fall in with tribes of young people who decided to spend that particular day at that particular area at the reservoir? And yet, what was so far-fetched about that? They *were* young and this *was* where young people in Nashville went on sunny summer afternoons, and her letter had indicated that she was in Nashville. So why not? Crazier things had happened.

Her dress was long and flowing and accented with a red sash that looped her waist. In Marty's mind that sash wound its way between the trees and reeled him in to where she was. He stood on the edge of the clearing and watched, with what must have been the biggest grin in creation plastered on his goofy face. And you know how sometimes when you awake gradually while dreaming you can continue to dream while thinking clearly about what you're doing? Mentally able to separate dream from reality while still dreaming? That's the way it was with Marty then. He was watching real people and simultaneously tripping out on acid visions. He knew all the people there. They were the whole tribe from Father's house: Lily, Rose, Petunia, Peter and Paul. And his old friend Chuck was there, too, back from Vietnam. And Maria, of course.

She saw him and smiled a glorious smile and danced over to near where he stood, and in a mad rush they were in each other's arms gripping one another in a desperate embrace. And time passed and they were in a house within a room, and they were naked, and he was drinking in the vision of Maria's perfect body, and they crawled into bed and made love for hours, and then they drifted off to sleep, and when they woke up it seemed like days had gone by. She told him about everything that had happened

since he left on the Mediterranean cruise, and she tried to explain —
although there was no way she could make him fully understand — that she
loved him still and would always love him, but that they could never get
back together. That was the part he could not comprehend.

"After you left," she said, "I was so depressed I came within inches
of taking my life. It was crazy, but I knew in my heart that you were never
coming back."

"Of course I was coming back. There was never any doubt."

"I know. I know. But I wasn't being rational. I was lonely and afraid
and guilty."

"Guilty?"

"Yes, guilty for leading you on that first night at the dance, guilty
for not telling you the truth about me and Billy and — well, just so much.
For leading you on. For pretending to be the perfectly nice girl you'd want
to marry. I'm so ashamed of lying to you. But I was blinded with love, and I
knew if I let you know the truth about me you would have run away. I feel
guilty for letting you marry me."

"Are you kidding? You did nothing wrong."

"Yes I did. I did everything wrong. Our whole courtship and
marriage was just a crazy dream. I was not the girl for you and never could
be. You were smart and talented. You were destined for college and a
successful career, and I was uneducated trash. I could never fit in with your
life. Didn't it ever seem strange to you that I never read anything or that
whenever you talked about books or movies or art I just kind of agreed with
whatever you said? Hell, I barely got through high school. I even cheated on
some of the tests, and Mallory White wrote papers for me. While you were
hanging out with the class president and star athletes and writing for the
school paper, I was dating a guy that played country music and whose life
ambition was to be a mechanic. My God, can't you see how different our
worlds were?"

He tried to tell her that none of that mattered, but she shushed
him. "What we had was romantic, and it was wonderful while it lasted, but I
knew — and I think you also knew, somewhere deep inside, that it was
never meant to be.

"I called my mother. I told her that I had to come home. I could not
bear the thought of staying all alone in that little apartment in Norfolk. She
called Billy Boone, and Billy came to get me."

Billy Boone. Of all the people in the world, naturally it would be Billy
who came to take her home to her mother. Marty knew her mother had lied
to him. He'd known it all along, but now he had Maria's word for it. Maria
said that no sooner had she and Billy packed her few belongings in the
trunk of Billy's car and headed west on Interstate 64 then Billy started
talking about Nashville, the country music capital of the world. Billy's real
ambition, of course, had not been to be a mechanic. It had been to be a
country music star. By the time they turned south into North Carolina, he
had talked her into stopping off for a few days in the country music capital,
visions of playing at the Grande Ole Opry in his head. Once they got there,

he refused to leave. He got a job working in a garage. And he started to work on her, too, trying his damnedest to convince her to divorce Marty and live with him.

"He could be terribly convincing," she said. "He always had been able to talk me into just about anything he wanted." She also said he could be nasty and scary, that she was afraid of him, afraid to stay with him and afraid to leave. They were still living together. "Like man and wife" was the way she put it, and Marty had the heartsick feeling that was never going to change. "So where is he now?" Marty wanted to know.

"He went to Memphis with a friend. They'll be home in another day or two." She said, "You better not be here when he comes home. If he comes home and finds you here he'll kill you."

He tried and he tried to talk her into taking him back. "We can go back home to Washington," he said. "You can be close to your mother. Or we can stay here, or live anywhere you like. And the past doesn't matter, and Billy Boone doesn't matter. All that matters is that we love one another."

But she would not give in. They talked until they were talked out, and then they fell asleep again. When he woke up, he was back in Father's house in bed with Marigold. She said, "Wow, man, that must have been some potent acid. You were tripping for like twenty-four hours, and then you slept another ten or twelve."

That was when he found out that instead of going to the airport as planned the day before, Marigold and the others had decided, along about the time he was ogling Orchid's breasts in the front yard, to head out to the reservoir. They were already there when the truckers arrived with Marty and Orchid. It was no coincidence that they had picked adjacent spots near the water. Those were their usual spots. Hallucinating on acid, Marty had mistaken Marigold for Maria. Maybe she played along and gave him the answers he wanted to hear when he thought she was Maria. Or maybe he'd just dreamed the whole thing. He had been so stoned he had no idea what was real and what wasn't. The one thing he knew for sure was that they did make love, and in Marigold's mind — despite everything she had said about sexual freedom — their consummation meant they were mated for life. Suddenly she was no longer the free spirit she had seemed to be.

In bed the next night, or sometime shortly after — time being an almost meaningless concept when you're doing a lot of drugs — she quietly started to cry. Her cry was so muffled that at first he thought she was moaning in her sleep. "What is it, honey?" he asked when it finally dawned on him she was crying.

"Nothing," she said. Then, "You'll see."

He wiped the tears from her cheek. She was lying stiffly on her back, her arms straight by her sides. He reached to hold her hand, and he felt something damp and sticky. He pulled back the cover and turned on the bedside lamp, and saw that there was blood on her wrists. She had cut both wrists and was lying there quietly bleeding to death. Or at least that seemed to have been her intention, but she had not severed the main artery, and the flow of blood was minimal.

He ran to the bathroom and grabbed a towel and rushed back and wiped the blood off. He saw that the cuts were not very deep. He ran back to the bathroom and rummaged through drawers until he found some gauze and tape, and then he rushed back to the bedroom to bandage her cuts. "Why did you do it?" he asked.

"Because you don't love me. I don't want to live if you don't love me."

"But I do love you," he said. "Maybe not the way you'd like, but I do love you." That was a lie and he knew it. But he had to say something, and that seemed to be the only thing that would keep her from trying to kill herself.

#

He stayed in the house with Marigold throughout the rest of the summer. On more than one occasion he tried, as gently as he could, to tell her that he had to go back home to Washington and that she could not come with him. But whenever he mentioned leaving she would get so despondent — more than once again threatening suicide — that each time he agreed to stay a little bit longer.

She did attempt suicide one other time. This time she took a whole bottle of aspirin, and they had to take her to the hospital. He was stuck with Marigold. To leave her would be to kill her. Or so he feared.

#

Steve and Mary came over one day and told them that the next day was Driver's birthday and they wanted to do something special for him. They said laughing gas was Driver's favorite drug, and they had secured a tank of the stuff and wanted to have a laughing gas party on their front lawn. It was crazy the way Steve said they got the gas, which he said was illegal to sell to just anybody off the street. He said they told the guy at the supplier they were sculptors and they needed it for an underwater sculpture project. Like the warehouseman they duped, Marty never questioned how or why they would use nitrous oxide in underwater sculpture, but he admired their cleverness in thinking that up and got a good laugh at the warehouseman who bought their story.

So the next day they all gathered on the lawn and passed around a hose, taking turns inhaling the gas. There was a lot of laughing. That seemed to be the only effect from the gas: about half an hour of silly giggling. Afterwards Steve hung around and talked to Marty for a while. Everybody else went inside. They remained seated on the grass. Steve said, "Man, you're about the weirdest guy I've ever met."

"Really?" he said. "Why's that?" He took it as a compliment.

Steve said, "Because you agree with whatever anybody says. Like you don't have any opinions of your own."

Marty thought surely he must be wrong, but he didn't want to argue about it. Steve was his new hero — a substitute for Chuck, who for all Marty knew, was buried somewhere in Southeast Asia. So if Steve, who flaunted his own weirdness, thought Marty was weird, maybe that was a compliment. Truth be told, Marty was something of a pushover. He always had been. He said, "Yep, that's me all over again."

#

A young guy called Buzz came to the house driving an invisible bike. He came flying up the sidewalk holding his hands out as if gripping handlebars and making roaring mouth sounds that vaguely sounded like a big Harley hog. He stood no taller than five-foot-three. Skinny, with knobby knees and elbows sticking out of a sleeveless shirt and cut-off jeans. Coarse red hair flowed across his shoulders. He said his lifelong ambition was to join the Hells Angels, but he couldn't afford a bike. Buzz had hitch-hiked from California. He said he hadn't eaten in two days. They invited him in and told him he could stay as long as he wanted to.

As was so common, they had beans and cabbage for dinner that night. And Father led them in prayer, and there was a lot of farting. When the farting started, Buzz went into a laughing jag and couldn't stop. Tears streamed from his eyes. Marigold whispered to Marty, "I feel sorry for him. He doesn't have a friend in this world."

After dinner she dragged Marty out on the porch as she had on his first night in the house. This time when she got him alone she said, "Father has asked if I'd be willing to welcome the new guy."

"Do you mean?"

"Yes. I mean share my bed with him. Ball him. Would you mind?"

"No, I don't guess so. I guess I can be cool about this. I knew it was coming sooner or later." Then he chuckled a bit at a thought he was entertaining and added, "Maybe he could ball you in an imaginary way just like he rides that imaginary Harley."

"Yeah, sure. But hey, I think it's pretty fucking far out that you're kind of a little bit jealous but still willing to let go a little. You're a sweetheart. You're the only one I love."

"Yeah, I get it. Ballin's just ballin'."

"Right on!"

So that night Marigold took Buzz into her bed. Early the next morning Buzz took off riding his invisible bike. Marigold took Marty by the hand and they stood on the porch and watched him run away. "He's a strange one," Marigold said. "He couldn't get it up at all. But at least I'm glad I was there for him. What about you? Where'd you sleep last night?"

He said, "I slept with Orchid."

"With Orchid, huh? Far fucking out. How was she?"

"OK."

"Just OK? Was she as good as me?"

"Not even close. You're much better."

"Oh, goodie."

"And you're not jealous?"

"Of course not. Why should I be?"

#

Marty got a part-time job with one of the many underground newspapers that were popping up all over the area. Not really a job; he didn't get paid, but there were free snacks in the office, and usually a joint or two passing around, and he didn't have to wear a tie or punch a clock. The paper was called *Fly on the Wall*. They weren't bound by deadlines, or even a publication schedule, but simply printed an issue whenever they could pull together enough material. It was printed on a mimeograph machine and distributed free of charge in head shops and at the food co-op and a few bars. A few advertisers who sometimes paid their bills pretty much covered the printing costs. Marty covered the local arts scene. He got free admission to plays and concerts. They even let him bring Marigold.

Gradually they began to separate themselves from the other people in the house. Getting stoned every night was getting old. They started going out more — not just to the venues he covered for the paper, but poetry readings and movies, or just taking long walks and talking about whatever popped into their heads. They talked a lot about their past lives. She told him that she had been an honor student in high school and had gone to college for one semester before dropping out. She said she planned to go back some day but not until she figured out what she wanted to be — a social worker of some sort, perhaps, but she wasn't sure. She said she wanted to make a difference. Her broad range of interests meant there was no shortage of topics they could talk about. In Marigold he began to see things he had missed in Maria. Maybe she never thrilled his heart the way Maria had, but she could converse intelligently about poetry and music and philosophy. He thought that maybe in the long run having such common interests might turn out to be more important than romantic attraction. If only she weren't so needy.

Marigold's real name was Selena Ballard. She had lived in Nashville all her life, and her mother still lived in town. She said, "I should probably visit her sometime, but I don't know. I don't think she really cares about me. After my daddy left, she started running around with men and drinking a lot, and I was just a burden to her. She didn't want me around anyway, and I had to establish my independence, so I cut her off. Still, I don't know, I guess I should go see her. She *is* my mother, after all."

"Let's do it," Marty said. "Let's go see her. You should never lose touch with your mother. God, I'd give anything if I could see mine. My parents were killed in a car crash when I was in high school. So believe me, I know, someday you'll regret it if you don't."

"Maybe. But crap, man, I don't know. She's freaking crazy. I mean it."

"Hell everybody's mom is freaking crazy. It comes with the job. How long since you moved out?"

"About a year."

She made it very clear that she wanted to see her mother, while insisting that she didn't. She brought it up three or four times over the next week or two. Every time Marty said, "Let's do it" and every time she said,

"Yeah, but not yet." Finally, Marty insisted, and she gave in, reluctant but relieved.

Mrs. Ballard lived in a small apartment over a barbershop in the heart of downtown. Steep metal steps in an alley led to her door. "This is where you grew up?" Marty asked as they stood at the bottom of the stairs looking up.

"Yep. This is it. Not exactly a suburban estate, is it?"

They climbed the stairs and knocked on the door. The door opened to the smell of bourbon and stale cigarette smoke. Mrs. Ballard was a slatternly woman with dark hair twirled up in curlers. Cat-eye glasses dangled from a chain around her neck. A scoop neck shirt revealed a deep cleavage liberally dusted with baby powder. "Hey there," she said. "Ya'll come on in."

Behind her was a television, a child on the floor in front of it watching cartoons. She looked to be about six years old, dull blonde hair, wearing shorts and a T-shirt.

Marigold said, "Hi, Mama. You surprised to see me?"

"Nah, I knew you'd come around sooner or later. Who's your feller?"

"This is Marty. Marty, meet my mother."

He said, "Hello, Mrs. Ballard. It's nice to meet you."

"Likewise. Call me Katy."

The child shot them a malevolent look, then turned her attention back to the television. "That there's Rebecca," Mrs. Ballard said. "She's my little angel." Then she said, "Ya'll want something to drink or anything? I got some beer if you want."

"Well yeah, I could go for a beer. Thank you."

She stood up and said, "How 'bout you, Selena?"

"No, nothing for me."

Mrs. Ballard shuffled into the kitchen, her fuzzy slippers never lifting off the scarred hardwood floor. Marigold stepped over to where the child was and tousled her hair, saying, "Hey there, kiddo." The kid slapped her hand away and didn't say a word. A moment later Mrs. Ballard slid back in with a can of Budweiser in each hand. She handed one to Marty. It was barely cold. To Marigold she said, "School's 'bout to start up again. You thinking about going back or what?"

Marigold said, "I don't want to talk about it."

"Well don't you think it's high time you did? Dropping out was the stupidest thing you ever did. I swear, Selena, I'll never know what got into you." Addressing Marty, she said, "Less than a year to go. Less than a year! And she could have had a scholarship to State. Throwing away a opportunity like that! I can't believe it."

"Can we just drop it?" Marigold scoffed. (Or Selena. Marty was trying to get used to the newly learned old name. Thrown off stride for a second by hearing her called Selena, he almost did not catch that her mother was talking about high school, not college.)

"What's she talking about?" he whispered.

Selena twirled her finger by her ear and mouthed the words, "She's crazy."

Ignoring her daughter and appealing to Marty as if he were the only voice of sanity, Mrs. Ballard said, "Youngun's these days. Humph! They don't know when they got a good thing. I'll tell you one thing, and you better believe it. Raising this hellion all alone weren't no picnic. She wasn't but six years old — same as that child there — when her daddy ran away and left me without a pot to piss in."

"Stop it now, Mama. Don't you start trying to guilt trip me. We didn't come here for any of that. We came 'cause we've got something to tell you. Something real important." She took Marty's hands in both of hers and squeezed as if trying to put up a big show of solidarity. She blew a stray hair from her eye and smiled at him, the biggest smile he'd ever seen on her face. She said, "We're going to have a baby."

"You're what!" Marty exploded.

Mrs. Ballard said, "I knew something like this was going to happen. I knew it. I knew it the moment you run off with those damn hippies."

"Aren't you happy for me, Mama?"

"Happy? Are you out of your mind?"

She turned her wrath on Marty. "You got my baby pregnant! You better make it right, young man. Elsewise she's going to end up all alone with a howling baby on her hands and dump the bastard on me just like her no good sister did."

Selena said, "Yeah, well that turned out just peachy, didn't it? Look at how dirty she is. And skinny. I bet you don't even feed her right. I'd never let you raise a child of mine."

Mrs. Ballard said, "You're just a child yourself. What the hell do you know about being a mother?"

"Probably a lot more than you. Couldn't nobody do a worse job than you."

It was like the fight between Maria and her mother all over again, back when Marty had proposed to her right after getting whacked over the head with a broom. He wondered if all girls had such screwed up relations with their mothers.

Mrs. Ballard said, "We'll just see about that when you have to face the reality of feeding and clothing a baby on what little money you goddamn hippies can make panhandling or dealing drugs or whatever the hell else it is you do."

The child started crying. Mrs. Ballard set down her beer and picked up the child and stroked her and said, "There now, there now."

Selena said, "I'm sorry, Marty. I should have told you sooner."

For a few minutes the only sound was the child crying. Her wailing gradually subsided. Mrs. Ballard set her down and said, "You go on outside and play on the stairs, honey."

She went out, sniffling. Mrs. Ballard turned her steely gaze on Marty and demanded to know, "What are you going to do about this? This girl is only seventeen years old. I could have you thrown in jail for having sex with a minor. That's statutory rape, I'll have you know. You best do what's right by her."

Marty said, "She told me she was nineteen."

"Well she's not."

"Well I didn't know."

"That don't matter. I want to know what you're going to do about this?"

"I'm — uh, I'll do what's right. I promise."

#

Back at the house later that night they excused themselves from the gathered group around the table and went into the room they shared to get ready for bed. They had not talked about what happened at her mother's. Selena sat in front of her dresser and began methodically brushing her hair. Marty was in bed sitting high against large pillows, not lying down. They were both naked in the humid night. They always slept in the nude. Their clothes, as usually, were tossed on the pile on a chair. Selena said, "I'm so sorry. I should have told you as soon as I found out. I don't know what I was thinking."

"Should have told me what, that you were pregnant or that you're jail bait?"

"Both, I guess."

"Well I think I know pretty damn good and well what you were thinking. You were counting on your old lady to insist I do the right thing, and that's just what she did. You were scared to tell me. That's why you kept talking about your mama. You were sneaky about it, too. You kept pushing around the edges of it until I insisted that we go over there. You wanted it to look like it was my idea so I couldn't accuse you of manipulating me."

Selena put her brush down and came to bed. "Give me a pillow," she said. She was softly crying.

Marty handed her one of the pillows. She fluffed it and leaned back into it. She said, "Please don't be mad."

"Why shouldn't I?"

"I know. You got every right."

"No. I'm not really mad." He reached over and wiped a tear from her cheek. He might have reminded himself that she could turn on the tears at will, but knowing that didn't keep him from being moved. He said, "I'm not mad at you, honey. But it just disturbs the hell out of me. The whole situation. What do you want me to do?

"I want you to be my man. I want you to take care of our baby."

"You expect me to marry you?"

"I don't know. I guess. Maybe. I know my mama does."

He swung around and put his feet on the floor and stood up. He started pacing the floor. He said, "There you go again. You're manipulating me. That's a threat. If I don't marry you, your mama'll have me thrown in jail. What kind of marriage do you think that'll be?"

She said, "I know, I know. I don't blame you if you hate me. I lied to you from the start. I kind of tricked you into bed right off, and then I used threats and pity to keep you around. But I'm going to tell you the whole truth now. Really, I am. And I wouldn't blame you if you didn't believe me, but I swear I just can't lie anymore. Mama was telling the truth when she said I'm only seventeen. I knew you wouldn't have anything to do with me if you knew how young I was. I dropped out of high school and left home. It was true that I had a scholarship offer. I was a good student and a good girl. I never did anything wrong. But then my sister got knocked up and ran off, and I ended up being the only one that paid any attention to little Rebecca. Mama put it all on me. She might have bragged about me getting a scholarship and all, but if I'd stayed at home she wouldn't of let me go off to college. She'd of kept me there like her slave, making me raise my sister's kid. So I took off. I might have lied about a lot of stuff, but I never lied about loving you."

He said, "I don't know why I should believe that. It looks to me like you just need a man to take care of you and I'm the most likely candidate. Of course you'd say you love me."

"Well it's God's own truth. I do love you, and I want to have your baby. I was scared to say anything when I found out I was pregnant, but it's a fact. I really am pregnant, and it's going to be your baby, and if we get married I promise I'll never lie to you again, I'll swear on a stack of Bibles, and I know you don't love me now, but you if you try you can learn to, and I promise I'll be a good wife to you."

#

Selena had grown up in the Episcopal Church. Since childhood she had loved the dark wooden pews, the stained glass windows, the elaborate rituals of the church. She said the church she went to dated back to the Civil War, and when she walked into the vestibule she always felt as if she were stepping back in time and into an enchanted world. "I would imagine the church was the doorway to Narnia. Those stories, they were my favorites."

As much as she loved the church, she avoided it after she left home. She was afraid the priest, Father Bell, would try and talk her into going back home. If he did, she didn't think she could refuse him, because he had been the only father figure she had ever believed in. For three months she lived on the streets of Nashville begging for spare change and sleeping whenever she could in one hippie crash pad or another. Finally she was taken in and given a home by the one they called Father. He replaced Father Bell in her heart, but not for long. After she reclaimed her old name, and after Marty agreed to marry her, she went back to Father Bell and the Episcopal Church. A wedding outside the church simply wouldn't seem real to her. The wedding was held in the church rectory. The only people in attendance were Steve from the band of truckers, the rectory housekeeper, and Selena's mother. Selena had asked Father to come, but he refused, saying, "The only true church is the sanctuary of the human heart. I will not darken the door of a temple where worship of money is the highest calling."

It was a brief ceremony. Afterwards they went out for dinner in a downtown restaurant with Steve and Mrs. Ballard. They spent that night in the house with Father and his disciples, and the next day they moved their meager belongings into a garage apartment a few blocks away on Linden Avenue.

Marty wanted to go back home. He started sending out resumes to newspapers back in Washington, and eventually he was offered a job as an editorial assistant on what was called the Living section of the daily paper in Olympia — a chance to go home again. In November he spent a hundred dollars on a 1963 Chevrolet with eighty thousand miles on it and prayed it would get them all the way across the country. They got as far as Oklahoma City before the transmission went kaput. So they put the junker in the hands of a local mechanic and checked into a cheap motel for the night.

They sat their single suitcase on the stand at the end of the bed and climbed under the covers still in their clothes, shivering. The radiator wasn't working. It made clanging noises but they couldn't feel any heat. Marty called the motel office to complain and the manager said someone would be by to check on it. Through the window he spied a flat horizon painted the pink of twilight. There were not other buildings in sight and very few vehicles swished by on the highway. He recalled that the only other time he had seen so much emptiness was while standing on the deck of a ship in the middle of the Atlantic Ocean. And he felt an emptiness inside as huge as the ocean, because as much as he had grown to care for Selena in the brief time since their wedding, getting married and having children with her had never been in his plans. Now he was facing a new life with a new family, and he had the nagging feeling a ship plowing the Atlantic was the perfect metaphor for his situation — no way to jump ship and no chance of changing course. But no sooner had he thought that thought than he was struck with another disturbing thought, which was that as weird as it might seem, he couldn't imagine any other course he'd rather take. Maybe Steve had been right that he simply floated with the current wherever it might take him.

Selena snuggled close, saying, "Warm me up. I'm freezing."

"Yeah, me too." Her body felt good next to his, soft and warm. She had put on a few pounds. When she first started putting on weight, he thought she looked better with a little more meat on her bones. Then, when it became obvious that it was baby weight, he thought that looked good, too, in a different way. He said, "Hey, you know what? We've never talked about baby names. Don't you think it's about time?" She was well into her fourth month by then. They could see the baby moving in her belly. "If it's a boy," he said, "I want to name him William, after my father."

"That's a good name. Would we call him Bill or Billy?"

"Not Billy. Hell no. I can't stand Billy." He thought about Billy Boone, the one person who, if he could have gotten his hands on, he would have choked the life out of. He still believed it was Billy Boone's fault that Maria had left him.

She said, "Won't people call him Billy anyway?"

He decided that was a nice bit of logic on her part, but he said, "Well I guess we'll just have to set them straight if they do. His name's going to be William. No diminutives, no nicknames."

"All right. William it is. Now what if it's a girl?"

"It's not going to be a girl."

"Well it might. Come on now, play fair."

"All right, if it's a girl, I'd like to name her Maria."

"Oh no, not Maria. Anything but that. That's your ex-wife's name, and you're still in love with her."

He was stunned to hear her say he was still in love with Maria. What had he even told her about Maria? He couldn't remember. He was even more stunned to think that not only did she believe he was still in love with Maria, she readily accepted it. At least in some measure. "I'm willing to live with her ghost," she said, "but I refuse to go through the next eighteen years addressing our daughter by her name."

"I'm not still in love with her," he said, "What makes you think that?"

"I can just tell."

"Well you're wrong. But you're right about the name. I should know better. What would you like to call a daughter?"

"I don't know. What about Mabel?"

"Yipes! That sounds like a name for some old busybody that sits on the porch all day shucking corn and meddling in everybody else's business."

"A name for a real Southern belle, huh?"

"Yeah, a very old Southern belle, a bell with a withered clapper. That's the last kind of name I'd want for a daughter."

Exaggerating her Southern drawl, she said, "Well now, ain't that all poetical of you. But I reckon you're right. We don't want to curse our daughter with a little 'ol Southern name."

"Right. OK. So how about Melissa? That's a nice name."

"I don't like it. How come we're stuck on *M* names?"

"Beats me."

"How about Marigold? You liked it when I went by Marigold."

"Maybe."

Eventually following the *M* line led to Marty suggesting the name Marianne, and he was surprised that she immediately said she liked it.

"I love it," she said, "Mary Ann."

"Yeah. But I want to spell it as a single name: M A R I A N N E."

"Oh, that's beautiful."

If it dawned on her what the first five letters of Marianne spelled, she decided to just let it go by.

The motel manager showed up to fix the radiator just about the time they concluded their baby name discussion. He tinkered with the radiator a while but couldn't get it to work, so he moved them to another room. Once settled into a room with actual warmth, they stripped out of their clothes and snuggled together under the covers, and turned on the TV. Flipping back and forth between the only two stations they could get, they caught the tail end of a news report about a bunch of Vietnam War veterans who were throwing away their combat medals. Marty jerked to sudden attention and shouted, "My God! That's Chuck!"

"Who?"

"Chuck. Chuck Nagel. God! He was my best friend since way back in elementary school. What have they done to him?"

Chuck looked to have lost at least forty pounds. He looked haunted, skeletal, angry. A scar ran from just under his eye to his earlobe. His eyes receded deep into the sockets. His hair had grown long and hung over the collar of a scruffy Army field jacket.

The news segment was over almost before it started. They didn't identify any of the soldiers by name and said little about why they were protesting. Simply that they opposed the war. There was no explanation of what changed them from warriors to anti-warriors. Marty wanted to know what Chuck had done over there. He wanted to know how he won his medals in the first place and why he now thought they symbolized something he could not abide.

Some man in a suit, maybe a congressman or someone from the Pentagon, said their actions were treasonous. With that, the newscast moved on to a story about Marlon Brando.

Marty shouted at the TV: "Is that it! Is that all you got to say?"

"Well yeah," Selena said. "They never tell the whole story."

#

After spending a good chunk of their savings on a rebuilt transmission, they got back in the car and drove through Texas and New Mexico, and halfway across Arizona, Selena keeping up a running commentary all the way. Her breathless commentary unwound in syncopation with the scenery of the great American frontier that spread out in receding ribbons on either side of the highway. She was fascinated with the high desert in Arizona. "Look at the colors," she said. "I never knew the world could have such colors — all these browns and tans. I'm used to green everywhere. I thought deserts were all sand. I never knew they could be so colorful. There must be a million shades of brown." She saw green, too, a soft, washed-out green unlike anything she'd seen before. "It's sort of like a green shirt washed with bleach. And look at the sky, how far you can see. I've never seen so much sky all at once. Back in Tennessee the trees blocked most of the sky."

"Yeah, I know. I was there, remember? It'll be like that again when we get to Washington."

She said, "You reckon we're going to see any cactuses? Or jackrabbits? Do they have them out here? I'd love to see a jackrabbit come hopping across the road. What about tumbleweeds? Do they have them? And what about Roadrunners? Are they even for real? God, I bet a hundred years ago there were Indians in war paint galloping across here. And settlers. Covered wagons."

Marty loved her enthusiasm, but after while it got on his nerves.

She kept crinkling the pages of the fold-out map, checking everything on the map against signposts they passed and telling him every ten minutes or so what was coming up next. "There's some mountains off that way, they're called the Dragon Mountains. Isn't that a great name? Then Benson's coming up next and then Green Valley, and then Tucson."

For Selena, the road trip was an adventure. It had started out that way for Marty as well, but after a few hours of North Texas and New Mexico he'd seen all of the barren West he wanted to ever see. He just wanted to get home. He resisted most of her pleas to stop for snacks or drinks or bathrooms. He remembered traveling with his parents when he was little. His dad never wasted a moment on the road. Snacks and drinks were packed in advance and consumed on the go, and if the old man needed to pee, he'd simply pull off on the side of the road, open both front and back doors to shield him from sight, and piss in the grass.

They spent their second night on the road in a motel west of Tucson, and headed out again just as dawn was breaking the next morning. Selena had picked up some brochures on Los Angeles tourist attractions, and no sooner had they hit the road then she started in with a breathless recitation of all the sights she wanted to see in L.A. — the La Brea tar pits, footprints of the stars in front of Grauman's Chinese Theatre ("They've even got Rin Tin Tin's paw prints") and the Hollywood Wax Museum.

Marty didn't want to do any of those things. The more excited she got, the pissier he got. But then he recalled something else about the good old piss-on-the-side-of-the-road days. He had hated his dad for never stopping to let him see the sights.

"Maybe we can stop long enough to get lunch," he conceded. "Maybe we can cruise through Hollywood. Take in some of the sights."

"Just drive through? You can't really see anything just driving through. What's it going to hurt to take a few hours to see things we may never get another chance to see?"

"What do you want to see some fucking fake mastodons stuck in a tar pit for?"

"I don't know. I just want to. Besides, you really need to get out from behind the wheel, stretch your legs a little. Non-stop driving ain't safe."

He hated to admit it, but she was right. He knew he shouldn't push it too much. And he was more curious about the tar pits than he was willing to let on. Plus he secretly hoped they'd get to see a real movie star. It wasn't that unusual in L.A., he'd heard, to bump into somebody like Marlon Brando in a restaurant, although he figured Marlon would never eat in any restaurant they could afford. So they spent half a day touring Los Angeles, which was mostly disappointing and boring. Seeing names and handprints of stars on the sidewalk was certainly no thrill, and the Wax Museum was dark and dingy. "They must keep the lighting low to hide all the imperfections in the statues," he whispered. "They're nowhere near as lifelike as advertised."

They killed a couple of hours in L.A., and then they hit the road again, headed north on I-5. They drove straight through the night and most of the next day. She begged him to stop in San Francisco, but by then he was too edgy for home. He said, "We'll come back sometime. Spend a weekend in San Fran." They spent one more night in a motel, in Eugene, Oregon, and then drove non-stop to Olympia.

After Pride

Everyone else had gone to bed. Marty and Chloe were seated on high stools at the island counter in William's kitchen, drinking beer. "This is good," Marty said. He took another sip of the cold beer and sat the glass on the counter top. He picked up a napkin, wiped the condensation ring off the counter and sat his glass of beer back down. "This really hits the spot. Maybe I'll be able to get a halfway decent night's sleep."

"I hope so. You need it." Chloe lifted her glass. "To sleep, blessed sleep."

"Amen." They clinked glasses.

Chloe crossed one leg over the other at the knee and rocked her long leg as if from a fulcrum. She wore red silk pajama pants. Fluffy red slippers dangled loosely from her toes. Marty noticed again what an attractive woman she was. She carried her age with dignity, her silver hair a badge of honor. Funny, he thought, how he seldom noticed the way she looked. Maybe they were too close to see each other. But now he looked closely. He saw the lines of worry and laughter around her eyes and noticed how blue her eyes were. He noticed the softness of her lips, a blush of blotted lipstick not successfully wiped off. Chloe was one of the few women he knew who regularly wore lipstick, the only other one he could think of being Barbara Morrow from the real estate agency next door to *The Sounder* office. He let his eye wander around William's kitchen. A pair of black-and-white drawings of naked men hung on the wall over the counter. They were cheap looking pictures, clumsily drawn. He figured Jake must have bought them. Or maybe they were a gift from someone they didn't want to insult by not hanging them. Surely William had better taste. Marty was the first to admit that he, himself, was deficient in artistic taste. How many times over the years had Selena begged him to take her to the art museums in Tacoma and Seattle? He had always resisted, but once he gave in he always enjoyed the museum visits. Selena would instruct him in the ways of observing art. He was always amazed at what a discerning eye she had, something he had first noticed when they drove cross country from Nashville. Back then she had pointed out colors in the desert that he never would have noticed on his own.

He returned his gaze to Chloe. He saw the strength of her jaw and thought: This woman is a rock. If there's anyone in this world I can depend on, it's her.

He said, "I keep thinking about Maria. God! It's the weirdest thing. I don't know where that comes from. How can I possibly think about my ex-wife when my current wife is lying up there in a hospital bed as dead as dead can be?"

"She's not dead."

"I know. But Jesus, you know what I mean. With all those goddamn tubes sticking in her — and here I am having dirty thoughts about Maria."

"You can't help what thoughts come at a time like this. They're just random. You're not being disloyal or anything."

He reached his hand out to Chloe. He gripped her leg above the knee and squeezed, paternally. He said, "It scares me to say this, but I think maybe it'd be best if she just went ahead and died. I'm afraid that if she lives, she'll be a vegetable. God, I can't stand the thought of having to tend to her day after day for years on end, having to feed her and wipe her ass. Oh shit. I must be really selfish to think like that."

Chloe tried to assure him that he was only being sensible, not selfish. "I'm sure she wouldn't want to live like that," she said.

They sipped their beers in silence for a while. It was past two o'clock in the morning. Marty laughed, bitterly. He said, "I just had another one of those random thoughts. I remembered the way Maria looked naked. What a body that woman had. I can't help it, you know. I never felt the same way about Selena. We never had that moment when two people collide and electricity fills the air. When we made love, it was — don't get me wrong, it was good. But it was never really exciting."

"That's hard to believe. She's one of the sexiest women I've ever known. Look at her eyes. The way she looks at you. I'd give anything to have a beautiful woman like Selena look at me that way."

Marty was surprised to hear that. Of course he knew that Chloe was a lesbian, but he'd always avoided thoughts of her as sexual in any way. But then he told himself that maybe, just maybe, he had never allowed himself to think of Chloe as a sexual being because of their closeness. If he ever let the thought of sex with her cross his mind, he quickly squelched it. It would be like lusting after a sister, if he had one. He never was comfortably able to wrap his mind around Chloe having relations. And in all the years she'd been renting a room in their house, she had never brought another woman home. Marty knew that sometimes she dated, but she never talked about her dates. As for Selena, he had never really thought of her as being sexy or beautiful either. She was just Selena.

Book Two
1971 to 2004

Baby Marianne clawed her way out through the birth canal. She poked her head out and screamed her outrage at the light of day. Outside of the hospital it was a balmy April afternoon. The giant firs sheltering the parking lot rippled in a gentle breeze. But inside the third floor delivery room a storm was raging. Hurricane Marianne. Letting everybody know it had not been her choice to enter this world. Five minutes old and already giving fair warning that when things didn't go her way she damn well intended to let somebody know about it.

The doctor cleaned her up, swaddled her in a soft blanket, and placed her at Selena's breast. "She's going to stop this screaming some day, right?" Selena quipped.

Marty laughed. "She better. If not, I'm going to ask for a refund."

"She's probably hungry," the nurse said. "And she doesn't like the light. For nine months now she's been in a place where it is warm and dark."

Selena freed her breast and guided the screaming baby to the nipple, and immediately her screams were replaced by suckling and gurgling sounds.

"This is patently unfair," Marty said. "She carries on like a holy terror and you give her a tit to suck on, but if I acted like that you'd tell me to grow up and behave myself."

"No I wouldn't. I've got two of them. You could share with your daughter."

"Thanks for the offer," he laughed, "but somehow that just doesn't seem right."

Then, with a mischievous sparkle in his eye, he said, "Hey, but what about at work? If I cried like a baby at work, you think maybe they'd give me a kind of editorial tit to suck on? Maybe treat me a little better? Maybe they'd offer me a promotion."

Marty was not exactly thrilled with his new job. Of course he liked the money, no doubt about that. Compared to working for an underground paper for fringe benefits and no pay, it was great. But he hated the corporate structure and the restrictions on what he wrote and how he wrote it. *The Olympian* was the only daily newspaper in town, and the locals pretty much despised it, derisively calling it the *Daily Zero*, even though, as corporate newspapers go, it was no worse than many another. Marty's job was the lowest position in the newsroom hierarchy. *Toady* or *errand boy* would have been a more descriptive job title than the impressive sounding *Editorial Assistant*. He sorted through news releases sent in by local arts and entertainment venues and put them in the hands of the appropriate editors and reporters. He made a lot of fact-finding calls, and he made a lot of coffee and ran a lot of errands. The coffee making and errand running were not in the job description when he signed on, but those were chores that naturally fell to him as low man on the totem pole. He didn't mind. He stuck with the job and eventually moved up to better positions.

Shortly after Marianne was born he got a promotion of sorts. They moved him to the copy desk where he worked from four in the afternoon until midnight, and sometimes much later, checking for errors. Dragging himself home after midnight, he would often find Marianne awake in her crib, fretting, but not loudly, her inner clock telling her it was time for Daddy to come home. He would pick her up, kiss her and stroke her back, and she would instantly fall back to sleep. He'd gently lay her back in her crib, tip-toe into their bedroom, get undressed and crawl into bed. Selena would stir, mumble something unintelligible, and flop an arm across his chest. Two hours later, Marianne would wake for her two-thirty feeding. Marty would get up and fetch her to Selena's breast. Sometimes Selena wouldn't even wake up. Marianne would finish feeding and fall back to sleep on her breast. Marty would carry her back to her crib, and Selena would sleep through it all. Other times she would wake up for the feeding and not be able to go back to sleep, and she and Marty would talk through the early morning hours while taking turns pacing the floor with Marianne.

It wasn't long before Selena got pregnant again. By the time William was born (Marianne was eighteen months old) Marty's job had become a little more interesting. He still read other people's stories and made them more readable, but he was also being handed the occasional assignment to fill in for feature writers. It was thrilling to see his by-line in print. He would see people reading the paper in coffee shops and look to see if they were reading his stories. He always wanted to saunter right up to them and say, "I wrote that." But he never had the nerve to actually do it.

Baby William was as placid as Marianne had been demanding, and even she had mellowed out considerably by the time her little brother came along. Marty and Selena marveled at the way their children seemed to trade personalities around William's first birthday. William, who had been so placid as an infant, became almost hyperactive as a toddler; and Marianne, who had been hell on wheels for the first year, became so calm and well behaved that they thought of her as a thirty-year-old in a child's body. Life around the Winters household was becoming routine. Marty and Selena were maturing despite themselves. While the children were growing up, Marty's hair was thinning and turning gray. He wore it long and tied in a pony tail, just like many other men in the growing ranks of ageing hippies. As for Selena, she looked nothing like the flower child of years past. She cut her hair short and wore smartly styled slacks and jackets. They had borrowed a shitload of money for Selena to go to college and get her Masters in social work, and they piled another shitload on top of that to buy a house overlooking the state capitol and Budd Inlet, the muddy southernmost tip of Puget Sound, just a few blocks away from Priest Point

Park. It was a three-bedroom, white clapboard house with a spacious deck out back that hung over the water.

Their life was not exactly what you'd call easy, what with Marty working weird hours and Selena in school, two kids at home, and a mailbox stuffed with bills at the first of every month. But they were happy. The house was a joy. They joined the local film society and had season tickets to the Little Theater. They threw parties on the deck. There was beachcombing with the kids and summer evenings watching lights over the water. Marty wired stereo speakers throughout the house and outside on the deck, so no matter where he went on the property he could listen to his collection of classic rock 'n' roll hits.

In 1976 a small group of local entrepreneurs started up a weekly newspaper and asked him to be their arts and entertainment editor. He jumped at the chance. It didn't matter that the pay was less than he was making at *The Olympian*. By then, they had a second income. Selena had finished school and was working as a counselor at the WomynsCenter — spelled with a *Y* and run by women for women. She wasn't very comfortable there. The feminists who ran the center were too militant for her taste, and she was the only non-lesbian on staff. But the pay was good, and the job would look good on her resume when she was ready to look for something more to her liking.

The founders of the newspaper, on the other hand, were more to Marty's liking. Their names were Mike and Reggie (they insisted on first names with everyone). They were former hippies who clung to the old values so long as they didn't interfere with making money. They told him their idea of how to run a weekly paper was to hire the best editors and writers they could find and give them free rein to do what they wanted. Marty's boss, the managing editor and the only person he had to answer to, was a guy with two first names: Ron David. He was thirty years old, a flaming liberal and an art lover. The first thing he told Marty was, "Mike and Reggie are not for sale. Not to advertisers and not to politicians. I expect your writing to be lively and factually accurate. But your opinions are your own."

He thought he'd died and gone to heaven.

#

A dozen years flew by. Marty became a fixture at *The Sounder*. Marianne and William grew up. Selena worked for six years at the WomynsCenter and finally quit to start up a private practice. And Chuck Nagel came back into Marty's life. After getting out of the Navy, Chuck had settled in Seattle's Capital Hill district, where he became, as he liked to put it, a professional rabble rouser. He worked in various capacities (fundraiser, lobbyist, clerk, publicist — sometimes for minimum wage and sometimes for no pay at all) for a succession of political action and social service agencies, most of which were connected with the peace movement or with gay, lesbian or transgender causes. Marty got it that Chuck's anti-war activism was an outgrowth of his service in Vietnam, but he couldn't figure out where his dedication to gay and lesbian causes came from. When he asked him, he said, "Because they get the shaft all the time, you know? I got to know some gays in the movement, and man you can't imagine what it's like to be them. Check it out. What if you couldn't have a picture of Selena at work? What if when you went places with her you had to pretend she was just a friend, because — I don't know, maybe because having sex or, God forbid, being married to a woman with dark hair was considered some kind of disgusting perversion? God help you if you ever dared to hold her hand or kiss her in public. Some self-righteous Neanderthal would smash your ass for it. Well that's what being gay is like, and that just pisses me off."

"Aw, man, you got to be exaggerating. That kind of prejudice might still exist in Holcom, Kansas, or Greenville, Mississippi, but not in Western Washington."

"You wish. Try getting outside your safe little liberal enclave in Olympia and you'll find out what the real world is like. You ever spend any time in Rochester or Chehalis? Shit, man, they got hillbillies down there that'll make you think you're in Mississippi."

It was during the time that the AIDS epidemic was really heating up and gay men were going to funerals every week when Chuck first called Marty to say, "Hey, man. I just wanted to let you know I'm back in the area." He was spending a lot of time in Olympia lobbying the legislature for money to fund AIDS research. Seattle was only an hour away, and they both commuted frequently, Chuck driving down to harass legislators and Marty driving up to cover arts events for *The Sounder*. When Marty was in Seattle they would often meet for lunch. Marty always paid. Chuck was always broke. Marty reminded him that that was how it had always been. "Even back in high school I always paid. And back then you had as much money as I did."

"Yeah, but I made up for it in Norfolk when you were married to what's her name and never had any dough."

When Chuck was in Olympia, Marty and Selena would often have him over for dinner, and many times he would stay overnight, sleeping on a mat on the floor in William's room. When he was on his own, Chuck survived on take-out and microwave meals, so naturally he loved Selena's home cooking. She was not exactly the best cook in the world, but she got by. She made some pretty good Southern fried chicken and cornbread, and her meatloaf wasn't bad. Standard meat and potatoes cooking. But the way Chuck raved about it, you'd think she was head chef at the Four Seasons.

Chuck habitually showed up about half an hour before dinner. Marty would usually offer him a beer. "Thanks, I'll get 'em," he'd say — an excuse to invade Selena's kitchen. He'd grab a couple of beers out of the 'fridge and pour them into tall glasses (Marty always just drank out of the bottle, but Chuck said that was uncouth). While waiting for Selena to put dinner on the table, he would often beg her for a little sample of whatever she was cooking, and inevitably rave about it. "You're a marvel. You're God's gift to mankind." — smacking lips and licking fingers, and often kissing her cheek or forehead. He was such an actor, a new aspect to his personality that Marty and Selena both found highly entertaining. Chuck was invariably gentle and flirtatious with Selena, courtly in an old world manner. She ate it up.

William loved him, too. Not quite into puberty yet, William was beginning to show signs that he would grow up to be the next Versace. He was fascinated with fashion. He pored over fashion magazines. Marianne was the one who brought the fashion magazines home, but it was William who wore the pages out. Marty and Selena suspected (were afraid?) that he might be gay. He could be as flamboyant as the most outrageous of drag queens, but only when he was in a particularly playful mood. Where he got that from, they never knew. It was not as if there were any drag-queen role models around, at least not that they knew of. The one thing that kept them from being convinced he was gay, even long before he came out, was that he was totally into sports, especially baseball. He could quote stats on the entire New York Yankees team, and he was an outstanding second baseman on his school and Little League teams. Marty couldn't understand how he could fold together these seemingly opposite characteristics. There was something about being stereotypically gay and loving sports that simply didn't jive with Marty's way of viewing the world.

"He's me," Chuck said. "Me at that age, exactly. Only he has the inner strength to be himself. That's a kind of strength I never had."

"Are you shitting me? God! I mean, yeah, you had the baseball in common. There was nothing swishy about you. You were rugged, almost ridiculously rugged. Let's face it, you were about as sensitive as a rutting hog or a lump of — oh, whatever."

"But what I'm trying to tell you is there's always been a strong feminine side of me that I never let out. I was scared to let it show. Well William's got that, too. There's a woman inside of him, and he's not afraid to let her out. More power to him. And he's still a damn good baseball player."

Selena said, "It's never too late. You can still let your feminine side out."

Marty said, "But don't start coming around here wearing a dress."

"Ah ha! Your insecurity is showing."

"Yeah, maybe. Seriously, though, I know that William might have some tendencies — You know. And that's all right. But if I had a choice between seeing him become a baseball player or a fashion designer, I'd feel a lot more comfortable with the baseball."

"And if he turns out to be really good at either one," Selena put in, "He'll make more money than we ever dreamed of."

#

One summer afternoon Chuck dropped by *The Sounder* office and asked Marty to join him for a beer at the Spar before going home. The lounge in the Spar was dark and homey. Photos of loggers lined the walls. Plush seats comfortably worn. They downed a couple of beers and then another, and then some friends came in and offered to buy more. Before long they were thoroughly soused. Chuck started reminiscing about Vietnam, something he had never done. The few times Marty had asked him about the war he had clammed up, but on this occasion he became unusually talkative, and as he talked he seemed to slip into another personality, the person he must have been in the jungles of 'Nam.

"We were elite guerilla fighters," he bragged, loud and slurring. "We were underwater demolition experts. Frogmen. Like what-the-hell's his name — the 'Sea Hunt' guy."

"Lloyd Bridges," Marty supplied. If it was ever on TV Marty knew it.

"Yeah, him. The Army's got their friggin' Green Berets and the Navy's got their SEALS. The Cong called us the men with green faces. They were scared to death of us. With good reason, too. We were assassins, is what we were."

He told about a lieutenant named Pechacek who was legendary among Navy SEALS. Marty thought for sure he was lying, so later he went to the library and looked the guy up. Pachacek got his brains blown out in 'Nam. Literally. They scooped his brains up and stuffed them back in the hole in his head and taped his head up. His buddies thought he was dead, so they left him like that. But he wasn't dead. Didn't say how they found him, but they did. They sent him back home. They brought him in a wheelchair to the swimming pool at the UDT school, and they picked him up and threw him into the pool. "He had rubber bands for legs and a neck as thick as a telephone pole," Chuck said, "and he just swam around and looked up at all the trainees and shouted, <u>Hoo-ah</u>! The guy was a vegetable but he was still gung-ho. He became a symbol for all the other SEALS. They wanted to be Pachacek."

"Jesus."

"Yeah."

"You wanted to be like him?"

"I don't know. Yeah, I guess. It was crazy times."

"I don't get it," Marty said. "I never did get it why you wanted to join the SEALS in the first place."

He shrugged his shoulders. He held up two fingers to signal the bartender to bring another round. Marty said, "I get it that you admire great courage, but Jesus Christ, man, when you put your life on the line it's got to be for something you believe in. Surely you didn't believe in that war."

"At first I did," he said. "But the truth of the matter is I did it for me, to prove I was a man."

"To whom?"

"To me."

"And?"

"And I figured it out that I had the guts, and I had the strength, but that wasn't what I wanted to be. I didn't want to be tough. I wanted to be soft and caring like — like — I don't know, like my mother, I guess. But what I figured out, what was really weird, was that soft was the one thing I didn't have the guts to be. Hard was easier."

#

"Dad, Mom. I got to talk to you," William said. It was the fall of 1989. William was sixteen years old, a freshman in high school.

"What is it, honey?" Selena asked.

"It's kind of hard to say. I think — no, I know. I'm gay."

Having suspected it for years, Selena was relieved to finally have it out in the open. She said, "I know, Honey. I've known it for a long time."

"What?! You knew? God, why didn't you say something?"

Not having an answer to that, she shrugged her shoulders. Then she proceeded to get so maudlin about expressing her love and acceptance that William said, "Jesus, if you keep that up I'm going to take it back."

Marty laughed at that, his first response of any sort. He accepted it, too, but with some slight reservations at first. "Are you sure?" he asked. "How do you know?"

"I just know, Dad. How do you know you're heterosexual?"

"Well that's a weird question. I know I'm heterosexual because your mother's a woman." He paused for a moment while the reverse side of that sunk in. Whoever William might be having relations with — he didn't want to think about it — must have been another boy. He said, "Oh, I get it. OK. But are you sure it's not just a phase?"

"No, Dad. It's not a phase. I'm queer. Get used to it."

The harshness of the word *queer* was upsetting to both Marty and Selena, but they soon learned that many young gays and lesbians preferred that term. To William it was empowering.

Even more shocking to Marty, it was along about that same time that Chuck came out as transsexual. As with William, it was something Marty should have seen all along. There had certainly been clues enough. All his volunteer work at the Gender Center should have tipped him off. And how many times in the last year or so had he talked about wishing he could embrace his feminine side? Marty remembered way back in the second grade when Chuck had told the whole class he wanted to be a ballerina. He had conveniently shelved that memory for almost forty years. But throughout most of those forty years Chuck had been the epitome of manliness.

"That's what's called overcompensating," Chuck said. "The sports, the weight lifting, the SEALS — those were all ways of fooling myself. But the baseball was for real. I really did love baseball. Still do. My heroes are Ted Williams and Christine Jorgensen."

He had tried for weeks to work up the nerve to tell Marty, finally bulling his way through with it with a show of bravado that may have been, ironically, his most macho act ever. Much later Marty got great pleasure in describing to Selena and the kids how Chuck broached the subject with him.

"He came down to *The Sounder* office to break the news, bursting in so suddenly that he startled the receptionist. I sighted him through my office door before he saw me. He shouted my name and then he spotted me. You should have seen the way he strode through the office to my door. About a million similes come to mind. He bore down on me *like a slinging scythe through tall grass, like a blitzing linebacker, like a mole plowing soft ground.* He planted himself in my doorway *like a stop sign, like a line of yellow police tape, like a boulder.* Before I had time to say hello —"

"Or think of any more similes," Selena interjected.

"Yeah, that too. He demanded that I go to lunch with him *right now.*"

In years to come he would describe that scene so often that his listeners started quoting all the similes before he could get them out. But in the days and weeks immediately after Chuck's big announcement he was too discombobulated to make light of it.

They walked to the Spar and grabbed a booth. Neither of them said anything until the waitress came over and took their order. Then, with that booming and magisterial tone Chuck was known to take on when the occasion was grave enough, he said, "You think I'm a man, but I'm not."

Marty laughed. "Oh, really? What are you then? A horse?"

"No, smart ass. I'm a woman. I'm really a woman."

"Yeah, right."

"I'm not kidding. I'm transsexual, male to female. On some level I've known it all my life, but it took until now to fully admit it to myself. But I'm going through with it now. All the way. I've already started the process of transitioning. I'm taking hormones, and I'm going to learn to live as the woman I really am, and I'm going to have the operation."

He was seated at attention, his massive hands like slabs of beef laid on the table, his shirt straining against broad shoulders, the old scar from Vietnam barely visible but nevertheless accentuating his rocklike jaw. Marty could not imagine a more manly man. He tried to envision him as a woman, but it was laughable. He tried to picture a pearl necklace wrapped around his big, corded neck, to imagine tapering red fingernails on the ends of his blunt fingers, pert little breasts resting on a chest that looked like it was made to wear medieval armor — hell, that looked like it was *made* of medieval armor. He couldn't picture it.

"You want to run that by me again?" he asked, trying to mask his astonishment with flippancy, not one-hundred percent sure Chuck wasn't putting him on.

"You heard me. I said I'm going to become a woman."

"Well please forgive me if I don't take this seriously," Marty said, venom in his tone. "I thought you were insane when you joined the goddamn SEALS and went off to Vietnam all gung ho to get your head blown off. But now I know you're really crazy."

He glanced around the restaurant. People sitting within hearing range quickly looked away. People Marty knew. Greg Nelson, a lobbyist for Native American tribes in the area, and Anita Warner, Artistic Director of the Capital Players. Marty was well known in Olympia. Overnight everyone in town, or everyone who mattered in his circles, would know that his best friend was going through the sex change.

Chuck also noticed that people might be eavesdropping. He lowered his voice. "I know I've got a long way to go. I couldn't pass for a woman now if my life depended on it. But I don't intend to pass. I don't even like that word. Passing is pretending to be something you're not. I *am* a woman. I intend to *be* a woman. I know it won't be easy. I've dressed in drag. I know what I look like in a dress."

"You have? Oh my God!"

"Not in public. I know it's not a pretty picture. I look like a cross between a football player and Tammy Faye Bakker. But I'm working on it little by little. I'm taking estrogen, and I'm going to have electrolysis to get rid of some of this nasty hair. I've already lost some muscle from the estrogen, and my breasts are beginning to grow. I guess I'll have to learn how to walk in high heels and stuff, but still. It might take awhile, but eventually, when I'm fully prepared, I'm going to have the surgery."

"You're going to cut your dick off?"

He thought he had whispered it softly enough that nobody would overhear, but he must not have because Greg and Anita at the next table hid their faces and snickered. Chuck said, "Yep. Cut that sucker right off. Add a little fold and tuck down there, sort of like genital origami, and, *voila*! I'll have a sweet little pussy."

"Oh shit, it hurts just to think about it."

"Don't be stupid. It's not like some dude's going to whack it off with a switchblade. We're talking about doctors and hospitals. Anesthesia. It won't hurt at all." With a sly smile he quipped, "Maybe I'll ask the doctor to save my balls, maybe put 'em in a sack and stick 'em in my pocket. I'm kind of used to playing with them."

Marty pushed away from the table. He started to huff off but changed his mind and sat back down. He said, "That's not funny, man. It's not funny at all."

"Sorry."

"So when did you make this big decision?"

"I don't guess there was any real when. It wasn't so much a matter of deciding as discovering. I've always known, as long as I can remember. But I guess I didn't understand what it was at first, and then I pushed it away and refused to recognize it."

"But you've always been so manly."

"Yeah, that's how I hid from myself. Didn't we just go over that? Weren't you listening? Going to 'Nam, man. Do you have any idea how many trannies and closeted gays join up? Do you have any idea how many volunteer for the most dangerous assignments, hoping deep, deep inside to come home in a body bag so they'll never have to face it?"

"Aw, come on. Surely that wasn't you. I can't imagine it."

Chuck said, "Who knows what unconscious motives any of us may have?"

Marty pushed away again, shaking his head in bewilderment. This time he stood up, folded his napkin and set it on the table. He said, "Look, I got to think about this. I got to go."

He turned and walked out of the restaurant. For just a second Chuck sat in shocked silence, the hurt plain on his face. Then he said to

Greg and Anita at the next table, "He stuck me with the bill. That wasn't very gentlemanly of him."

Pushing his way past the counter, Marty rushed past two other people he knew, quickly acknowledging their greetings and apologizing for his rush. "Sorry. Can't stop and chat now. Gotta run. See you later."

He headed toward the bridge, walking right past *The Sounder* office without even slowing down. He kept saying to himself, "How in the hell am I supposed to wrap my head around this shit?" He thought it was bad enough that he had an openly gay son. What was he supposed to say about that? Wouldn't people wonder what he must have done to make his son gay? Now, on top of that, he'd have to explain a transsexual best friend. He looked at his reflection in a store window and consciously straightened his shoulders and lengthened his stride.

He took a short walk along the boardwalk at Percival Landing. He stopped by the play area and watched the kids climbing over the jungle gym equipment. He saw mothers seating at the molded plastic tables watching their children climb on the plastic playground equipment. Was that something new in the world, he wondered, or simply something he'd not paid attention to? He remembered that such playgrounds had been around since William and Marianne were kids. When he and Selena used to take the kids to McDonalds, they had always gobbled down their burgers and then rushed off to play on the climbing toys and slides, all of which looked just like the ones at Percival Landing, which, in turn, looked just like similar playgrounds all over the world. When did they take over the world? he wondered. What was the old saying — the more things change the more they remain the same? Maybe a gay son and a transgender friend were bulwarks against homogeneity. He knew that he would have to get rid of whatever reservations he might have and fully accept them both for what they were, embrace them and support them. Show them his love. He knew he could get his mind in the right place without too much strain. He also knew that his heart would be slow to follow, but eventually it would.

A homeless person who had been seated on a bench near the playground stood up and shuffled over to Marty and asked him if he could bum a cigarette. "Sure," Marty said, fishing out his pack of Marlboros and tapping out a cigarette. "You need a light?"

"Yessir."

"OK, here you go." He pulled out his disposable lighter and fired up the man's cigarette, cupping his dirty hand to shield the flame from the wind.

"You wouldn't happen to have a couple bucks, would you? For a bite to eat."

"Sure. I can let you have a buck or two." He pulled out his wallet and fished out two dollars, carefully shielding the wallet so the man couldn't see how much more money he had in there.

Seated on another bench on the boardwalk no more than twenty yards away was Marty's ex-wife, Maria. He didn't see her. She had her nose buried in a paperback romance novel. Had he seen her, he would have been surprised first at her being there and second at the fact she was reading anything at all, even a romance novel. But she had spied him first and had turned her back to him before he spotted her. Maria had seen Marty three other times since coming home to Olympia, one other time on the Boardwalk, once in a theater lobby and once at the Spar. Each time she had wrestled with contradictory urges to approach him and to run and hide, and each time she had hidden. She knew that avoiding him was not only silly, it was useless. Sooner or later they would bump into each other or somebody would tell him his ex-wife was back in town. Olympia was too small a town for it not to happen. She rationalized her avoidance in a number of ways, none of which, she knew, made any sense. The truth was, she was ashamed of the way she had treated him, and she was afraid that if she got to know him again she would fall in love all over again — forgetting that she had never really loved him when they were married.

She stood up and walked into the nearby public bathrooms to wait him out, hoping he wouldn't linger long and wondering exactly what it was she had once felt for him and what it was she might feel for him now. That was something she had been trying to understand for years. It was not love, she knew that. But it was something very much like love. It was not raw sexual desire either, although it was very much like that, too. Raw sexual excitement was what she had had with Billy Boone. But what Marty had stirred in her smelled the same. It was the overwhelming flattery of his desire for her, the power of being able to excite such ferocious desire in a man.

And, of course, Marty was such a catch. Successful and responsible. A devoted family man. Billy Boone had turned out to be a first class asshole, as she knew he would. And a string of men since him had produced not a single winner. Now she was married to another man she did not love. She cringed away from his touch and was somewhat revolted by his naked, flaccid body. Luckily for her, he hardly ever wanted to have sex, and he was filthy rich.

Maria washed her hands. She studied her face in the mirror, satisfied that she still looked good. If he did chance to see her, she thought, at least he wouldn't be seeing some middle age hag with drooping skin and even droopier tits. She had had both upgraded, as it were, at a substantial cost to her husband.

She peeked out of the bathroom and saw that he had left.

#

Marty's whole family — some more willingly than others — got involved in the project of helping Chuck through the transitioning process, teaching him/her how to dress and walk and talk. It became a nightly ritual at the Winters house: trying on dresses, experimenting with makeup, talking about bras and pantyhose and lipstick. When dressed as a woman, Chuck started going by the name Chloe. That took a little getting used to for Marty, but it came naturally to Selena, who loved teaching Chuck how to become a more convincing Chloe. Marianne, on the other hand, wanted to distance herself from the whole project as much as possible. She resented

Chloe's invasion of their home. "Are we going to, like, just devote our lives entirely to Chloe? It's like, go shopping with Chloe, teach Chloe how to walk, teach Chloe how to talk. I can't take any more Chloe."

"What's it to you?" Marty wanted to know. "You're never here anyway."

It was true. Marianne managed to spend most of her time away from home — out on a date with Randy Green, or out at some school function such as working on the yearbook or planning the senior prom, or spending the night with some of her girlfriends. When she was at home, she mostly kept to herself. Marty had grown accustomed to her sulking. He easily made light of it. But what seemed to be open hostility toward Chloe was something new that he didn't know what to make of. There were times, however, when she could suddenly reverse herself and be as sensitive to Chloe as she was, normally, insensitive to anything outside her own sphere of self-interest. There were moments when she was more understanding than anyone else in the family. This keener Marianne said, "You guys are all into making her into a believable woman. It's like you think she can't be real if she can't pass as a woman. But she *is* real. She is what she is, a woman who happens to look masculine. God knows she's not the only one. So what if she's not really comfortable wearing a bra or applying mascara? Big deal. Maybe she'll never look like a movie star, but that doesn't make her any less a woman."

"That may be true," Marty said, "but she *wants* to become more feminine. If that's what she wants we should help her. Besides, you don't like her anyway, so what does it matter to you?"

"I do too like her. It's just that, well, I don't know. It's just weird having her here all the time. It's like all of a sudden the Chloe project has taken over our lives." They were standing in the kitchen. Marty was sloshing the dregs of his coffee, long since gone too cold to drink. Marianne was making a tuna salad sandwich. She slapped it together and gobbled it down in a few hasty bites, tossed her paper towel in the trash and brushed crumbs from the front of her blouse. She said, "Hey, I got to go." She gave Marty a peck on the lips and rushed out the back door. Marty was left standing alone with the taste of tuna on his lips. He wiped his mouth with his sleeve and refilled his coffee cup. He thought a moment about what she had said, and decided she had been pretty astute in her judgment. He made a mental note to tell her so the next time she deigned to come home.

Marianne had always been the queen bee of the Winters family, the perfect child who seemingly escaped her mother's womb all grown up, the smart child who made straight A's all through school, and the levelheaded older sibling who had always kept her fun loving little brother in line. She thought of herself as the true mother figure in William's life, because they had done a lot of their growing up with both parents out of the house — Marty at work and Selena in school and later working fulltime herself — and William had always teetered right on the edge of being out of control. If it wasn't for her, she was convinced, William would have probably killed his fool self or got himself in real trouble with some of his wilder shenanigans

— riding his bicycle like a race driver down the rainslick hill on San Francisco Street or skinny dipping with his buddies in Long Lake after the public swimming area closed down at night or, after he came out as gay, wearing pink triangles and rainbow stickers at school, as if daring anybody to say something. She kept him in check, talked him out of risky acts and told on him as a last resort. And what thanks did she get for all that? She got ignored at home, that's what she got. William at least got punished when he misbehaved; that was better than no attention at all. Now in her senior year in high school, an honor student and one of the most popular girls in school, she thought she should be honored at home as well.

It was a week before Halloween, dinnertime. The family plus Chloe and Randy Green were gathered at the dining room table on one of those rare occasions when everyone was at home at the same time. Selena came in from the kitchen carrying a cut glass salad bowl and set it on the table. She had picked up fried chicken dinners from KFC on her way home from work and slipped an apron over her dress before tossing the salad. Marty said, "Here's June Cleaver serving dinner."

"Yeah, right," Selena said. "And it seems we have Eddie Haskell here as an honored guest." She was referring to Marianne's boyfriend, who, while spooning a heaping serving of mashed potatoes onto his plate, looked up at Selena and smiled. He had no idea she was making fun of him. Randy was a handsome young man with almost too perfect manners.

"So where's the Beaver?" Marty put in. "That ought to be William, but there's no friggin' way William could pass for such an all-American boy."

"He looks more like that weird little girl on "The Addams Family," Marianne said.

"Well screw you, Miss America."

William had lately taken to dressing all in black, with ripped jeans and a profusion of symbols penned and sewn to his jackets and backpack — the colorful symbols of gay pride and the more mysterious symbols that Marty was not familiar with but suspected came from Pagan religious practices. On this day he was not only dressed all in black, he was wearing black eye makeup and dark, plumb colored lipstick. Marty thought he looked like an androgynous vampire. He wanted to make a wisecrack about them all being ready for Halloween, but he refrained out of fear of hurting someone's feelings. He was never sure of what to say in front of Chuck/Chloe or William, always afraid he might inadvertently offend one of them.

Even though Chuck had started going by the name Chloe full time, Marty still had a hard time thinking of her as a woman. He was still Chuck to Marty. Probably always would be. As for William's bizarre get-up, Marty had no idea how to react to that. He summed up his frustrations with both kids with a single epitaph: *teenagers*.

Selena asked William about the pink triangle pinned to the back of his shirt. "It's what the Nazis forced homosexuals to wear," William said. "Yellow stars for Jews and pink triangles for queers."

"Then that should be a hateful symbol to you," she said. "I don't understand why you'd want to wear it."

"Because."

Marianne said, "They think by appropriating hated symbols and making them their own they can like take away the sting."

William glared at her. "I can speak for myself."

"Then why don't you?"

He gnashed a drumstick and glared at her.

"Well if you ask me, it's like wearing a target on your back," Marty said. "I really don't think you should wear it."

"Yeah, well I think you're just scared I'll embarrass you."

"No. I'm afraid that gay-hating bigots might beat the crap out of you. And if it embarrasses you that I worry about you, that's just too damn bad. You're still my son. I still love you. No matter how much black crap you put on your face."

William tried unsuccessfully to hide the smile that broke on his blackened lips.

Selena said, "Maybe we should change the subject." She tried to start up a conversation about the "lovely" Halloween decorations she had seen in the mall.

Marty said, "God, you really are June Cleaver."

"Well screw you," Selena said, but not in anger. Everybody laughed.

Marianne said, "I bet June Cleaver never said that."

Soon the kids excused themselves and went into their respective bedrooms and put on music that the adults could hear through their doors — Guns 'N' Roses from William's room and Tracy Chapman from Marianne's, blending together into white noise to the three adults in the front room.

"Well, that was weird," Marty said.

"What?" Chloe asked.

"Our dinner conversation."

"Oh."

Marty said, "I have to confess, I'm not too crazy about having to be politically correct in my own home."

"That's life," Chloe said.

"You're no fucking help."

Just as Selena had made "Screw you" sound totally inoffensive, Marty's "You're no fucking help" carried with it the implied qualifier: *but I love you, anyway.* They were all driving down roads that had no maps. Chloe had begun to live full time as a woman. It was part of the requirement for undergoing sexual reassignment surgery. It wasn't easy. She had to present herself as a woman in public when clearly she didn't yet look the part. "I thought Vietnam was scary," she said. "Hell, 'Nam was nothing. But going into the ladies' powder room at J.C. Penny's, that scares the bejesus out of me." So far she had avoided public restrooms, but she knew she wouldn't be able to forever. She also had to get a psychiatrist to diagnose her with Gender Identity Disorder, a term she despised. "Disorder my ass," she said. "I'm getting my gender identity *in* order for the first time. Pretending to be something I wasn't for more than fifty years, that was a disorder."

"It's a bunch of poppycock, if you ask me," Selena said. "You shouldn't have to prove anything. If I wanted to go get a boob job, I wouldn't have to convince a psychiatrist I needed it."

But Marty wasn't so sure. He said, "Maybe they're just trying to keep people from making too hasty decisions. After all, it's not like you can say, 'Oops, I changed my mind. I want my dick back.'"

"Believe me," Chloe said, I'm not going to want my dick back."

#

Their lives became centered on the Chloe project. It was like a nightly performance of *My Fair Lady* in their living room. And what a strange and bumbling Eliza Doolittle Chloe was — lurching in evening gowns, wrestling with the Rube Goldberg complexities of women's undergarments, and laughing wonderfully at her ineptness. At first, Marty and Selena stifled their laughter, but Chloe let them know it was all right to laugh. She even made fun of herself, aping a growling, knuckle-dragging football player when Selena accused her of walking like a linebacker. But she applied herself with determination as Selena patiently taught her how to demurely cross her legs when seated, how to apply makeup so she didn't look like a man in drag, and how to speak with a breathlessly husky voice.

"The thing you have to remember," Selena said, "is that there are plenty of masculine women out there who are still sexy. That's the look you have to go for. Subtle but businesslike. Avoid heavy makeup and dress in suits and pants."

"Suits and pants? What's the fun in being a woman if I can't wear dresses?"

"But nobody wears dresses anymore. Except for transvestites, and I really don't think that's the look you want to go for."

"For parties they do. For special occasions. Haven't you ever watched the Academy Awards? You don't see starlets on the red carpet in pantsuits."

"Maybe. But normal women don't dress like starlets on the red carpet. Have you ever seen that much cleavage on Fourth Avenue or even at the fanciest local restaurant? I don't think so."

"Well I don't care. I want to look fabulous. I want pink boas and plunging bodices."

"Yeah, and a twenty-four-inch waistline," Marty said. "Sorry, honey. It'll never work."

"You're just a spoilsport. I think I'd look lovely with décolletage. Besides — Ha! — you just called me honey. That proves I can pull it off. Next thing you know, you'll be trying to look down my blouse."

Marty thought, if you only knew. He had caught himself trying to look down her blouse more than once — more out of curiosity than prurience, he told himself. But still, when he confessed it to Selena he put it this way: He said, "I accidentally got a big glimpse of much more cleavage than I should rightly be allowed to see. I should have looked away, but I didn't. Now I'm a little bit ashamed of myself." But he knew good and well that was an outright lie. He wasn't ashamed at all, and he couldn't imagine why he should be.

On the subject of what kind of feminine look Chloe should be going after, Selena said, "Think of it as Katherine Hepburn versus Marilyn Monroe. Pants suits are Katherine Hepburn and dresses are Marilyn. Believe me, honey, you'd better go with the Hepburn look."

#

The first few times they went shopping for Chloe she dressed as a man, with jeans and a loose shirt, and a vest to hide her burgeoning breasts. She was not willing to face the ridicule she expected to run into, not to mention the real danger she might be in, if she dared to try on anything in a store dressing room. Selena and William accompanied her on shopping excursions. Chloe presented herself to the sales clerks as Chuck and told them they were shopping for his twin sister. "She's as big as me. Twins, you know."

One day they drove thirty miles south to Centralia, a town famous for its factory outlet stores. On the drive down, William asked, "Are you going to use the shopping-for-your-sister story again?"

"I might, and I might not."

"I know," Selena said. "We'll tell them we're a film crew making a comedy about a drag queen, and we'll tell them you're the star of the film."

"Maybe they'll ask for my autograph."

William said, "That's crazy. You'll just start laughing and blow the whole thing."

Selena, who was not known for having a sense of humor or a sense of adventure, said, "Don't underestimate your mother, young man."

They arrived at the first store in a party mood, having spent the last ten minutes playing out the movie fantasy, and immediately began rummaging through racks of blouses. A sales clerk approached. She looked to be about sixteen years old. She was nearly as tall as Chuck, and almost as masculine looking, with slim hips and a flat chest. She spoke with a Southern drawl. "Hiya. Ya'll need help with something?"

Selena shushed her with finger to lip. She whispered, "Keep it down, please. We don't want to draw any attention. This is Chuck Nagel, the famous actor."

"Oh wow! You really a film star? What you been in?"

"I'm not really a star star. I'm always the sidekick, you know."

"Oh yeah, right. I know. Hey, I think I seen you. Weren't you in that movie with Dustin Hoffman?"

"Yeah, I was his buddy." Struggling mightily to keep from laughing.

"Are ya'll somebody, too?" she asked William and Selena.

Selena said, "I'm Marigold Ballard, wardrobe mistress for Fox Studios, and this is Billie Bonney, Best Boy."

"Damn. I ain't never met real Hollywood people before. What's a best boy, anyway? I always wondered about that."

"It's best that you don't know," Selena said. Then she gently placed her hands on the clerk's face and turned her to face her, as if she were a mother forcing a child to pay attention, and again she shushed her, saying, "Please, keep it down. We don't want to cause a scene. If word gets out that Chuck Nagel's in here it'll be a riot. Now here's the situation. We're doing a comedy. It's about a football player that pretends to be a woman. He, uh—well, he wants to spy on his girlfriend, see. He pretends to be a new girl in town. It's Chuck's first leading role, and it's going to make him the biggest star in Hollywood.

"Well how come you're up here instead of down there in Hollywood?"

"We're filming in Seattle 'cause, uh, the football player in the film, Chuck's part, he plays for the Seahawks ."

"Oh."

"He's the left fielder," William said.

Selena said, "We need women's clothes that will fit Chuck. We need you to help us pick out some blouses, and then we need you to stand guard when he slips into the dressing room to try them on. We mustn't cause a scene. Do you understand?"

"Oh yeah, yeah. I can do that."

They succeeded in finding three nice blouses there. Selena thanked the sales clerk and slipped her a ten dollar bill. "That's for keeping quiet," she said.

As soon as they stepped out the door, the clerk picked up the phone and quickly called her girlfriend who worked next door. So the girlfriend met them at the front door all aflutter to help in any way she could.

"It was a thoroughly successful shopping spree," Selena declared half an hour later while they were eating ice cream at a Baskin Robins.

The next time they went shopping, Chloe decided to take a chance on going as a woman. "Sooner or later I've got to do it," she said.

They went to one of the large department stores in the mall. Chloe was nervous. While fingering the sleeve of a dress in the full figure department she sensed people staring at her and looked up to see two teenage girls with their heads together looking in her direction. She hurried away, and spent some time browsing shoes and accessories. "What are you doing?" Selena asked her. "You hardly looked at that dress before hightailing it over here. And I thought we were going to shop for bras."

"I'm hiding from a couple of nosy teenage bitches, if you must know," Chloe hissed in a kind of stage whisper. "They give me the creeps."

"You can't let them scare you."

"I know. I know. OK, let's do it."

They ambled over to the lingerie department, and Chloe picked out two bras. With Selena carrying the bras, they returned to the full figure section, and Chloe picked out two dresses and tried to slip unnoticed into a dressing room. That was when the store manager, an officious looking, baldheaded pig in a gray suit with a pink tie, shouted at Chloe. She had noticed him earlier. He had followed them from the lingerie section. "Stop! What do you think you're doing?"

"I'm just—"

"I see what you're doing, you sick pervert. Put the merchandise down and get out of here before I call the police, and don't you ever come back." To Chloe and Selena and William it sounded like he was shouting through a megaphone. Every eye and every ear in the store seemed to be focused on them. The teenage girls who had spooked Chloe took advantage of the distraction to stash merchandise under their shirts and slip away.

Chloe hastily shoved the bras and the dresses into the manager's hands and rushed out of the store with Selena and William fast on her heels. As they ran out the front door, they heard a customer exclaim, "Well I never!"

"My God," Chloe said once back in their car and headed home, "That made me feel dirty. It's not fair. Why should I be made to feel dirty just for trying to be myself?"

"You shouldn't, honey. That fat pig of a manager, he's the one who should feel ashamed," Selena said.

Selena was driving. She drove down the hill and across the bridge into downtown and up Fourth Avenue. After a few blocks, she made a sudden turn onto a side street and announced, "I'm going back to give that son of a bitch a piece of my mind."

"Oh, don't do it," Chloe said. "I'd be mortified."

"Well you don't have to come in with me. You can stay in the car if you want."

"Oh no. If you're going to do it, I've got to witness it."

"Me too," William said. "We'll stand back and listen from a safe distance."

She drove back to the mall and marched back in the store and confronted the manager. "That was my sister you kicked out of here. And embarrassed no end. All she wanted to do was try on a couple of dresses before she bought them. She can't help it that she looks kind of manly. I don't know what you thought was going on, but I can assure you we'll never shop in this store again." And she turned and walked out of the store.

Outside, William shouted, "Way to go, Mom!"

#

Eventually Chloe became feminine enough that she could present herself as a woman in any setting — feminine enough that, if she wanted to, she could shop the ladies' department in any store in town. But she never got over her dread of dressing rooms and public restrooms, and she never felt completely natural when shopping for clothes — not that shopping was an everyday event. Throughout the eighteen months leading up to her operation she went on maybe six or seven shopping excursions, and she always had Selena and William along to give her courage and help her make wise choices. William had an unerring eye for fashion.

Back at home after their shopping trips, Chloe modeled her new clothes for everyone's approval. William orchestrated the fashion shows, turning them into fun theatrical events complete with spotlights (a standing lamp held in his hand) and background music (hits from Broadway musicals played on his boom box). He announced each new ensemble as if Chloe were gracing the runway at the unveiling of the latest line by Giorgio Armani.

Marty grumbled. When he was there. Often he was not around for the fashion shows in his living room, because he had to work late, but when he was at home, he just wanted to zone out in front of the TV, not watch Chloe strut her stuff.

The mock fashion shows in the living room were mostly a three person party, with Chloe, Selena and William whistling, applauding and laughing. Marty and Marianne pretended to be aloof, disdainful of the whole thing, but once in a while they would relent and get into the campy spirit of it, joining in on the whistling and applauding. Once or twice Marty even broke out a bottle of wine to make it a truly festive event. Chloe was always into it, strutting into the living room with head held high and twirling in front of the TV before sashaying back to the bedroom to try on the next outfit. Gone was the broad-shouldered athlete; in his place was an overgrown little girl playing make believe. Magic hovered in the living room. With every change of outfit Chloe became more fully the woman she had often envisioned herself to be, more glamorous, more sure of herself. Marty was amazed at the transformation in his old friend, and he wished nothing but happiness for her. Still, he could not help but think that Chloe and William and Selena were deluding themselves. He remembered the old Chuck, the hulking man-boy from high school who once did a thousand sit-ups in the school gym and did a bunch of push-ups with Joel Carpenter sitting on his back. "Damnitohell!" Marty shouted, "I miss my old pal Chuck."

"I know you do," Chloe said.

But every day there was less of Chuck in Chloe. Selena did a great job of teaching her how to apply rouge and lipstick so it no longer looked like stage makeup, and with practice and coaching Chloe developed a kind of whispery voice reminiscent of Lauren Bacall. The daily injections of estrogen were having their desired effect. She was casting off bulk like last year's fashion. Granite muscles were becoming firm but supple sinew. But Marty wondered if a stranger seeing Chloe on the street would see her as a woman. He wondered how many people would see her the way that department store manager had, as some kind of sicko. What was it he had thought, anyway? That Chloe was a man pretending to be a woman so he could sneak into the ladies' dressing room and get a peek at women in their underwear? He wondered how many people might want to hurt her simply because she symbolized some kind of challenge to their precious beliefs about the proper roles of men and women. He had talked about it with Selena, actually putting down his book to talk in bed. Selena could count on her fingers the number of times he had done that. Usually she couldn't even get him to put his book down for sex. He blamed her for their diminished sex life, but he was the one who wouldn't quit reading until after she was too sleepy. "What do you think?" he asked her, "Can she pass in public or will people just think she's a big old drag queen?"

"It's hard to say. She looks pretty girly to me, but I imagine she's always going to have to put up with stares and whispers."

They brought it up with Chloe, tentatively, afraid of touching a raw nerve. "We fear for you," Selena said. "We don't want you to have to put up with — I don't know — whatever kind of crap you're going to have to endure."

"There's no way to avoid it," Chloe said. For almost fifty years as man and boy she had cultivated a tough persona. Masculine movements were ingrained in her bones. There was no way she could erase all of that in a few short months. There was little she could do about big hands, slim hips and broad shoulders, or a chiseled jaw. Her estrogen regimen helped a little, but the changes were limited.

"I know I'll never be mistaken for a supermodel. "I'm too old to change that much. I guess people will always do double takes when they see me. That's just something I've got to live with."

That conversation took place on a cool fall evening in front of their fireplace. Outside, a dreary drizzle dampened their deck, and lights across the water appeared as if seen through a theatrical scrim. William had walked out on the deck to bring in another stack of firewood, not so much because of the chill in the room, which central heating took care of quite nicely, but for atmosphere. Catching the tail end of their conversation when he came back in, he jumped in with, "Just be glad you're not in high school."

"Why? What's so bad about high school?"

"You catch it coming and going. There's not a day goes by without somebody calling me a fag."

"Since when?" Selena asked.

"God. I don't know. Like forever."

"They call you fag?"

"Yeah. Fag and queer and fruitcake and lollypop."

"Lollypop?"

He told them that kids at school had been teasing him and even threatening him all year. He tossed a stick of wood in the fireplace and bitterly joked, "Toss another faggot on the fire."

Selena said, "Why haven't you told anyone?"

"I have. Nobody listens. I told my homeroom teacher and the guidance counselor and the principal. You know what the principal said? He said I shouldn't flaunt it."

"Flaunt it?!" Selena screeched.

"Yeah. How lame is that? The goddamn bigots threaten me and the fucking principal says it's my own damn fault. They called me faggot right in front of Mr. Ramsey in Algebra, and he pretended he didn't hear it. That ain't the half of it. Here's the worst: in the locker room a couple of guys they —" He hesitated, embarrassed to say it in front of his mother, and then blurted out, "They pulled their pants down and flapped their damn dicks in front of me and said, 'Lick it, queer boy.'" William's jaw quivered as he said this. He bit his lip. His face reddened in ugly splotches. "I was afraid they were going to force me. And the coach, the goddamn coach, the adult who's supposed to protect us — he laughed at me. It was just one big joke to him."

"Well he'll be laughing with a broken jaw when I get through with him," Marty said.

Selena said, "Calm down, Marty. Don't you go off half cocked. I know you. You'll just make things worse. Let me handle it."

William said, "I don't want anybody *handling* it."

"I'm sorry," Selena said, "but I can't just let this go."

"Oh please, Mom, no."

But Selena would not let it go. Early the next morning she called the principal and made an appointment to come in and talk to him. She had to reschedule her two o'clock client. At the school, her anger simmered while the principal made her wait in the outer office as if she were some truant student. Once inside, she told the principal everything William had told her. The principal said, "I understand your anger, and believe me, we do not tolerate that kind of behavior. Unfortunately, we can't prove the other kids are intentionally harassing William. When I confront them, they say William starts it. His homeroom teacher says the other kids probably do pick on him, but he's never been able to catch them actually doing anything. Besides, boys get picked on for all sorts of reasons. They get picked on for wearing glasses or being fat. It's all part of growing up. I'm sure you understand." He was a little man with a few wisps of brown hair combed across a red skull and a crooked clip-on bow tie on a collar that was a size too large. On the wall behind him was a poster with a picture of a marching drummer boy in a Revolutionary War uniform and the printed legend: *March to the beat of a different drummer*.

Selena said, "What about the incident in the locker room?"

"Coach Larson said William made up the whole thing."

"Well he's got to be lying," Selena said.

The principal said, "You may be right, but we have no proof. It's William's word against three upstanding students and a coach."

"Well I know my son, and he doesn't lie."

The principal adjusted his bowtie. He looked out the window and then back at Selena. He said, "I hate to say this, Mrs. Winters, but every parent whose child gets in trouble says that. I know my child. He doesn't lie. But they're kids, Mrs. Winters. They all lie."

Two days later, a bunch of kids, both boys and girls, grabbed William and forced him into the boys' bathroom. They forced him to the cold tile floor, and while the boys held him down, the girls pulled his pants off. One of the girls straddled him, hiked her skirt up and rubbed her crotch against his face. They said they were going to make a man out of him. William couldn't bring himself to tell his parents the humiliating details. Instead, he told Chloe, and she told Selena.

Once again Selena went to the school to plead with them to please protect William from the constant harassment. This time she met with both the principal and the school counselor. "Do you know what they did this time?" she asked, and she told them about the incident in the bathroom. She felt she was getting somewhere with the principal, finally, when he asked for names. But when she gave him names he said, "The Ponder kid, maybe. I wouldn't put anything past him. But that girl is on the student council. She's one of our best students. I know she would never do such a thing."

#

Marty was working late that night, something he was doing more and more often. Around eight o'clock Barbara Morrow from the real estate agency next door poked her head in and said, "Hey Marty, buy me a beer?"

"Sure. Why not?"

Marty and Barbara had been friends since the seventh grade. Her name was Barbara King then. They had dated off and on throughout junior and senior high, but had broken it off shortly before Marty started dating Maria Perez at the end of their senior year. Two years out of high school she married Evan Morrow, a car salesman from Yakima who was elected to the state legislature on a Republican ticket. Their marriage lasted slightly longer than his two terms in the legislature.

Marty grabbed his coat and hat, and they walked to the Spar and squeezed into a booth in the lounge. He ordered a dark porter for himself and a light ale for her, their usual. "How're things at home?" Barbara asked.

"Weird."

"Really? Weird how?"

He told her about Chloe and the nightly fashion shows, and about William coming out and the harassment he was having to put up with at school. "That is pretty weird," Barbara said. "I don't really get the gay stuff and all. I mean, I don't think it's right. The Bible says it's a sin, but I've known gay people and they're probably a hell of a lot less sinful that a lot of other people I know. If that's what they want to do, I guess it's their right. Live and let live, you know?"

"Well you knew Chuck back in high school. He was a good guy."

"He was your best friend. Everybody knew that."

"He still is. Only he, or she, is Chloe now. I kind of understand what's going on with her. And William, well he's my son, after all. I love him. I always will. But Selena, she's the one I can't figure out, the way she's embraced the whole gay movement. It's like this whole new thing for her, like she's got to be the den mother to the whole gay and transgender community. It's kind of got my head spinning. I love them all, I really do. But it seems like sometimes I don't even belong in my own house."

"Well you can come home with me anytime," Barbara teased. That had been a running joke with them for a long time, and neither one of them quite knew if they were kidding. He said, "One of these days I'm going to take you up on that."

"Promises, promises."

They finished their beers and Marty said, "I guess I'd better get my ass home to my wife where I belong." They hugged goodbye. She squeezed hard, and their lips met. They always hugged goodbye, and often kissed as well. But chastely. This time there was a hint of something more. She held the kiss a moment longer and ran her tongue inside his mouth.

When he went home, Selena told him about the latest incident with William. "They held him down and the girl forced herself on him. Maybe there wasn't penetration of any kind, but if it had been a boy doing that to a girl it would have been attempted rape."

"That's exactly what it was," Marty said. "I guess we need to report it to the police, since the school obviously won't do anything about it."

"I think so, too," she said, "But maybe you'd better be the one to do it. You have friends on the police force."

"Not really. There are some cops that went to school with me. We're not exactly what you'd call friends, but I can talk to them."

Later, in bed, he spooned close against her backside and reached around and slid his hand under the waist band of her pajamas and down between her legs. She said, "Not tonight, OK? I'm really tired."

"OK," he said. But he wondered, if not tonight, when? When he tried to count up how long it had been, he couldn't remember.

#

The police were no help. The officer Marty talked with said, "Unless we have witnesses come forth or catch someone in the act of assaulting your son, there is nothing we can do, and that doesn't look very likely. It looks like the school's put up a solid front to hush it up."

Later, Marianne argued with her parents about it: "Every time you talk to the principal or to the cops, word gets around, it just makes the bigots want to do more. And William's not helping matters either. I hate to side with the school on this, but he does flaunt it."

"What do you mean?"

"I mean if you think he acts like a drama queen around here, you ought to see him at school. He purposely antagonizes people. And how do you think that makes me feel? I'm his sister, after all."

If anyone in the family had their finger on the pulse of the school population, it was Marianne. She worked on the school yearbook and was on the student council. She knew the girl who had allegedly straddled William and rubbed her crotch against his face. She said, "I can't believe she'd do anything like that." Normally Marty would take her side on such issues, but in this case he was beginning to wonder if she wasn't more concerned with her popularity at school than with her brother's safety. He hated that she was being tarnished by the same brush that painted a big target on William's back, but he sometimes wanted to choke her for being so self-centered and, he thought, shallow. And even if she was right about William making matters worse, what could he do? Go back in the closet?

The bullies weren't likely to let him off that easy. They had it in for him. Sooner or later it was going to turn violent. They all saw it coming, but they had no idea what to do about it. Selena suggested sending William to a different school, but William refused to transfer. He said he had every right to go to his own school.

#

"Everything turned to shit all at once," Marty grumbled. He was talking to Barbara at their usual haunt, the lounge at the Spar. "Talk about your winter of discontent. Oh man."

It had been a nasty winter with no sign it was going to let up anytime before late spring. And it wasn't even Christmas yet. Two weeks of solid rain around Thanksgiving had turned to intermittent snow and freezing rain with blustery winds. The Winters family had been without electricity for two days because of downed trees on power lines. There were threats of outages in the pocketbook as well. At *The Sounder* office rumors of layoffs floated about, and Selena's hours at the Womyns Center had been cut back. Money was tight already, and Marty resented it that Selena had kicked in a good chunk of money on Chloe's new wardrobe. The one bright spot was that William hadn't reported any new instances of harassment at school. But everybody suspected the harassment was continuing; it had just reached a point where he no longer bothered to talk about it. And as if all that were not enough to make their lives miserable, Marty and Selena were misfiring in their sex lives.

"When I'm upset or worried about something — money or the kids — I tend to seek sex for comfort. But, of course, that's the one time Selena's least interested in sex."

"With me and Evan it was just the opposite. I was the one that wanted comfort sex, but he never wanted any kind of sex at all."

"Sorry to hear that."

"Yeah. Well, you saw how long that marriage lasted."

They clinked glasses in a mock toast to shared misery.

They were interrupted by a voice he could never forget. "Marty. My god, it's you."

He looked up and saw her. Approaching from behind his back but reflected in a mirror was the familiar figure of his ex-wife. He turned to face her just as she reached their booth. "Maria! I don't believe it."

"Oh my god, it's been so long. How are you? You look great."

"You too. What a surprise. Are you living here now? Here, sit down. Join us." He scooted over to make room for her in the booth.

"Oh no, I can't. Well, maybe just for a minute." She slid into the booth next to Marty.

Like a well cared-for classic automobile, Maria's beauty shone through the ravages of a life that had included bouts of mental illness and a string of bad love affairs. Over the past few years she'd been variously diagnosed as bi-polar and borderline schizophrenic, or simply situationally depressed. More than one therapist suspected that she used mental illness to gain attention or sympathy from them or to get men to pull out their wallets. As for her current husband, Michael, she freely admitted to the other wives she met at the county club and the yacht club, "I married him for his money. I gave up on love a long time ago. But Michael, he takes good care of me. Maybe he's not so much in the romance department, if you know what I mean, but if I want me some good loving, I can always find that. There's no shortage of hot young studs in this town."

(The women with whom she confided such personal tidbits were among a small group of wives who called themselves golf widows; they all led lives they hated but put up with because their husbands were rich.)

Maria's clingy skirt rode up on her thighs as she scooted close to Marty on the vinyl seat. He noticed that she was wearing some kind of tights underneath the skirt that made her legs look like polished bronze. Her hair was silvery. He spotted the diamond on her finger, noting that it probably cost more than he made in a year.

Despite her cold-hearted manipulation of other men, she had never been proud of the way she had used Marty. And, as she confided to the golf widows, "He may have been the only one I ever really loved. It was disgusting the way I used him. I'm so, so ashamed. I treated him like shit, I really did. I walked all over the poor guy, and he didn't deserve that. But I think I really did love him, or as close to real love as I'm capable of. I tried my best to be a good wife to him."

Knowing from a very early age that she had no marketable skills and considering herself lucky to have even graduated high school — "Lucky, hell. I cheated my way through. I had boys doing homework and writing papers for me. I had 'em eating out of my hands." — at a very early age she had it figured out that her only chance in life would be to hook up with a successful man, and who could possibly have been a more obvious candidate than the boy voted Most Likely to Succeed by his classmates? Marty Winters.

"He was a nice enough guy," she told the golf widows, "but kind of boring. And he had never given me a second glance. I admit I wasn't exactly in his league. I mean, he may not have been exciting, but he was classy, you know? I thought he was going places, and I wanted to go with him."

Her only weapon in the battle of love, she thought, was a knockout figure. She knew she could never bob and weave with charm and wit, but she could sucker punch him with her heaving bosom. She knew how to make the boys want her. She had already wowed half the boys in school. But Marty seemed mysteriously unaffected. Actually, she had no idea just how deeply he was affected or how hard it was to hide it. But it was precisely that, not letting it show, that drove her crazy. Just as Billy Boone's aloofness to her charms had cast a spell on her. If she hadn't gone after Marty for his potential as a way out of what she saw as a dead-end life, she would have gone after him because he presented a challenge. She determined to make him notice. That was midway through their senior year in high school. She started wearing the sexiest clothes she could find in the used clothing stores in Olympia or shoplift from the fancier department stores in Olympia and Tacoma. And she put herself in Marty's view whenever she could. She started attending pep rallies and other after-school programs where she knew he would be, eating at a table next to him in the cafeteria, brushing against him in the hall — all while wearing revealing clothing that pushed the limits of what was allowed in school. Some of the teachers complained, and she was called into the principal's office and given a warning. "We do not dress provocatively in this school, young lady," Mister Madison told her, and she replied, "Maybe *we* don't, but I do. And the last time I checked this was still a free country."

She laughed about it later with Billy Boone: "All the time old man Madison was getting on my ass for wearing sexy clothes he was looking up my skirt and sweating like crazy. The horney old bastard."

In her English class, she told Mrs. Robinson she was having difficulty hearing and asked if she could move closer to the front of the classroom, a maneuver that placed her right next to Marty. That set up her most daring move. It was a Friday afternoon near the end of the school year. She slipped into the girls' restroom right before her English class, and pulled off her bra and stuffed it in her book bag. Braless then, with breasts barely covered by a sleeveless blouse, she took her seat just ahead and to the right of Marty, and leaned forward in such a way as to completely expose her left breast to his view. She could feel the air on her naked skin, the tingle of nerves where her nipple kissed the fabric of her blouse. She cut an eye in his direction to assure herself that he was, indeed, captivated by the sight. He was transfixed. An eighteen-wheeler could have run into the side of the building and he wouldn't have turned to look. When Mrs. Robinson called Marty to the board, he didn't hear her at first — she had to repeat his name, much to the delight of the rest of the class. He hesitated and stumbled getting out of his seat, and held a sheet of paper in front to hide his erection.

But not even such blatant sexual allure could entice Marty to come on to her. Of course not. She scared him half to death. He fantasized about her. He jerked off to visions of her. But he would never ask her on a date. She was, in short, too much for him. Besides, everyone in school knew she was Billy Boone's girl.

As far as Billy was concerned, her pursuit of Marty Winters was a game. She could flirt with Marty all she wanted. If she succeeding in getting him in the sack, so what? It was just a game, and she'd always come back to him. She was his girl and always would be. They both treated it like a lark. In fact, she made a bet with Billy that she could get Marty to ask her out. She even bragged to Billy about flashing Marty in English class. "It gave him a boner," she boasted.

"Well la de da, you can give him a boner. But he ain't never going to ask you out. He'd be embarrassed for his society buddies to see you out together."

But soon after that came the graduation dance and the magic mood of artificial stars flashing on the deep dark walls of the Chalet in the park, and Marty asked her to dance, and his arms reached around her as if they were made to encircle her waist, and his cheek rested wetly against hers in the humid night, and she smelled his mixture of sweat and aftershave, and as they swayed to the strains of "Smoke Gets in Your Eyes," she felt like the hero of a storybook who had finally arrived home after an arduous journey — or, more accurately, like the lovesick maiden who had waited for her hero to return home.

Maria never intended to fall in love with Marty, and if anyone had asked her a month before the graduation dance, she would have scoffed at the very idea of falling for anyone. What others called falling in love, so far as she was concerned, was a sickness she was completely immune to. That was the line she handed out. But what a lie that was. She was no more inoculated against the lure of romance than the most chimerical of her teenage classmates. She described her romance with Marty as something that happened to her. She said, "One moment we were dancing, and then walking around the park at night, holding hands — nothing at all sexual. Not like with Billy at all. And then the next thing you know, I'd packed my bags and moved clean across the country to marry him. But our marriage was doomed all along. I knew it from the start. For one thing, Marty never knew anything about me. He never suspected I was using him to escape a dead-end life. The damn fool even believed me when I told him I was a virgin, despite the fact that I had the worst reputation of any girl in school. We'd been married a good week or two before it ever dawned on him to ask me why I didn't bleed the first time we made love. Maybe he thought about it but was afraid to ask. Anyway, I told him I busted my cherry riding a bicycle, the oldest story in the books, and he never doubted it. Another thing was, it didn't take me long to figure it out that he wasn't ever going to be rich. Most likely to succeed, my ass. All he wanted to do was write stories. He was going to become a reporter. Shit. Mechanics make more money than reporters. But the main thing was — God, how gullible Marty was! He never ever suspected a thing — I never broke it off with Billy Boone. All the time me and Marty were dating, Billy was waiting for me at home. To Mama, it was like we was married, me and Billy. Shitfire! We slept together for two years right there in Mama's house, with her in the next room. And that was at a time when such things were not tolerated. Mama might not have been much of a mama, but at least she wasn't uptight about sex. Me and Marty would go out on a date, and we'd smooch and stuff, and I'd give him this line about how I wanted to save my virginity until our wedding night, and then he'd take me home and I'd go to bed with Billy. Meantime, Mama never knew a thing about me dating Marty. Not until the night he proposed. So Mama really freaked out about that. As far as she was concerned, I belonged to Billy."

Billy followed them to Norfolk. He rented a room behind the market down near the beach, not two blocks away from them. He had another girlfriend while he was in Norfolk, a Navy wife whose husband was overseas. Maria knew about his other women, and put up with it. That worked out well for her because she had to be with Marty most of the time. She and Billy had never been exclusive anyway.

Almost immediately after Marty's ship sailed for the Mediterranean, Maria took off with Billy Boone. "It was the weirdest thing," she said, "I fell apart when he left the apartment that morning. I wasn't expecting that. It was like some horrible fear washed over me, and I burst into loud sobs. I was heartbroken to see him leave. But it only lasted a few minutes. I cried it out, and then I set about packing."

Within minutes after Marty left home that morning, Billy Boone pulled up in front of their apartment with a U-Haul trailer hooked behind his fifty-five Chevy. They hastily packed her belongings and took off for Nashville.

She stayed with Billy in Nashville for about three years. Billy went from job to job, getting fired from one car repair shop after another for such things as stealing parts and cheating customers. Maria had a string of part-time jobs. She worked as a sales girl and a waitress. She lied her way into a job as a dental assistant, but quickly got fired when it became apparent she was not qualified. She tried going to cosmetology school once, but that lasted only a week. Their nights were spent in bars where Johnny Cash was king of the jukebox and where musicians played for tips. Both of them had numerous lovers. They had an understanding that sexual dalliances were permissible so long as they took place outside their own apartment. "Anywhere but my bed," Billy said. "Yeah, and anybody but that stupid blonde that works behind the lunch counter at K-Mart," she countered.

They each caught the other breaking the anywhere-but-home rule. He came home once at lunchtime and found her in bed with another man. He was a bony man with thinning hair who wore his glasses even while making love. Billy grabbed the guy by his skinny upper arm and snatched him off of her. There was a popping-cork sound of wet bodies pulling apart. He fell onto his knees on the floor, and Billy jerked him to his feet. With a tight grip on the man's arm, Billy kicked his ass three or four times, kicking sideways like a soccer player while the man ran in circles trying to get away, shouting, "Yow! Yow! Ooh, stop." Billy was just toying with him, but the situation grew serious when Maria screamed, "Let him go!"

Billy let go of the lover and swirled around and took a big swing at Maria, barely missing the side of her jaw with his fist but grazing her face with his arm. She crumpled backwards to the bed. Her lover scooped up his clothes and ran into the bathroom, slammed the door shut and locked it. Maria clambered off the bed with arms swinging, shouting, "You ever hit me again, you son of a bitch, I'll kill you."

Billy grabbed her wrists and held her off until she calmed down. The man in the bathroom shouted from behind the locked door, "I'm dressed now. I'm leaving. Is it all right to come out? You're not going to hit me again, are you?"

Billy said, "No, I'm not going to hit you." And Maria said to Billy, "If you ever hit me again I'm leaving you."

"That's all? While ago you said you'd kill me."

"Well, I changed my mind. But I swear to God I mean it, I'll leave you for good if you ever hit me again."

He said, "I never took to hit you. I missed on purpose. I just wanted to scare you."

What finally caused their irredeemable split was the one time she caught him with a lover at home. The lover he brought home for sex in their bed was another man. "He hated queers," she said. "I didn't get it. How could a man who hated queers have sex with one of 'em?"

She said there had been clues all along that Billy's sexual orientation was not as perfectly straight as he claimed, but that she had never given it much thought before — clues like the way Billy and Chico used to look at each other back in high school; and clues such as the way, when he talked her into a group grope (her term), Billy seemed more interested in watching the other guys than in doing anything with her. She remembered when they broke into the high school and he planted a gay magazine in the teachers' restroom. "He wouldn't of had that magazine in the first place if he wasn't just a little bit interested. Anyway," she said, "catching him with that guy was the last straw. I left Billy shortly after that. I went back to Olympia and lived with my Mama until I was able to get a job and get out on my own."

To the ladies in the golf widow club Maria's life was juicy and romantic. Accept for the borderline poverty, she had lived the kind of adventurous life they dreamed of. But after Billy Boone and Marty Winters her life settled into a kind of drudgery not unlike their own. In the early eighties she got a job in a restaurant and married the manager. He had teenage children and a drinking problem. The marriage lasted less than a year. Then she got a job serving drinks at Raven Crest Country Club. Michael Delgato was a regular customer, a heavy drinker and a big tipper. He proposed on their second date. She finally found a successful man who could keep her in style.

But Marty had been much on her mind since she returned to Olympia, and marrying Michael hadn't changed that. Naturally she knew Marty was in town. She sometimes read his articles in *The Sounder,* and she often kept an eye out for him knowing eventually she would run into him, as she did.

#

After Maria slid into the booth next to Marty and across the table from Barbara, it took him a moment to shake off the shock of seeing her. And then he said, "Oh, this is Barbara. Barbara Morrow, an old friend. You might remember her as Barbara King from high school."

"Yes, of course. It's good to see you."

The two women reached across the table to shake hands.

"So what's going on with you?" Marty asked.

"I've been back here for awhile. I'm married. My husband is Michael Delgato. He's — well, we — uh, I don't know how to explain it. It's a life unlike any I ever expected. Very respected and upper crust. Grownup children and even grandchildren from his previous marriage, and a big old yacht moored down at Percival Landing. And Michael works about a million hours a week. I hardly ever see him, to tell the truth. But it's OK, I guess. What about you?"

"Well, I'm married, too. We have a boy and a girl, both in high school. And I'm working as entertainment editor for *The Sounder*."

Of course Maria knew all about Marty, but she pretended to know nothing about what he may or may not have done since their separation. She queried, "And you two, you're —"

"Just friends. Our offices are in adjacent buildings. We're kind of break buddies."

They talked for a few minutes, and then Maria said, "I meant it when I said I could only stay for a minute. I'm meeting some people down at the yacht club. Business partners with Michael."

"Well look, it was great seeing you. Maybe we can get together sometime and catch up on old times."

"Yes, I'd love that. I'll give you a call. Can I reach you at *The Sounder* office?"

"Yeah."

She stood up. Marty stood up as well. Maria said, "Is it permissible to give an ex-wife a hug?"

He hugged her, and then she turned and walked away. He watched her traipse past the counter and then sat back down. Barbara said, "Jesus! You're totally smitten with her."

"No I'm not."

"You are. It was written all over your face. I saw how you checked out her ass, too, when she was walking out."

He made light of that by saying, "You ought to see the way I check yours out when you're not looking."

"Well I should hope so. But seriously, I remember you telling me about how she left you and how you were obsessed with her for a long time after. Seeing her now, after all this time, must do something to you."

"It's true that I was obsessed with her for the longest time. I mean, there's something about your first true love, if that's what it was with her. But the thing is, the kind of relationship I have with Selena is much more satisfying over the long haul. More down to earth. I think I'm better off with her. I know I am."

"Shucks," she teased, breaking the serious mood, "Just when I thought you were falling for me."

#

The snow started around nine o'clock in the morning. Small flakes that turned to water the instant they touched ground but that, within an hour, began to stick. By noon the flakes were as large as quarters and blowing hard. Mike, one of the co-owners of *The Sounder*, buzzed Marty and asked if he could come to his office and talk. Mike's tone of voice, right off, told him it was going to be bad news. When he opened Mike's office door and saw his partner, Reggie — who never came to the office — he knew for sure it was going to be bad. He just didn't know how bad. Mike told him they had to cut the entire editorial staff with the exception of the managing editor. "We've got to cut everything. We're going to shrink the paper down to twelve pages (it had been between twenty-four to twenty-eight pages). And we gotta let everybody else go except just Amy and Milton putting the pages together, and freelancers to handle all the stories. We hate it. We'd do anything to avoid it, but there's nothing we can do."

"We're bleeding money here," Reggie put in.

Marty knew better. He could count. Even conceding that ads were down a little, and expenses had gone up, he knew Mike and Reggie were not hurting. They still had their BMWs and country club memberships, and Mike wasn't about to sell his boat. They were more in the league with the rich new husband Maria had bragged about, and Marty resented them saying they were bleeding money, as if they had the slightest idea what it was like to barely scrape by. They at least offered to keep him on as a freelancer. His first impulse was to tell them to shove it, but he squelched that impulse. Barely. "Shit, man," he said, "I don't know what to say. It just seems like there must be some way to work it out where you can keep me on. I've been with you from the beginning. I'm like a member of the family." Mentally he said, "Yeah, like when was the last time you invited me to dinner."

"We can give you freelance work," Mike said. "That's the best we can do. "But I promise you, you'll be our number one guy. And if we ever get back on our feet financially so we can hire more staff, you'll be the first one we call."

That was what kept him from telling them to stick it up their collective asses, the slim possibility that some day they might offer him his job back. In the meantime, until he could find another job, freelancing was better than starving. It meant about one-third the pay and a complete loss of benefits, but it was better than being fired. At least there would be some income while he tried to figure out what to do next.

Christmas lights sparkled on clean white snow that evening as he drove home in the early dark. He pulled into the driveway and got out and kicked snow off his shoes before entering the house. Inside, Selena and William and Marianne were trimming the tree. "It's a white Christmas," Selena chirped. "Come celebrate with us. We have eggnog."

He could not bring himself to tell them he had lost his job. Spirits in the Williams household had been gloomy enough of late. He wasn't about to destroy this little moment of joy. He thought he would tell Selena when they were alone in bed later.

Even Marianne was home, with Randy, to join in the ritual of decorating the tree. Selena dragged out boxes of lights and ornaments that had been accumulating over the years. William threatened, as he did every year, to throw away the pipe-cleaner ornaments he had made in first grade; as always, Selena said, "These are precious. We can't throw them out."

Marianne and Randy popped corn to string on the tree, and ate most of it. After they finished trimming the tree they all got a little tipsy on the eggnog and later huddled under blankets on the couch to watch *It's a*

Wonderful Life on TV. Marty choked up as always when Zazu said, "Look, Daddy, every time a bell rings, an angel gets his wings." Marianne laughed at him.

At bedtime Marty was still thinking he would tell Selena he'd been laid off, but first he just wanted to read a little bit. He always read in bed. He turned on his bedside lamp and pulled up the covers, and stuck a book in his face. When Selena came in and started changing into her pajamas, he tilted the book to peer over it as she stepped out of her clothes. She was still a sexy woman, despite a bit of thickening and drooping. She crawled under the covers and snuggled next to him. She scissored his thigh with her legs and slithered insistently. She said, "Put the damn book down, would you?"

"Are you trying to tell me you want to do something?"

"Yeah, if you remember how."

"OK. Just let me get to the end of this page."

Later, she said, "Talk to me."

"About what?"

"I don't know. Anything. Just talk. We never just talk."

"We talk all the time."

"No we don't."

What was he supposed to say? *Oh, by the way, I got sacked today. Merry Christmas. We're probably going to be homeless soon. And by the way, did I tell you I saw my ex-wife the other day? She still looks sexier than you ever were. I ran into her while I was having drinks with an old girlfriend, who happens to be quite a looker herself.*

Minus the sarcasm, he could not think of anything he could talk about that she would be interested in. Would she like an intellectual discussion of the teenage musicians he did stories on — stories she never read — or the boring conversations he had in *The Sounder* office? He didn't think so. Selena simply wanted attention. They'd been having the we-never-talk talk since their earliest days together. It always went from "We never talk" to "You could show a little affection once in awhile, you know." He knew she was right. He withheld affection. He always had. He didn't know why. In his school days, long before he met Selena, he had been terrifically affectionate, and he had never hesitated to be demonstrative with Maria. With her, it had been all about holding hands and petting and pampering. But they had been awfully young, and they never talked much, either. Maybe it was a man-woman thing. Thanks to lessons learned from William and Chloe, he had begun to scoff at gender stereotypes, but it certainly seemed true that men never seemed to be able to talk about their feelings, the one thing women seemed to think was all important. He tried to think of something loving to say. His mind went blank. He studied patterns cast on the wall by the light of a streetlamp that shone through their bedroom window. Selena said, "Never mind," and turned her back to him. She pulled the covers to her chin and mumbled "Goodnight."

Hours later he was still staring at the wall, unable to sleep. He kept thinking about how he was going to support the family, and how he was going to break the news to them. Would he be able to find another job? If he did, would it mean moving to another city? Maybe even another state? There was only one other newspaper in Olympia, and the chance of them having an opening was slim. Could he stay at home and make enough freelancing? Would they have to sell the house and move into some cramped little apartment? He couldn't imagine losing all they'd put into the house over the years — the new roof, the repairs to the deck, the hot tub. He imagined what it would be like living in a two-bedroom apartment downtown, one of those in the old hotel building with windows overlooking Sylvester Park, where he often saw makeshift curtains flapping. Marianne would get the extra bedroom, one half the size of her current room, and William would have to sleep in the living room. Or maybe they'd have to live in the mobile home park near the mall. Trailer trash. Marianne would be devastated. She'd be ashamed to face her friends. William, on the other hand, would be the responsible young man coming to the family's rescue. He'd want to quit school and get a fulltime job to help out. Flipping burgers at McDonalds. And Chloe would want to help, too.

The thought of Chloe wanting to help, wanting to be a part of the family, inspired a new idea. Chloe could move in with them. They could convert the family room into an apartment for her. She would have her own bathroom and a separate entrance. It would be perfect. She could rent it for less than she was paying in Seattle, and she wouldn't have to commute as often, since most of her work was in Olympia. Half the time she stayed over anyway, sleeping on the convertible couch in Marty's office. She was probably there now. She had gone out after the tree trimming, and Marty couldn't remember whether she was going home to Seattle or out with friends in Olympia.

Marty liked the idea of renting a room to Chloe so much that he started to wake Selena and tell her about it. She'd been flailing about in her sleep, maybe having disturbing dreams. But finally she had settled into a deep sleep. She looked so peaceful it was as if forty years of care had been washed away. Her skin had a pearly sheen. Sometimes in her sleep she looked unbelievably beautiful. He was tempted to kiss her and stroke her hair, but he didn't want to disturb her. He turned his back, and she responded by spooning against him.

He didn't think he had gone to sleep at all, but the glowing digits on the clock on the bedside table showed that three hours had passed. He heard a noise coming from the direction of the kitchen. It was a knocking sound. Like something bumping against a wall. At first he thought it might have been William up and raiding the 'fridge. Or maybe Marianne and her boyfriend. They had gone out earlier, and he sometimes stayed over, especially on nights like this when the weather was bad and they had been out late. Marty could picture them giggling and smooching while spreading sandwich makings all over the kitchen counter. But there was no giggling. The sound he heard was more like a small animal scratching at the back door. He thought maybe it was their neighbor's cat. He crawled out of bed and shuffled to the kitchen, feeling his way along the hall, wondering what he could find to hit the damn annoying feline with. He got to the door and pulled it opened, and Chloe tumbled in as if she had been a bag of garbage propped against the door.

He flipped on the light switch just as Selena came in to see what all the ruckus was about. Chloe was on the floor clutching at her blouse where it was ripped from her collar to beneath her breasts. Her face was bruised high on one cheek, and a dark smear of blood ran from her lip to her chin. Marty stood immobilized with shock. Selena said, "We've got to get you to a hospital. Get the car, Marty."

Chloe said, "Wait, wait. I'll be all right. Just help me into a chair."

"OK, but we're still taking you to the hospital," Selena said as they helped her to her feet and into a chair.

"Well you're not dressed, and I'm not going to any damn hospital looking like this."

"I'll clean you up," Selena said. Turning to Marty she said, "Bring me my purple blouse, the one William gave me last year. She can wear it."

She dampened a washcloth at the sink and began to clean the blood off Chloe's face. Marty rushed to the bedroom and quickly returned with the purple blouse. Chloe said, "It's not as bad as it looks. It's just my dignity that's beat all to hell." She ripped apart what was left of her shirt and exposed her breasts (her bra had also been ripped away). She cupped her breasts in her hands and lifted, as if offering them for inspection. "They said they wanted to see if they were real. Look what they did. There were only two of them."

"Two tits?" Marty asked, incredulous.

"No, you idiot." She laughed despite her tears, and wiped snot with her sleeve. "Not two tits," she started laughing even louder, a hysterical cackle that subsided into a bitter wail. "Not two tits, but almost the same — two boobs. Two boobs with a half a brain and a switchblade knife." She pulled the now tattered shirt across her chest and clutched her ribs. She took a deep breath. She said, "They weren't all that big or tough either. I could have killed the little snots if I'd taken a mind to."

She was noticeably calming, and Marty and Selena could see she wasn't hurt nearly as badly as they had first thought. Merely a busted lip and a black eye. Nothing worth rushing her to the emergency room. She just needed to be comforted.

Selena helped her into the purple blouse and buttoned it. Chloe held her hands out palms up. "Look at these hands. I know it's a cliché about people trained in hand-to-hand combat, but it's true: these hands are lethal weapons. I could have destroyed those little punks, but I didn't. I'm not a fighter any more. That's great, isn't it?" She was truly enchanted with that bit of self-discovery. "I'm a woman now, and I reacted like a woman. I didn't even think about fighting back. I balled up to protect myself, and I cried and begged for mercy."

"That's what women do? Ball up and beg for mercy? Hell, I know a couple of women who would have beat the crap out of them."

"Well I don't know what kind of women you hang out with down at *The Sounder*, but I'm a lady. I don't engage in brawling."

"At least they didn't beat all the rancor out of you."

Selena put on a pot of coffee. They sat at the table and drank. Outside the smeary kitchen window, dawn was rising with the tide. William wandered downstairs in his underwear. Barefoot. "What's going on?"

"Get some clothes on. It's twenty degrees and you're half naked."

"The house is heated. What's happening?" He spotted Chloe. "Christ, girl, what happened to you?"

"Two idiots with testosterone for brains."

Across the still gray water of Budd Inlet, white light reflected off the snowy hillside. Marianne and her boyfriend shuffled in, murmuring to each other about being hungry, pulling up short when they saw everyone in the kitchen. "How come everybody's up so early?"

"Chloe brought us a little excitement to kick off the holiday season."

"Oh crap. What happened?"

Everyone chimed in, "Two idiots with testosterone for brains."

Selena and Marty started work on a big breakfast while Chloe told everyone what had happened. She had gone to a bar for the first time dressed as a woman. Two men started flirting with her. At first, she played along. She was flattered. But gradually they began to notice things that looked suspicious. "You sure got big hands, girly." Then one of them noticed her Adam's apple. "Hey, what gives? Chicks don't have Adam's apples." She tried to explain that, in fact, some women do have Adam's apples; they just tend to be less noticeable. But the guys weren't listening. They were beginning to get the idea that the woman they'd been flirting with was not a woman.

"I don't get it," Chloe said. "I guess they couldn't tell the difference between a transvestite and a transsexual. To them, I guess I was just a freak, half man and half woman. It pissed them off that they'd been coming on to me, and at the same time, I think it kind of turned them on."

While they ate breakfast at the dining room table, Chloe told how the guys had started making nasty comments, how they put hands on her in places they had no right to touch, how she tried to escape, and how they followed her out of the bar and trapped her between cars in the parking lot and beat her up. Wolfing down her toast and eggs and delicately dabbing the corners of her mouth with a napkin, and then draining her second cup of coffee with pinky extended, Chloe said, "It was not an auspicious beginning to my life as a woman."

"Maybe you should hold off awhile," Marty said, "or not go out alone. Next time you might get really hurt.

"If I do, I do," she said. "I'm not going to spend the rest of my life in hiding, and I'm not going to pretend to be something I'm not."

"Are you going to report it to the police?"

"I don't think so. There's not much chance they could ever catch the bastards, and I'm afraid telling it to the cops would be too humiliating."

#

The next day Marty asked Chloe if she would consider moving in with them. Naturally, she thought he had asked because she had been beat up. She got all huffy, thinking he was trying to play big brother to her now that she was newly weak and vulnerable.

"You think just because I grew me some tits I'm not safe living on my own?"

"Your words are sarcastic as all get-out," he replied, "but it's hard to hear them through your swollen lip."

She said, "Touché" or something more like <u>Toufee</u>.

"Yeah, I'd say you can use a little protection. Especially since you're too ladylike now to use your famous lethal weapons to protect yourself. But that's just a part of why I want you to live with us. We're going to need to rent out a room because I just got laid off down at *The Sounder*. We're going to need the money."

"Oh no," she said, "That's terrible. What are you going to do?"

"I'm going to keep working on a freelance basis while I look for another job. And I guess we're going to have to tighten our belts a little."

"What about Selena? How did she and the kids react when you told them?"

"I haven't told them yet."

"Oh shit."

"Yeah. But back to the room deal, renting out the old family room might be a life saver for us. And let's face it, if we have to open our home to a renter, I can't think of anybody I'd rather have. And I know Selena and the kids will feel the same way."

"In that case," she said, "I'd love to live here. But I think you'd better talk it over with Selena before we make it official. I'll save your butt and not tell her you talked to me first."

"Wouldn't be the first time you've saved my ass."

When Marty told Selena he had lost his job, she calmly said, "There goes the European vacation." It was a joke. They'd never talked about going to Europe. When he said he had invited Chloe to move in with them, she said, "That's a lovely idea. It would be wonderful having her here."

"Wow!" I thought for sure you'd panic," Marty said. "The old you would have, back in Nashville when you were Marigold, or even the young Selena from when the kids were little."

"Well that's not me. Hasn't been for a long time, in case you hadn't noticed."

#

Marty was at home working on an article he hoped to sell to *Seattle* magazine when the phone rang. He thought about ignoring it, because the only calls he ever got at home were from sales people. But he picked up anyway. "You're not at work," the voice on the other end said. It was Barbara Morrow.

"I'm working at home."

"What's going on? You haven't been at work in weeks."

"I got fired." When she didn't respond, he gulped air and said, "They laid me off. And then they asked if I'd keep working on a freelance basis."

"So they kicked you out of the banquet and handed you table scraps on the way out?"

"Yeah, that's about the size of it. And wimp that I am, I took it."

"Oh, you poor baby. You need a drink, and a big hug. Why don't you meet me at the Spar? My treat."

He tried to beg off, but she insisted. It was early afternoon shortly after the Christmas holidays. The kids were back in school, Selena and Chloe were both out, and Marty was home alone. He decided that a cold beer and a little tender loving care from Barbara might be just the thing he needed.

Marty and Barbara were the only customers in the back lounge at the Spar. Big Gerty, the waitress who had been there since before Marty was old enough to drink, was listlessly shooting pool by herself. Without looking up from the table, she said, "You know where the taps are. Help yourself."

Marty stepped behind the bar and filled their glasses — a little too thick on the head. The beer foamed over the rim and wet his hand, and when he and Barbara took sips they both ended up with beerfoam mustaches. They were seated in a booth facing each other with knees touching underneath the table. They made small talk while they emptied their glasses. Marty scooted out of the booth and back to the bar to fill their glasses. When he came back, he slipped in beside her. They drank three beers each, more than Marty was used to drinking on an empty stomach. Their bodies were touching from knee to shoulder. She reached down and stroked his thigh. The gesture seemed not intentional at first. Their conversation was all about him — his family, his problems. Barbara was a listener and a toucher. She seldom had much to say. She was all about dispensing comfort. Marty had long since learned to accept that a touch from Barbara, which from anybody else would be sexual, should be taken as innocent affection. But this time her touch was sexual, too. It might have started as a reassuring pat on the thigh, more motherly than wanton, but the message she seemed to be conveying through her fingers grew hot and insistent. When, halfway through the third beer, her hand reached his crotch, he was hard as rock.

"This is nice, he said, "but we probably shouldn't keep it up."

"Probably not," she said. "I hope you know that I'm just being playful when I flirt with you." She removed her hand.

The thought flickered across his mind that he and Selena had never engaged in this kind of sex play.

She said, "Speaking of flirting," have you seen Maria again?"

"No. She said she was going to call, but she never did. That's probably best."

"Well I might as well tell you. With you and me, if it went further than playing around — I mean if we ever wound up — you know, doing it, it would just be for kicks. I don't want to be a home wrecker. God, if you and Selena ever broke up and I thought for a moment it was because of me, I'd be devastated. I'm not out to steal you away from her. Really, I'm not."

"I know."

"I like Selena. I want you to be happy together. But if you're not getting what you need from her — sexually or emotionally or whatever—"

She trailed off, not knowing how to complete that thought. He laughed at her. He said, "I know, honey. And believe me, I'm as flattered and tempted as can be."

"Then why are you laughing at me?" She stiffened in a huff — put on or not, he could not tell.

"I'm laughing because I never saw you get tongue tied before."

The phone behind the bar rang, and Big Gerty laid down her pool cue to answer it. "It's for you," she said, holding out the phone for Marty.

He mumbled, "Shit. I got to start going to a different bar. Too many people know they can find me here." And then he took the receiver from Gerty and said, "Yeah? Hello. What? Oh no! I'll be right there. I'll call Selena first, and then I'm on my way."

"What's wrong?" Barbara asked.

"It's William. He's in the hospital. He got beat up."

#

Marty and Selena arrived at the emergency room at the same time. William was sitting up in bed when they got there. His face was mangled meat. His lips blue, swollen and cracked, his nose swollen to twice its normal size. Bandages encased his chest and ribcage. But he greeted them with a smile and a self-deprecating quip. "I forgot to duck."

He had been walking home from school when it happened. Normally he would have caught the bus, but the sun had peeked out that morning for the first time since before Christmas, and he had felt cooped up all day while waiting for school to let out. He took the bus downtown, and then headed on foot for the boardwalk at Percival Landing, where he stopped at an espresso shop for an iced mocha. From there he cut across port property toward home. Over his shoulder he spotted a couple of boys quickly catching up with him. When they got to within about thirty yards of him they slowed down and kept pace, and started taunting: "Hey queer boy. Hey ya little fag!"

To his parents he said, "I don't even want to repeat most of the stuff they hollered at me. It was pretty sick stuff."

He said they were playing some kind of sick game, one of them taunting and teasing in a playful manner and the other threatening him. One of them was a skinny boy with red hair cut so close to his scalp it looked like his head was carrot colored. He was the teaser. He said, "Hey sweet thing, I got a big juicy dick for you. Hey, chicky chicky chick, come and get it." The other one, taller and much heavier, shouted, "You and all your faggot friends are dead meat. We don't allow your kind around here" — changing his tone of voice to quote, quite smugly and quite authoritatively, from the Bible, "If a man lie with mankind, as he lieth with a woman, he shall be put to death." — then back to his menacing tone for, "You're dead, you fucking queer bastard. You're dead goddamn queer meat!"

William knew who the boys were that beat him up, not by name, but he had seen them before. He said, "I think they're a little bit older, maybe nineteen or twenty. They used to be students but they dropped out. But I remember they came around once and passed out some religious tracts on campus."

He knew better than to antagonize them. He ignored their goading and kept walking. They followed him for blocks, continuing to shout insults and taunts. At one point they started picking up rocks and throwing them at him. He started to run. They ran after him, jogging at first and letting him get farther ahead, but then speeding up and catching up with him, only to slow down and keep apace a few yards behind. "They were like cats playing with a mouse," he said. "I was the mouse."

He cut across a vacant lot behind a boat dealership. They followed. They caught up with him. They shoved him to the ground and kicked him in the face and kicked him in the ribs and in the groin. He balled up to protect himself as best he could. They beat him until they wore themselves out. Before they turned to run away, one of them said, "This was just a warm-up."

"You're lucky, kid," the ER doctor said. "There are no internal injuries. Nothing's broken. In a few days you should be good as new." They cleaned him up and bandaged him and gave him pain relievers and sent him home. At home that night, everyone catered to him, especially Marianne, who brought him extra pillows and blankets while he watched TV on the couch like some potentate who expects to be waited upon. The assault was briefly mentioned on the evening news. The news anchor called it a gay bashing.

"If I had any doubts about being out to the whole damn town, it's a little late now," William said.

"Look at it this way," Marty said, "It takes somebody special to be outed on the six o'clock news."

"Right," William said through split lips.

Selena made hot dogs for dinner. Marianne helped William's plate and served it to him on a tray, rushing back to the kitchen to get him another soda when he finished off the first one in a few great gulps. After dinner, she made a run to the video store to rent *The Sound of Music*, which she hated but William couldn't get enough of, and she made popcorn for everyone. Trying to chew the popcorn hurt William's lips, and the salt stung; but he loved the big helping of ice cream with chocolate syrup Marianne served him. He also loved the novelty of her pampering him.

The next day a Channel Four reporter interviewed William. The segment aired that night, and within half an hour a woman called asking permission to organize a rally to display community support for William and "send a message to the bigots that they are not welcome here."

Marty recognized her as soon as she said her name: Karla Schoenberg. They were used to seeing her on the local news as leader and spokesperson for whatever group was up in arms at any given time. She was also known as a rather otherworldly poet who read regularly at Ground Zero's open mic nights.

"We don't want the rally to be confrontational or anything like that," Karla said. "It would be dignified and solemn. I'm thinking of a parade of lights, bringing light to the dark of night, fighting hatred with love."

"A nighttime procession?"

"Yes, we'd gather at Sylvester Park at dusk, and walk down to the lake with lanterns."

Marty said they would have to talk it over. "This touches us all, so I think the whole family needs to agree to it."

"Yes, of course."

"OK, then. Can we talk it over and get back to you?"

"Yes, but quickly. We should do it while William's assault is still on people's minds."

They had a family pow-wow that night to talk about the plans for a rally. Selena was all for it. She was ready to lead the charge. William was a little more hesitant, but he agreed. Marianne, as expected, had her doubts. She said, "It'll make William a poster child. They'll just be using him to further their agenda."

"What agenda?" William asked. "Who is this *they* you're talking about?"

"You know who I'm talking about. The gay community."

"There's no community," he said. "Hell, I hardly know any other gay people. And there's certainly no agenda. You hear people at school use terms like gay agenda, and you just spout it right back without even thinking about it. That's not like you."

Marianne started crying. She wiped her tears on her sleeve. "I know. I'm sorry. I guess I did kind of speak up without thinking. But this stuff scares me, OK? I'm really scared. I don't want to stir up any more trouble."

Selena said, "Let's everybody just calm down and think this through rationally. OK? I think we all kind of agree that we should do this, but only if we all feel comfortable with it. Above all, we need to know that we can count on one another."

"I didn't agree to anything," Marianne said.

Selena said, "I think it really ought to come down to what William wants to do." Turning to William, she said, "It's up to you, honey. But take your time. Don't think you have to make a decision right now."

"But I already have, Mom," he said. "They shouldn't have the right to beat us up. If we don't stand up for that, it will never stop."

#

Sylvester Park was a throwback to the kind of small town parks featured in movies set around the turn of the century, nestled smack in the middle of downtown with a white gazebo in the middle and heavy maple and oak trees standing sentry around the perimeter. During the holiday season, a lighted Christmas tree stood in one corner and tiny white lights circled the block like strings of fireflies. Because it gets dark so early in the Northwest and because the city leaders feel the need to bring light into the darkness, they always leave the Christmas lights up until well into February or March. In the summertime, there were weekly concerts in the park — rock and folk and jazz, but always culminating with the local symphony orchestra playing the *1812 Overture* with a volley of cannon fire, cannon courtesy of Fort Lewis.

About two hundred people gathered around the gazebo. Karla opened the ceremony with a fiery speech about how being silent in the face of bigotry and oppression only encourages the oppressors. She spoke glowingly and lovingly of William's courage and thanked his family for standing by him. What does she know of William's courage? She doesn't even know us, Marty thought. But he is courageous. Really. And yeah, I guess she can see that.

The minister from a local church, who also served as president of the local chapter of PFLAG, Parents, Family and Friends of Lesbians and Gays, gave a short speech saying that "we" (meaning the responsible adults in the community) must love and respect all of our children regardless of race, religion or sexual orientation. Chloe whispered to Selena, "What about gender identity?"

"Give him a break," she whispered back. "He's trying."

The mayor also spoke, saying that when the people who attacked William were caught they would be severely dealt with. "Crimes of this nature are not only crimes against an individual. They are intended to send a message to the wider community, and we must send a message in return that such bigotry is not tolerated in our town." That drew wild applause.

A representative from the school board stepped up to the microphone to say they would not tolerate bullying of any sort, and William whispered, "Bullshit."

Thankfully, there were not many speakers, and they kept it short. After the last speaker spoke, Karla and four of her volunteers wandered through the crowd in the park handing out candles in white paper bags, each set in a little origami boat. Silently, everyone walked the two downhill blocks to the lake with their lighted candles. They looked like some kind of mystical medieval procession out of a Bergman movie. People in the group whispered to one another in awestruck tones of how beautiful the procession was. Marty also thought it was beautiful, but in an eerie sort of way. As he looked at the candle holders, one by one, spreading left and right to form a semi-circle of lights that stretched about two hundred yards along the banks of the lake, he shuddered at the thought that the event was like a funeral procession and the funeral could easily be for his son.

Everyone set their candles on the water and watched them slowly drift away from shore. Many of the candlelit boats tipped over, and their flames were extinguished. For each dead candle and how many more, a life snuffed out by bigotry. Stupidity. Marty looked at the people spread along the water's edge. Most were black silhouettes, but every thirty yards or so small clusters of people were washed with soft light from poles that circled the paved portion of shoreline, the lake itself and the surrounding park too perfectly symmetrical and pristine, looking like a stage set. In one of the farthest of these lightwashed groups, Marty thought he spotted Maria dressed in white and swaying as if to music — playing through earphones or perhaps the music of her mind. He was reminded of the time twenty years earlier when he thought he saw her dancing beside the reservoir in Nashville. He whispered to Selena, "This is déjà vu."

"What do you mean?"

"It's like when we were in Nashville tripping on acid. I saw this then."

"Saw what?"

"A whole scene like this, with water and lights." He almost reminded her that he had seen a vision of Maria at the time, but realized how foolish it would be to bring that up.

"In your acid-rattled brain, maybe," she scoffed.

More than half a lifetime had gone by, and he had to remind himself that the event he was recalling had been the lead-up to making love to Selena for the very first time — making love to her, in fact, in an acid-induced hallucination during which he thought Selena (or Marigold as she was known then) was Maria. A short time after that, while smoking a joint in their shared bed, he had made the mistake of confessing to her that he actually thought he was making love to Maria. She slapped him, and immediately blubbered, "I'm sorry. I didn't mean to slap you. But you didn't have to tell me that. I know you're never going to love me like you loved her, but you don't have to keep reminding me."

She would not speak to him for days afterwards. And the incident was never again mentioned. And in a moment of thoughtlessness, here he was reminding her again.

There was no official end point to the candlelight procession. The crowd broke up little by little. Slowly people wandered away from the water. Marty scanned the departing figures for another glimpse of Maria, but did not see her. Everyone walked back to their cars in silence.

Back at the Winters home, they wound down by analyzing the event. They agreed that Karla's speech was powerful and heartfelt, and that the lighting ceremony was moving.

"I liked the mayor's speech," Marianne said.

"Yeah, I just hope he meant what he said and the authorities follow up," Chloe said.

As for the other speakers, they pretty much agreed that most of them had meant well but would soon forget the whole episode, having satisfied themselves they had done the right thing. Chloe said, "I think the PFLAG guy has a really good heart, but he's probably not aware of what's going on all around him."

William said, "From what I hear, all those people do is get together and cry about how they'll never have grandchildren."

"I don't think that's true," Selena said. "Maybe some of them are like that. But at least they try. They're not like the parents who reject their kids and kick them out of the house when they turn out to be gay. I've heard that's a lot more common than you might think. "

"The mayor and that lady from the school board were just trying to make political points," William said. "They don't really care about the shit that goes on at school. They close their eyes to bullying all the time. They don't want to see it. And if the school or the cops really wanted to catch the guys that beat me up, they could."

The Olympian and The Sounder both did nice write-ups about the rally, but their articles stirred up controversies that perhaps should have been expected but weren't. Over the next few weeks both papers were deluged with letters to the editor. A surprising number of them criticized the family for being so public about William's homosexuality. They said they were "airing their dirty laundry." The typical rant claimed that William had brought the beating on himself by not hiding his homosexuality — this after graciously conceding that no one deserved to be beat up and the perpetrators should be punished (with an implied "but let's just not talk about it"). "God forbid we should acknowledge homosexuals exist," William said.

A lot of the letter writers made the typically illogical leap that said making an issue of gay bashing was somehow tantamount to glamorizing the so-called gay lifestyle. "If we allow them to teach our children that homosexuality is normal," one of the more outrageous but not atypical letters said, "the next step will be to encourage sexual experimentation between young boys or, worse yet, between men and boys. There's no telling what else it could lead to. Can anyone spell bestiality?"

In the following months Selena repeatedly called the police department to ask why they hadn't caught the perpetrators. "We gave you a good description," she said. "One of them had a tattoo of a heart on his cheek. Surely you should be able to identify him by that. And William knows they used to go to his school. How hard can it be to find them?"

"We're trying, Mrs. Winters," a policeman told her. "You're right that that's a pretty unusual tattoo. It's pretty rare to get a tat on the face. Sooner or later we'll spot him. Probably when he gets picked up for something else."

A few weeks after the rally Karla Schoenberg dropped by unannounced to ask if Marty or Selena would be willing to speak at a school board meeting.

"About what?" Marty wanted to know.

"About your experience."

They were standing in the doorway. Marty had purposely not invited her in because he didn't want to encourage her to linger. But Selena said, "Don't stand out here like a stranger. Come on in."

Marty said, "I don't get why you'd want us to talk to the school board. Won't that just stir up more hullabaloo?"

"The bigots have already stirred up enough hullabaloo. The way to diffuse that bomb is to talk about it openly and honestly. Ignoring them and hoping they'll go away doesn't work. Silence will only lead to more attacks on innocent people like your son."

"That sounds an awful lot like a litany of bulleted points," Marty said. "I'm sorry, but I'm just not ready to jump into anything like that."

"Well I am," Selena said. "If talking about our experience will help, then you just tell me where you want me to speak. Kiwanis Club, Daughters of the American Revolution. I don't care. You name it and I'll be there."

Selena was more riled up than Marty, and was proving to be surer of herself than he was, which really surprised Marty. Self-assurance had never before been a Selena trait. She spoke at the school board, and after the meeting one of the board members asked if she would speak at the Rotary Club. Then the guy from PFLAG called and invited Marty and Selena to their next meeting. So Selena dragged Marty to a PFLAG meeting, and then another, and they were asked to join the board. (Selena accepted the invitation, but Marty didn't.) Soon she was a full-fledged activist. She joined in the fight for gay rights with the same fanaticism she'd displayed back in 1970 when she joined up with a bunch of religious nuts in Nashville, and Marty surfed along in her wake. He gave her his full support, but never stepped up to take a leadership role. She spoke at schools and civic clubs, and she lobbied legislators for bills outlawing bullying in the schools and discrimination in jobs and housing, and joined with Karla in leading sit-ins at the state legislature. She wrote letters to the editor and started e-mail chains and appeared on local-access TV shows, and she even went on the offensive against certain gay and lesbian support organizations that she viewed as being wishy-washy on certain issues — issues she had not even been aware of a few months earlier. She was especially fierce in her condemnation of gay and lesbian groups that were less than inclusive of transgender people. Some of the leading gay politicos were afraid that championing transgender causes would alienate some potential supporters. Selena railed against those people, saying, "My god, that's like Jews being afraid to speak out against Hitler or blacks against the Klan 'cause they're afraid of pissing off folks in the middle."

Her face was all over the news. Politicians were on their best behavior around her — even the most diehard conservatives managed to sound like bleeding hearts when talking to her — and she became a mother figure to gay and lesbian kids whose parents had rejected them. She was like a rock star to them.

Meanwhile, Marty kept looking for work. Half-heartedly. He felt that he had to if he wanted to keep up with the mortgage and car payments. On his more optimistic days he thought they'd be able to continue living comfortably on their reduced wages, but on other days he was haunted by horrible visions of losing their home and being forced to live in a cramped apartment, of having his car repossessed and having to stand outside in the rain and cold for a city bus to cart him around — but to where with no job? His job hunt was futile. The only newspaper jobs were in Seattle or

Portland or even farther away. He did apply for one or two jobs in Seattle, but secretly hoped he wouldn't get them. With two kids in high school and Selena's part-time work and fulltime activism in the area, he wasn't about to abruptly uproot the family and move up there; and commuting every day would be torture. Nor was he willing to take a fulltime job that would mean he'd have to completely give up writing. He was determined to keep working as a writer, and that, for the immediate future at least, meant freelancing at *The Sounder*. Once or twice a week he went into the office and got the office manager to find a computer temporarily not in use so he could write his stories for the week. He felt like he wasn't really working there, like he was an intern or cub reporter — Clark Kent demoted to Jimmy Olson's job.

#

On a gorgeous day in June, Marty found himself at *The Sounder* office with nothing much to do, shuffling notes from one spot on his desk to another, wondering if maybe he should go on home or perhaps take a walk to the Spar and have a beer. If Barbara had been in her office next door and free to go with him, he would have gone for a beer, but she was out of town. He picked up notes on a story about a local record producer who'd made quite a mark on the Indie music scene and started to read it, but he couldn't focus. His hands were shaking. He needed a vacation. What he wouldn't give for a week away from everything! He wandered up front and asked Margie the receptionist to step outside and have a smoke with him. He had quite many times but still gave in once in a while, usually bumming a smoke from Margie.

They stood on the sidewalk by the front door and puffed on their cigarettes, not talking. When they were done they snuffed the butts out in a bucket Margie kept by the door for that purpose. Back inside, he again read through his notes on the record producer, but still he couldn't concentrate. He heard the phone ring up front, and then his extension started blinking. He picked it up. "Yeah?"

Margie said he had a call on line two. "OK." He punched two. "Hello. Marty Winters."

"Hi Marty. "It's me, Maria."

He didn't know how to react. After bumping into her at The Spar, and after she failed to call as she said she would, he had once again written her off. What could she possibly want now? How was he supposed to act? What was he supposed to feel? Could she possibly want to rekindle their love life? He had to admit that he sometimes still thought about it. But she was married now to some unbelievably wealthy businessman (he had bothered to check around), and he was happily married as well, which she surely knew.

He was so stunned that for a long moment he didn't respond at all. She was blabbering something about William and the assault, which she'd read about in *The Olympian*, and then she stopped and said, "Are you still there? Are you listening?"

"Yes, I'm still here. I'm just shocked is all. I can't believe it's really you."

"I know. Me either. I mean, I can't believe I'm really talking to you. Even after seeing you the other day. I should have called you right away, but I didn't know if I should. And then I was embarrassed 'cause I hadn't. Hell, I should have called you ages ago. I should have answered your calls and letters after I left you way back when — oh hell, Marty. I was such a fool. I should have never left in the first place. Oh Marty, I am so, so sorry. You have no idea. I just want to let you know that I owe you an apology. The way I left you was pretty shitty, I know. I wasn't in a very good place then (she'd picked up some psychobabble along the way). We were both pretty young and I was—"

He interrupted, "It's OK."

"No, I—"

"Really. It doesn't matter. I'm glad you called. It's nice that you wanted to — you know—"

Changing the subject, she said, "I was sorry to hear about your son. Did I tell you that already?"

"Yes, you did. But thank you."

"It's very admirable that you and Selena have used your tragedy to do good." More nervous chatter filling in the blank spaces.

"Thank you," he said perfunctorily. Something about the way she uttered Selena's name disturbed him. It sounded like she was casually speaking of an old friend, and she didn't even know Selena.

She said, "I really want to talk to you in person. Can we get together? Maybe over coffee or drinks?"

He said, "Yeah, I guess so. When?"

"How about right now?"

They agreed to meet at Budd Bay, a casual restaurant overlooking the docks at Percival Landing. Nervous about meeting her, he turned the short drive down to the waterfront into a long drive through the past and the idea of Maria, climbing the hill to the old neighborhood (a mere six blocks but world's away from where he now lived), past the house where Maria had grown up (recently repainted, the yard now littered with a tricycle, swing set and sandbox), down the winding hill to East Bay Drive, and then a short drive along the water's edge, past the boat yard where William had been attacked, and then on to the boardwalk that edged its way from the market on Fourth Avenue, past the yacht club (where he knew Maria and her husband moored a big sailboat) and a string of boutiques and cafés, and on out to the working port area where big ugly cranes loaded and unloaded big ugly cargo ships.

The café was in a lowslung building situated on the boardwalk halfway between the yacht club and the industrial port. It was sparsely crowded, two or three people at the bar and a couple eating sweet rolls at one of the patio tables. He asked for a patio table and was seated under a large umbrella sporting an advertisement for some kind of wine he'd never heard of. He ordered Guinness Stout and sat facing the parking area where he could watch for her. She parked her silver Chrysler Town and Country minivan, climbed out and walked into the restaurant. He had not taken a good look at her at their recent meeting. She looked exactly like the twenty-year-old Maria, and yet totally different. She had gained weight, but not much, and her now silvery hair was shorter than he had ever seen it, put up in a poofy seventies style. She wore glasses with jeweled rims and what appeared to be some sort of short beach robe, a pale lemon color with a sash belt. It was open just enough to reveal ample cleavage — a glimpse of either a bikini top or a yellow bra; he couldn't tell which. His first thought was My God, it's Mrs. Robinson's English class! She's trying to turn me on! But then he rationalized that they were, after all, on the waterfront near where her yacht was moored. Swimwear would not be completely inappropriate. Nevertheless, he felt an unmistakable spark of the old electricity.

They shook hands awkwardly and then, embarrassed at the formality, hugged each other -- a tentative hug at first that quickly turned into a strong embrace as their bodies recognized one another and, confirming to old habit, molded to one another as they had thirty years before. Slowly they pulled apart to look each other in the eye. She slid her hands down the length of his arms, gave his hands a quick squeeze, and then let go. He noticed the watch on her wrist. A Rolex.

"You haven't changed a bit." Her voice sounded much huskier than he remembered.

He said, "Bullshit. I got a beer gut and lost my hair."

"So you got a little older. We both did. But you're still the same. Besides, you've got a little bit of hair left up here (she reached twirl a wisp of hair). I think it's cute."

"Well you're looking pretty good yourself."

"Now you're the bullshitter. I'm old and fat and ugly as homemade sin."

"No, no. You look beautiful."

She ordered a glass of red wine. He ordered another Guiness. He asked where she'd been all these years, and she said she'd spent a number of years in Nashville, "with Billy Boone. I'm sure you remember him."

"Oh yeah, I remember him all right."

She shrugged her shoulders and gave him a look that said, "What can I say? I was young and stupid."

He said, "I was in Nashville, too. I went there looking for you and found Selena, the mother of my children."

"You went all the way to Nashville looking for me?"

"Yes, I did."

"Well you're lucky that you found her instead of me. I was no good for you. I never was, not from the start."

"But you were."

"No. No I wasn't. You're just trying to be gallant like you always were, but I know what's what. Look. Here's the thing I have to explain. I was pretty messed up when we got married, but I didn't understand it at the time. And when I left you, well that was sudden and cruel. I've been wanting for years to apologize, but I just never felt like I could face you."

She ran her little finger around the edge of her glass in a gesture he remembered from all those years ago. She licked the corner of her lips and then daintily dabbed at her mouth with a napkin the same way she had back then. She said, "I left you because I was mentally unstable, and I didn't want you to know. I didn't want you to have to be my nurse. If you'd known what terrible shape I was in, you would have sacrificed yourself to take care of me. I know, 'cause that's just the way you were. And I wasn't about to let that happen. Besides, I didn't have a shred of self-esteem back then. Surely you remember that. I didn't think I was worthy of you."

She looked down at her lap. They remained silent for a few moments. She looked back up and said, "I've been bipolar — manic-depressive — since early childhood. But I didn't know what was wrong with me back then. I just knew I wasn't normal. They didn't diagnose it until much later. When I was a child, I just thought I was bad. My mother said I was born bad, and I believed her. I had these wild mood swings. There were times I'd do anything just for a little excitement, and then I'd crash, and for days on end I couldn't do anything but sleep and cry. I was really fucked up."

(When they had been together, Maria had never used that expression. There had been a time when she could not force herself to say the word. "Come on," he had teased her, "It's just a word. It won't hurt you," and she had said, "Fuh-fuh — I can't," and he had laughed at her. Could she have ever really been that innocent? Such innocence, affected or not, had been a big part of her charm.)

"It was the manic part that was attracted to Billy Boone, 'cause he was the same. Bone bad and frantic. You wouldn't believe the things we did, crazy, wild and dangerous things like playing chicken in his car, driving eighty miles an hour right at oncoming traffic, swerving at the last second. It was a huge adrenaline rush. And breaking into homes, stealing worthless little trinkets, riffling through people's private stuff — God, you wouldn't believe all the perverted sex toys and pictures people had, even way back in 1960. And speaking of sex— oh geez, even now I'm ashamed. But surely you must have suspected I wasn't a virgin. Well anyway, I'm not going to give you details, but the point is we did some pretty wild things that I never would have done if I hadn't been manic-depressive."

She ordered another glass of wine. Marty switched to coffee. "It's a little hot for coffee, isn't it?" she asked, flipping her hair back in a jaunty gesture that was new to him. Somehow he found that reassuring. At least she had developed some new habits in thirty years.

He said the heat didn't bother him.

She said, "You have to understand that I didn't know what was going on in my head at the time. I didn't know I was sick. I thought maybe I was crazy, not clinically, not like it was something that could be treated, but just plain nuts. And I thought I was just naturally bad. See, when you're a kid and you're taught that you're bad you do bad things, 'cause that's what you think you're supposed to do. I knew I couldn't ever get married and have a regular life. But then when I met you at the graduation dance, and there were such sparks between us — and there were, weren't there? — I thought maybe I could start over, be a new person. Be normal. And when I found out you thought I was just a regular girl and not the wild slut everybody said I was, I couldn't believe it. It was like a golden opportunity for me to be like everybody else. I pretended to be a girl you could fall in love with, and it worked for quite a while. But then when you went on that cruise I became so depressed I wanted to kill myself."

Instinctively he reached for her hand. She let him hold it for a few moments while tears pooled in her eyes. She said, "I guess it's all water under the bridge now, but I had to tell you. I know I treated you like crap, and I just hope you can forgive me."

He said he had forgiven her long ago.

"What happened after you left?" he asked.

She said she had hooked up with Billy again ("How could I have been so stupid?") and stayed with him through years of drinking and abuse, while he tried to make it as a country and western star. "He stayed drunk most of the time. He and his buddies would go off to play some gig or go fishing, or just get flat out drop dead drunk and stay away from home for days at a time. It didn't matter to him if I didn't have any money or any way to get around while he was gone. To him, I was just like some kind of mongrel dog he kept around the house and sometime remembered to feed. It was just pure out emotional abuse, and I was willing to put up with that for a while. But when he hit me, that was the last straw. I packed my bags and hightailed it out of there, and I haven't seen him since."

He asked how she was doing now, and she said her job and her marriage were wonderful. "I have three beautiful children and two grandchildren. I don't get to see them very often, but often enough." She reached into her purse and pulled out photos. Her husband and her grown children and her grandchildren all looked like perfect people out of a magazine spread. Marty had the weird feeling that they weren't real, that she'd hired actors to pose for the pictures. He handed the photos back, and glanced around at the boats and the water and the strollers on the boardwalk. To their left, the capitol dome loomed on the horizon, an otherwise splendid vista of downtown Olympia marred by one extremely ugly building that housed the state Department of Corrections. To their right, the craggy, snow-capped Olympic Mountains floated above a wash of low clouds on the horizon. The café patio where they were sitting was separated from the boardwalk by planter boxes filled with flowers of every imaginable color. Children and families and lovers strolled by on the boardwalk. Two young women passed by, holding hands, apparently a lesbian couple and from the look in their eyes very much in love. As had become his habit of late when seeing lesbian or gay couples, Marty tried to make eye contact and flash them a reassuring grin, figuring they probably got enough looks of the other kind. He sensed Maria tensing up, which he attributed to a gag reflex when faced with an outward show of affection between gay couples, a reflex she probably wanted to conquer but couldn't. But she nodded in greeting and then looked back at him with a weak smile. Give her credit for trying, he thought.

"Are you done with your coffee?" she asked.

"Yep. All done."

"Then come with me. I want to show you our boat."

They left the café and she led him along the boardwalk to the gated and locked piers at the Olympia Yacht Club. She stopped and dug keys out of her purse, unlocked the gate and opened it, saying, "Come on. It's right down here."

He followed her to a sleek, ocean going yacht that was large enough for a family to live on. She climbed onto the deck, turned, holding one hand on a line, and held out the other hand for him. He took her hand and hopped onboard. He followed her down the ladder into the overly warm cabin. Ahead of him, she twirled around and her beach robe fell open, and she shucked it off. Just as he had suspected, she was wearing a butter colored bikini identical to the one she had ordered from Fredericks of Hollywood in the summer of 1961 and worn one time only on the beach at Ocean View. He stared with unabashed craving at a body that had held its shape through the years. Other than a hint of cellulite and a barely noticeable widening of her hips, her body looked absolutely as sensual as it had when she was twenty years old. She placed her hands on her midsection and slid them upward, lifting her breasts and shedding the bikini top. He looked up; their eyes met. There was no denying what they both wanted, and he knew in a flash that he would not resist. She reached her hands out to him and he grasped them, and they pulled together and their lips met, and they made love in the hot cabin of the yacht paid for by her obscenely rich husband.

When he got home, Selena wanted to know where he had been. "I called the office hours ago and they said you left."

"Yeah, I had an interview with Jeff Kelo from Kelo Records. He's a long-winded bastard. It went a lot longer than I thought."

#

Marty finally found a part-time job to augment what little he was making as a freelancer. It was a night job at a center for troubled teens. He had high hopes for the job at first, with visions of setting up arts projects, maybe doing some theater with the kids, and a writing workshop. But he soon discovered that pretty much all he could do was play policeman. He spent most of his time at work trying to prevent arguments and insults and the constant rumor mongering that could potentially escalate into fights.

He was paid for twenty hours a week, but put in closer to thirty, working mostly nights and weekends. He came home late, worn out and keyed up from the kids' high energy level and the constant noise. During the day when he tried to write, he could barely concentrate. He started taking his work to the Spar, writing on a laptop in the back room while smoking and drinking. Sometimes Barbara would join him. Once they went in her car to one of her properties and tore each other's clothes off. Panting in a pool of sweat afterwards, Marty said, "I guess that's been a long time coming, huh?"

"Yeah. To tell you the truth, I'd just about given up on ever getting you in the sack."

"Yeah, well I'm no pushover but I can be had. God, I was faithful to my wife for thirty years, and all of a sudden I'm turning into a whorehound! Excuse me if that casts aspersions on you."

"No offense taken." Barbara swung her legs off the bed and pushed herself up. He watched her walk naked to the bathroom. He followed. They washed up in the double sink and dried off with his and hers towels belonging to people they didn't know. She said, "So tell me, whorehound, who else are you doing?"

"My ex wife."

He wondered if he should feel guilty, but if anything, he felt liberated. All his life he had tried to do the right thing. Just doing a thing and not caring whether it was right or wrong felt pretty damn good.

#

That summer Marty, Selena, William and Chloe went to the local Gay Pride parade. Marianne went, too, but with Randy, not with the family. Olympia's event was nothing like the big ones they had seen on TV in places such as San Francisco and New York. There were no floats, but only two or three cars flying banners and maybe a few hundred marchers. Three women wearing T-shirts with cut-off shorts and leather jackets were the token Dykes on Bikes, a group of traditionally big, bold and practically naked Harley-riding lesbians who lead off the parades in some of the bigger cities. The women in the Olympia contingent were more modestly dressed than the big city Dykes. There was even one woman on a tricycle wearing a frilly pink dress and sporting a sign that said *Dyke on a Tryke*. Before the parade started, the bikers cruised back and forth on the street in front of the capitol rotunda, where everyone was gathering. Assembled on the grass nearby were various groups with their marching banners representing PFLAG and the Rainbow Coalition and a couple of the more progressive church groups in town — Metropolitan Community Church and Unitarian Universalist. Candidates for various political posts mingled in the crowds handing out flyers.

Marty parked a few blocks away and the family walked up the hill to the capitol campus. "Look for Marianne up by the rotunda," Marty said.

William said, "If she actually shows up."

The sun was bright, and there was a cool breeze. It was the kind of day when you just knew in your soul nothing could possibly go wrong.

Sprightly family groups anxious to get to the start of the parade route stepped onto the grass to pass them by. A lively band of drummers stationed near the capitol steps pounded out lively rhythms. Two teenage boys running up the hill rushed past, and one of them bumped Marty off the sidewalk. "Sorry, man," he shouted over his shoulder. He was wearing a T-shirt emblazoned with the old Olympia Beer logo changed to read *Olympia Queer*.

William grabbed Marty's forearm and squeezed. For no more than a second or two, Marty took it as a loving squeeze, but the pressure quickly became alarming, and he realized something was dreadfully wrong. He looked at William's face and saw it was blanched white. He followed the direction of his eyes and saw two shave-headed young men wearing denim jackets with the sleeves cut off. They stood by the walkway leading into the capitol grounds holding signs that said *AIDS is God's punishment for homosexuality* and *Faggots=Death*. One of them sported a tattoo on his shoulder of Jesus on the cross, and under it a swastika. A small red heart dangled just below his earlobe. At first Marty thought it was an earring, but it wasn't; it was a tattoo. In a barely audible choked voice, William said, "It's them. Those are the guys that beat me up."

Marty's heart pounded and his hands began to shake. A fury as great as any he had ever known boiled in his heart. He jerked out of William's grasp and rushed at the two men like a runaway train. He attacked those guys for assaulting his child. He attacked them for the injustice of losing his job and for all the pent-up anger he had for the kids at the teen center. He attacked them because his oldest daughter was becoming a self-centered debutante and because his best friend was seen by most of the world as a freak of nature. He attacked them because they were a burning symbol of everything hateful in this world, from the Spanish Inquisition through slavery and Jim Crow lynchings to the gay bashings that seemed to be the latest favorite activity of the bigots of the world. In red raging fury he plowed into them and sent them both sprawling on the grass, and he jerked the sign away from one of them and raised it above his head and was bringing it down like a spear aimed right at the rotten red heart tattooed on the one man's cheek when Chloe, with all of her feminine beauty and the strength and agility of a Navy SEAL trained in hand-to-hand combat, grabbed the sign away from him and pinned him to the ground and, while still holding Marty, turned to the two Nazis and snarled, "Get your chickenshit asses away from here and don't ever come back."

They fled as fast as they could, and Marty was left shaken and breathless, overwhelmed by the enormity of what he had done. Even more, of what he might have done.

That moment ripped at his soul. In his mind, the blunt post to that signboard had been carved to a point, and he aimed it at the vampire's heart.

"Shit. We let 'em go," Chloe said.

"What?" He was discombobulated. He was on his back on the sidewalk with the disgustingly bigoted sign still clutched in his hand and a six-foot tall transsexual woman straddling him.

Chloe said, "We let 'em get away. We had them in our clutches. We could have turned them into the cops, but we let them go."

"What the hell," Marty said. "I scared the shit out of myself, you know? I didn't know I had it in me to be so vicious. If you hadn't grabbed me I would have killed that kid." He spoke between gasping breaths. He said, "It scares me to think about what I might have done. But in a way it felt pretty damn good."

Chloe laughed. She said, "Yeah. It's called vengeance, and it's pretty sweet. But you got to control yourself a little bit, too."

Chloe helped Marty back to his feet. They continued up the slope to join in with the marchers. They lined up behind the PFLAG banner and started the march from the capitol to Sylvester Park. Selena held his hand. When they got near the park they were met by a smattering of supporters who lined the sidewalk and cheered. By then Marty's hands had quit shaking and his breathing was back to normal. They spent a pleasant hour or two in the park chatting with friends and listening to political speeches and music. Later, back at home, Marty said, "I bet those guys will never tell their friends they got scared off by a middle-aged woman in an Isaac Mizrahi party dress."

Chloe said, "By a *beautiful* middle-aged woman in an Isaac Mizrahi party dress."

Pride

Marty's sixty-second birthday coincided with the Seattle Pride celebration in June of 2004. Life around the Winters household had settled into familiar patterns of work and TV, interrupted by meetings and political rallies and an occasional dinner out. Marianne and William had both long since moved out, Marianne with her husband and twin boys in Portland and William with his husband, Jake, in Seattle. Chloe was a good thirteen years post-op, and Selena had been one of the area's leading activists for well over a decade.

Selena was asked to serve as Grand Marshal of the parade in Seattle, so they decided to combine the parade and Marty's birthday into a single celebration.

They asked Marianne and her family to come up from Portland, but Randy had a business conference that weekend, and Marianne — who had finally gone back to school to get her nursing degree after giving it up for marriage and children — was preparing for an exam. "I'm sorry, Daddy. I'd love to be there," she said, "but I just can't. This exam is really, really important." (He wondered why her generation thought doubling modifiers made things bigger.)

William and Jake had been married in a beautiful ceremony two years earlier, and had recently moved to Seattle. Jake worked for Bistro Pagliacci, a small restaurant on Capitol Hill near the start of the parade route. So they definitely planned to be there. They planned to meet at Pagliacci's for breakfast.

Selena and Chloe arose with the sun and whipped up a breakfast-before-breakfast — coffee and bagels to keep them going until they could eat a real breakfast three hours later with William and Jake. While Marty read the morning paper and drank a second cup of coffee, the women fussed over the dresses they planned to change into in the ladies' room at Pagliacci's before the parade. Selena's was a simple red cocktail dress with a deep V neck and a gold band below the bustline that she had picked up at a second-hand shop. Chloe's outfit was a sequined white gown with a plunging neckline topped with a fiery red cape. As a theatrical touch just for the occasion, she had purchased a wig streaked in rainbow colors.

They headed north on I-5 in Marty's old Honda. Traffic was surprisingly sparse. A light rain was falling when they got to the Capitol Hill area around eight in the morning and started rounding block after block in search of a parking spot. Many people had claimed their spots the night before, and many of those who lived in the neighborhood had out-of-town guests, so parking spots were hard to find. They finally found a space about six blocks away from the restaurant and near the park where the parade would end. Despite the cool and damp, and the early hour, the streets were crowded with revelers, many of them in outlandish costumes with an abundance of exposed flesh. They seemed oblivious to the cold. Marty pulled his light jacket tight and hunched forward against the rain, serious doubts in his mind about the Channel Five weatherman's prediction that by the time they finished breakfast the sun would be out, and by the time they gathered in the park after the parade it would be a comfortable seventy degrees.

Pagliacci's was crowded and loud. Every table was full. People shouted at one another and screamed into cell phones. Dishes clattered and clanged. Extra chairs had been pulled up to seat three and four at tables for two, and up to six at tables for four. A line at the only restroom snaked past their table and out the door. Selena, Chloe, William, Jake and Marty occupied the one table in the restaurant that was actually intended for six. The bags containing Selena and Chloe's dresses occupied the sixth chair. Half the people in the place came over and introduced themselves to Selena, having seen her picture in the paper many times, not to mention on all the posters and ads leading up to Pride. A tall and very polite young man approached Selena and asked, "Are you a PFLAG mom?"

"Yes, I am," she answered.

"Every year at Pride I try to get a hug from a PFLAG mom."

Selena stood up and stretched on tip-toes to hug the young man. A pretty gay boy wearing a fishnet tank top and nipple rings asked Chloe if he could sit in her lap for a picture. He called her grandma. Another young person, this one a woman who sounded like she'd just come off a ranch somewhere in Texas, leaned over and kissed Marty's cheek and said, "That's for being a daddy who likes his gay son, unlike the bastard that kicked me out when I told him I liked girls."

"She works here," William explained, "So she knows who you are."

The breakfast and the walk from Pagliacci's to the staging area was a whirlwind of dizzying activity. Marty actually heard very little of what anyone said. Over the past few years he had suffered significant hearing loss and had begun wearing hearing aids, which tended to be useless in places where there was a lot of ambient noise. He guessed at what people were saying, nodded and smiled, shook hands and hugged people, and uttered remarks that could be appropriate to almost anything. At the staging area, Selena was introduced to the driver who was to chauffer her in a classic Packard convertible. He handed her a lavender rose corsage and said, "You need to sit on the back of the back seat and wave continuously. You might want to practice the wave." He demonstrated, and all joined in practicing the side-to-side wave.

Selena held the corsage up to examine it. "These are beautiful," she said, "But how do I put them on? There doesn't seem to be a pin."

"I can run and get a pin," William said.

A woman standing nearby said, "I have pins," and reached into her purse. She pulled out a little satchel filled with a whole assortment of pins, needles and paper clips and said, "Here. Let me do it. I'm good at this."

Selena's silvery hair glowed an almost golden blonde in the sunshine that made its appearance just on schedule. The lavender and buttery yellow of her corsage set off the rosy tones of her cheeks. Marty thought she looked more beautiful than ever. He watched other groups in the vicinity gear up for the parade. Nearby was a group of burly men all decked out in what appeared to be Viking costumes, with lots of fur and leather and studded balls and chains and massive swords. Their pants were cut to expose vast expanses of butt cheeks, some quite firm, round and attractive, and others disgustingly flabby and hairy. Just past them was a float celebrating breast cancer survivors. It was festooned with pink ribbons. Beyond them was a contingent of cowboys and cowgirls on horses.

Marty loved the colorful getups, but he thought the best of all was their own dear Chloe with her rainbow wig and fluffy red bolo, and the brilliant crimson cape that flowed down to her calves — beautifully turned calves, he noticed, accentuated by the high heels she had finally mastered. It seemed a lifetime ago when he had had difficulty seeing her as a woman.

Two kids wearing black berets and black arm bands with a large red letter Q approached. "Hi there," one of them said to Selena. "We're with the Q-Patrol, security for the parade. You're Mrs. Winters, right?"

"Yes. And this is my family," Selena said.

"Nice to meet you folks," the young man said. "I just wanted to tell you that we're here for your protection. Look for the Q armbands and call us at any sign of trouble."

"OK, I will," Selena said.

"Good. We hope you have a wonderful Pride day."

They split in opposite directions and took up positions blending into the crowd about twenty yards away.

Marty told Selena they would meet her in the park. They left her by the car and made their way through the crowd to a spot on the corner near where the parade was scheduled to start. Their intention was to watch the start of the parade until PFLAG groups from all over the state came by, and then join in to march with the Olympia group. Standing on the curb by a gas station at the beginning of the parade route were the usual hecklers with their hateful signs: *Repent, Adam and Eve not Adam and Steve, AIDS is God's Cure for Homosexuality*. The first time Marty had ever seen them, years before, he had tensed up and his hands had started shaking. They reminded him of the neo-Nazis that had attacked William. They keyed the same memories for William, but they didn't bother him as much as they did Marty. He squeezed his father's hand and said, "Just ignore them, Dad." That was then. Now, after years of attending the parades, they had become accustomed to the mostly silent protestors. They always claimed the same spot near the beginning, and were seldom spotted anywhere else along the route or at the celebration in Volunteer Park. A few people always heckled them and a few talked with them as friendly rivals, but most simply ignored them.

The parade began as it always did, with the mighty roar of some thirty or forty motorcycles driven by the Dykes on Bikes in their leather gear, many with their partners hanging on behind and, as usual, a few wearing nothing but leather thongs and boots, with inch-square strips of duct tape covering their nipples, a concession to local law. Typically, the topless bikers swapped their duct-tape pasties for the little stickers PFLAGers handed out that said *Somebody in PFLAG Loves Me.* The Dykes on Bikes were the unofficial leaders of every Pride parade. Boisterous cheers went up from the crowds lining both sides of Broadway as they sped back and forth in a deafening roar for what seemed to be almost a full half hour. They roared past so fast that Marty was amazed they never crashed. What a horror that would be. When the Dykes finally quit circling the rest of the parade took off: electioneering politicians, church groups, commercial businesses promoting their goods, Seattle Quake Rugby, the Kings Wrestling Club, the ACLU, Seattle Men's Chorus, Rainbow Family Coalition, West Seattle Fire Department, the city employee's union, rhythm bands, lesbian sororities, a gay kennel club, cross dressing soccer clubs and classic car enthusiasts. As each new group passed, the crowds roared their approval.

When the PFLAG contingent came by, Marty, Chloe, William and Jake fell in with them and marched to Volunteer Park, waving at the crowds that lined both sides of the streets.

In the park they met up with Selena and wandered through the throngs checking out the many vendor and information booths. They ate gyros from a vendor in front of the art museum (closed for the day), and then went with Selena to the stage area in the meadow and claimed a spot where they could sit together on the grass close up front. There must have been five thousand people in the meadow, seated on the grass, many with blankets and folding chairs and ice chests. The sun blinked on and off as wandering clouds paraded across a blue sky. Bits of paper blew hither and yon in the ebb and flow of a swirling wind.

The program opened with musical performances by the Seattle Men's Chorus followed by a couple of rock groups that drew enormous applause from the crowd. (Chloe pronounced them mildly talented at best, and Marty told her she was being overly generous; but the younger people seemed to love them.) Selena was scheduled to be up next. Before bringing her on, there was some shuffling of equipment and concomitant shuffling within the crowd. The rock groups had apparently brought their own followers who now left, and other people took their places. Both Marty and Chloe stood up, and Chloe wandered a few feet away. Marty looked around and spotted members of the Q-Patrol nearby. Their presence was a relief. Chloe claimed a spot in the shade of the only tree in the field. Marty saw a man wearing a camouflage T-shirt and red baseball cap about thirty yards off to his left. A cold shudder ran through him. For a brief moment he thought he was one of the guys who had assaulted William. He thought about telling one of the Q-Patrol to keep an eye on him, but decided he was being paranoid.

Onstage the Mistress of Ceremonies, radio disc jockey and locally famous drag performer Mother May Belle, was starting her introduction of Selena: "Boys and girls, it is now time to meet the wonderful Grand Marshall of Pride 2004. You all know her, or you damn well should, because she is our champion and our best friend, the person who — more than any other person in the state of Washington — is responsible for securing equal rights and protections for our gay, lesbian, bisexual and transgender brothers and sisters. Let's give a great big Emerald City welcome to Selena Winters."

The applause was loud, but not exactly what Marty and Chloe would have called thunderous. Almost lost behind the podium, Selena held up her hands and called for quiet. When the crowd settled down, she said, "Thank you. Thank you so much for that warm welcome. It's wonderful being here in Seattle on this special day. It's especially wonderful being here with my gay son and his partner (interruption by applause) and with our transsexual housemate (more applause), and with my husband, Marty. He's straight, but don't hold that against him."

There was an appreciative chuckle from the crowd. That was when Marty saw the man pull out a gun. It was the man with the camouflage shirt and red cap — the one he thought looked like one of William's assailants. One of the Q-Patrol people stationed another ten yards farther out spotted the gun at the same instant, and immediately rushed toward him. And, at the same time, Chloe leaped through the air like an outfielder diving for a line drive. It all happened in a blur.

Marty shouted, "Gun!" just as the man pulled the trigger. He heard the bang and caught sight of a confusing blur of movement. He ran to the stage area where Selena was crumpling to the boards. Marty felt like he was slogging in cinematic slow motion, his arms and legs held back by invisible wires, people on the grass like boulders in his path to be leapt over or skirted around. Reaching the stage area in a few long strides that took seconds but seemed to take forever, he caught Selena's falling body just as she hit the boards, and he cradled her in his arms. Suddenly William appeared next to them, and he was wailing. Policemen patrolling the crowd quickly blocked access to the stage area. Chloe fought her way to the edge of the stage. A policeman held her back. "I'm family," she beseeched the cop. "Marty, tell them I'm family." But the only thing Marty could hear as he cradled his wife in his arms was William's wailing. A slow river of blood coursed down one limp arm and onto the old wooden slats of the outdoor stage.

The crowd parted to make way for an ambulance that pulled onto the grass and up to the stage. Uniformed medics scrambled out of the ambulance and quickly unloaded a gurney. There were two men and a woman, each with radios and an array of medical equipment strapped to their belts. The men hustled to the stage and lifted Selena to a gurney, hooked oxygen to her nose, and carried her into the ambulance. The woman asked Marty for essential information, scribbled notes on a pad and radioed the hospital. Everything happened fast, fast. And yet, to Marty, it took forever.

At the hospital Marty was told that Selena's chance of recovering was slim. She had a blood clot in her brain that would have to be removed. There had been extensive damage, extensive bleeding. She might not ever wake up.

Policemen questioned Marty. "What did you see?"

"I saw the shooter. He was wearing a shirt like — what do you call it? Like the Army — a camouflage shirt. And a red cap. He had a tattoo of a heart on his cheek. I've seen him before. I recognized that tattoo. I saw him pull the gun and shoot, and then he was gone. Just vanished in the crowd."

Chloe interrupted. She said, "I saw him too. I recognized the bastard. He's the same Nazi creep that beat up William. He had that same heart tattoo."

"And who are you, m'am? And who is William?" one of the cops asked.

Marty said, "She's Chloe, our housemate. William's my son." He pointed at William, who was seated nearby.

Some time later the young doctor came back into the family room and told Marty he had successfully removed the blood clot but that Selena was still unconscious. He suggested if the family members had anyplace to stay overnight they should do so. "Get a good night's rest," he said. "You need it. There's nothing you can do here."

By that time Marianne had driven up from Portland with her twin boys. Everyone went to William and Jake's house. The gathering there was like a wake, with everyone eating and drinking and laughing and crying, and reminiscing about old times. It was terribly, terribly gloomy, and many a joke was told. Marty drank the last of William's beer, and Jake hiked to a nearby store and brought another six-pack. Old tales about William and Marianne's childhood were repeated. Sometime around midnight Marty fell asleep in his son's favorite easy chair.

Back at the hospital the next morning, Marty pulled a chair next to Selena's bed and held her hands and talked to her, not bothering to let go her hands to wipe the tears that dripped from his eyes from time to time. He didn't believe she could hear him, but he kept talking just in case. He apologized for every time he had been cruel to her and every time he had failed to love her.

Later that day the police asked Marty and Chloe to come down to the police station to look at photographs. They explained that the heart tattoo they had seen on the shooter was a common tattoo worn by many members of a hate group known as the Nation. The heart tattoo was visible on five of the mugshots they were shown. Neither Marty nor Chloe were able to positively identify the shooter. Later, when they were alone, Chloe said, "Oh God, I'm so sorry. I thought for sure I would recognize him, but they all look alike."

"I know," Marty said. "It's like the stereotypical racial thing where you can't really see members of another race; you just see their skin color and not who they really are. I thought I would never forget that one guy, the one at the capitol that day, but he could have been either one of the two in the pictures."

"I should have just picked one at random and sworn he was the one. God knows every one of those bastards is guilty of who knows how many atrocities. It would have been better to nail one of them, even if he was the wrong one."

Suddenly incredulous, Marty mused, "You know what I just realized?"

"No, what?"

"They're all too young."

"Too young?"

"The shooter, the guy in the park, and all of the men in the mugshots, they were in their twenties — early thirties at the very oldest. The men who assaulted William were about the same age, but that was fifteen years ago. None of them could possibly be the same."

"Shit. You're right."

Marty wondered if Chloe really meant it when she said it would be better to see one of those hate mongers prosecuted, even if he were the wrong one, than for no one to ever be punished. He wondered if she could really do it if given another chance — if *he* could. One thing was certainly true: he still wished he could get his hands on the guys who beat up his son. He often fantasized about beating the shit out of them. But would it really bring about closure, whatever the hell that may be, to see someone punished?

#

Marty lost track of time. Morning and night seemed the same, asleep and awake, seated in a chair by Selena's bed while tubes in her mouth and chest kept her alive, while doctors and nurses checked their instruments and read their charts, his children hovering and solicitous but helpless. Marianne and Jake cooked for him and made sure he ate. In the hospital they saw to it that he got up from his chair from time to time to walk around. They encouraged him to get outside for fresh air and sunshine. William took him to the hospital cafeteria for coffee. They sat at a table and drank from paper to-go cups. The coffee was watery. "This is the worst coffee I ever drank," Marty said.

"Even worse than when you were in the Navy?"

"Well no, but my taste buds were not exactly refined back then." That was the first thing he had said since Selena was shot that even approached being clever or engaging. William tried to draw him out more.

"What was it like? The Navy?"

"Well, there was lots of water. Don't you think we ought to get back upstairs?"

"There's no reason to hurry."

"There might be. She could wake up. I'd hate for her to wake up alone."

As long as Selena remained unconscious, Marty was a semi-conscious zombie being led around by his children. William and Marianne and Chloe escorted him back and forth between home and hospital, from Selena's room to cafeteria, and on short walks around the hospital neighborhood. When he was with Selena he stared at instruments for hours. He might as well have been watching one of those test patterns like they used to run on TV when he was a boy. He had no idea what he was looking at. But he knew what a flatline was, and at least he hadn't seen that. Yet. Selena's hand in his hand was weightless and cold. Out her window he saw urban buildings through a scrim of gray mist. He wondered what day it was. He decided it must have been the fourth day after Selena was shot. The young doctor walked in. Marty stood up. He was habitually deferential to authority. "Sit down," the doctor said.

He sat on the edge of Selena's bed. He said, "She's not really alive. You understand that don't you?"

"Yes, I do," Marty said.

He waited. The doctor didn't say anything more. Marty asked, "Are you saying we should unhook the machines?"

"That's not for me to say."

"It's for me to say."

"Yes."

"All right. Let her go."

#

Back home in Olympia, while visitors visited and the family made plans for the memorial service, Marty stayed glued to his favorite old chair, his feet kicked up on the ottoman. That chair had been new when William was a baby. No one but Marty had sat in it for years. But Marianne and William had loved it when they were little. They called it their sick chair. It was comforting to curl up in Daddy's chair when they were sick. Over the years that chair had molded itself to the contours of Marty's body. It was upholstered with a white fabric printed with green tendrils of ivy, worn down on the arms and stained with food and drink droppings. Seated in it after Selena's death, Marty looked older and smaller. He hadn't shaved in days. People handed him plates of food and coffee and water and beer. He picked at the food and drank the coffee and beer. Water glasses sweltered in their rings on the folding tray next to his chair. Conversations swirled around him, and half the words went unheeded. He nodded and answered yes or no when asked, "Are you all right, Daddy? Do you need anything? Did you get enough to eat?"

They talked about the killer. Marianne and William asked Chloe if she was sure she hadn't recognized him. "What if you looked at the pictures again?" Marianne asked. "Don't you think maybe a second look might jar your memory?"

"No," Chloe said. "It's useless."

It was the morning after Selena's memorial. Huge crowds had filled the ballroom in the hotel and filed out at twilight for a candlelight vigil that mirrored the one after William's assault. They marched to the lake and tossed her ashes on the water. Chloe said, "The service was beautiful, don't you think?" She was wearing an old chenille bathrobe and no makeup. It was one of the few times since she transitioned that she had allowed anyone to see her without makeup. She had not fixed her hair either, and Marty noticed for the first time how thin her hair had become.

Marianne said, "You're changing the subject. I want to talk more about the killer."

"There's nothing more to say," Chloe said.

"Well I think there is. I think you're scared to identify the killer. I think you're scared because if you identified him and he got off, he might come after you."

"That's not right," William said. "You've got no right to accuse her of being afraid. And besides -- my god -- what's wrong with being afraid of people who kill people?"

"I'm not afraid of them," Chloe said. "You don't know very much about me. You don't know that there was a time when I could have and would have killed them with my bare hands if I'd had the chance. I'm not that person anymore. Normally I couldn't hurt another person no matter how bad they were. But if I could identify the person who shot your mother, believe me, I wouldn't hesitate."

William said, "It wouldn't bring Mama back anyway."

"It doesn't matter," Marty said. "Nothing matters. Except that we're still a family, and we've got to quit blaming each other for stuff."

Everyone's nerves were on edge. Throughout the day following the memorial there were flare-ups over mundane things such as the kids making noise or Jake using Marty's favorite cup — "Hey, I didn't know. It's just a cup."

Marianne and Chloe wound up in the kitchen at the same time. They made valiant efforts to work together, but clashed over everything. When Marianne started to make a fresh pot of coffee, Chloe said, "That's not enough coffee."

"Well some people would rather not drink coffee you can stand a spoon up in."

"And some people would rather not have brown water in their cup."

Marty came in and took the coffee scoop away from Marianne and said, "Here, let me do it. You two can do the dishes."

"All right."

They started rinsing and stacking dirty dishes in the dishwasher. Chloe handed Marianne a platter, and Marianne handed it back and said, "Do you call that clean?"

"No. If it was clean I'd put it in the cabinet, not in the fucking dishwasher."

"Well you have to rinse them better than that or the old food will just cook on."

Chloe said, "You never have much liked me, have you?"

"What? Where the hell did that come from?"

"I don't know. But it's true, isn't it?"

"Are you serious? No, no. I never disliked you."

"Well you've certainly never acted like you like me. Not since I moved into this house."

Marianne stoppered the sink, squirted liberal amounts of detergent, and turned both spigots on high, determined to thoroughly wash the dishes before putting them in the dishwasher. She said, "Oh gosh, that was like — I was seventeen years old. I was all wrapped up in myself and worried about pimples and whether or not to let Randy go all the way. And then you came barging into our lives."

"Barging?"

"Yes, barging. Christ! You were a fifty-year-old transitioning transsexual and I was a teenage girl who always had to be the center of attention. You just rocked my world. All of a sudden, nobody noticed me."

"That's what it was all about?"

"Yeah. Pretty stupid, huh?"

"Yeah, pretty stupid."

Marty looked at his daughter and smiled. For someone elbow deep in dishwater, Marianne looked particularly striking in her black slacks and sleeveless white blouse with the high ruffled neckline. No matter where she was or what she was doing, she always looked like a businesswoman on the job. She wiped dishes with a sponge and handed them to Chloe to put in the dishwasher.

Chloe said, "If I was stealing your thunder back then, I was totally unaware of what I was doing, and I'm sorry. But as well as I remember, everyone respected you. You were like the star student at school and the ideal daughter at home. You were popular and respected."

"Yes, I know. But what can I say? I was a teenager, unstable by definition. The way I remember myself back then, I was trying really, really hard to find myself, and I was much less sure of myself than I might have acted. And I was so in love with Randy. God! I mean, wow, do you even remember what it was like when you were that age? He was pressuring me to have sex, and I wanted it so badly."

"I don't want to hear about your sex life," Marty said.

Marianne ignored him and continued talking to Chloe. "He was pretty damn good in bed, if you want to know, but I was afraid that was all he wanted me for — and I didn't know if I should talk to Mom and Dad about my feelings or not."

"No, and you still shouldn't," Marty said, trying unsuccessfully to inject a note of humor.

And again Marianne ignored him. "I was like super, super needy. And then here you came into our lives all aflutter with talk about dress styles and bras and electrolysis. Talk about needy! You were going through the drama of transitioning from male to female, and you just dominated everyone's lives for awhile there."

Chloe expressed shock. "I never knew," she said. "I guess I was pretty much wrapped up in myself."

"With good reason. I guess you were kind of a teenager too. Psychologically. At fifty you were just becoming yourself."

The coffee finished brewing, and Marty poured a cup. Marianne said, "As if changing from a man to a woman right under our noses wasn't enough to make my petty problems, well, petty, you went and got yourself beat up."

"Like that was my fault."

"And then William got beat up, and it was like the whole family centered on the two of you, and I didn't even exist."

Marty spoke up. "We knew you existed, Honey. But when people we loved were getting beat up, it was kind of hard to show you the attention you needed."

"I know that, Daddy. That was the worst part then, and it still is. I knew exactly how petty I was being. But I couldn't help it. I resented Chloe and William both, and I felt terribly guilty about it." Turning to Chloe she said, "And for all these years I've blamed you for usurping what I thought was my rightful place in the family. I guess I was a self-centered brat."

Chloe laughed. She said, "You were that, but hey, so was I. You shouldn't feel guilty. Those were natural feelings. I had feelings like that, too, when I was a teenager. You said I was a fifty-year-old teenager, and you were right. I was a teenager for thirty years. Inside I was just like you, a girl who wanted to be pretty. But on the outside I was a boy trying to be a man."

She trailed off into silence and stood for a moment staring at the glass she held in her hand. "I don't want to belittle the things you were going through back then, but you can't imagine — nobody but another transsexual can know what it was like being me. Try to picture me playing baseball and trying to prove to everybody how manly I was — obsessed, really, with proving my manliness, while all the time I was watching Gloria Small and Cynthia Drake in the stands and thinking I'd sell my soul if I could only wear Gloria's sweater or have Cynthia's hair."

Marianne dried her hands on a dishtowel before giving Chloe a hug. Marty pushed open the door and carried his coffee back to his chair in the living room.

#

By noon the next day, the old house was as hollow as a jack-o-lantern after Halloween. The creaking of boards on the deck out back reminded Marty of his old Navy ship when it was anchored off the coast of Naples. Marianne and her family had left for Portland right after breakfast. William and Jake had driven back to Seattle late the night before. Chloe washed the breakfast dishes and then loaded a bag of clothes and toiletries into the back seat of her new Miata and took off for the coast. She just needed a few days alone, she said. Marty reheated a cup of coffee in the microwave and carried it out to the deck. Morning fog still floated above the surface of Budd Inlet. He could barely see the farther shore. The deck planks under his feet were wet with dew. He took a sip of coffee. It didn't taste very good. Then the phone rang. He pushed himself up from the canvas deck chair and went into the kitchen to answer it. "Hello."

"Marty, it's me. Maria."

"Oh hi."

"I just heard about Selena. I'm so sorry. Is there anything I can do?"

"No, no. I'm all right. I don't need anything."

She said, "Well I just have to do something. I cooked lasagna for you. Please let me bring it over."

Marty had a pretty good idea that Maria had never in her life cooked lasagna. He figured she had probably bought a heat-and-serve dish from Safeway and put it in a Pyrex dish. His refrigerator was already loaded with casseroles people had brought over. One more couldn't hurt.

"Yes, of course," he said. "That's very nice of you."

She showed up an hour later carrying the lasagna dish and looking like she'd just stepped off her boat, wearing shorts and a halter top, her hair grown longer since he'd last seen her and hanging loose. "Are you hungry?" she asked. "Let me just pop this in the microwave for two minutes and we can have lunch. Show me to your dishes. Where would I find a table cloth? We can eat out on the deck."

He'd never known her to be such an efficient little homemaker.

She spread a cotton cloth on the glass-top table on the deck, dished the hot lasagna on plates and carried them out. The sun had finally burned off the fog, and the sky was an endless expanse of blue. A racing shell cut through the water like an arrow. Students from the college practicing. Waves gently lapped rocks on the shore. "I can't tell you how sorry I am for your loss," she mumbled around a mouthful of pasta. "I know you loved her very much."

"Yes I did."

After a few more bites she said, "It's been a long time. I've missed you."

They finished lunch and Maria went into Marty's kitchen and picked a bottle of Pinot Noir from his wine rack. She said it was the perfect after-lunch wine. He had no idea where she had got that notion, but it was a pleasant enough wine.

She said, "I know how terribly, terribly hard it is to be alone. You know Michael left me."

"No, I didn't know."

"We're divorced now. It's been over a year. Did you realize it's been longer than that since we were together? So anyway, yeah, I know. The fear of growing old all alone haunts me, as I know it must haunt you."

"Yeah, it's rough. But I'm not alone. I have Chloe."

"But you're not sleeping with her, are you?"

"No."

"Well you need more than just a friend. You need someone who loves you in every way. And so do I. We don't have to be alone anymore, Marty. We're free to be together again."

Marty snapped, "Could you at least wait until Selena is decently buried?"

Perplexed, Maria said, "I thought she was cremated."

"She was. That was a metaphor."

"I don't understand."

"No, you wouldn't."

Maria stood up. She walked to the edge of the deck, turned back toward Marty with her back against the rail. A slight wind teased her hair. The thought crossed Marty's mind that she was posing. She was beautiful, as beautiful as the sail boats that glided past on the water behind his house, and he no more wanted to be with her than he wanted to sail one of those boats.

She turned to face him again but looked down at the deck. "You don't have to be so nasty. You never talked to me like that."

"I'm sorry. I just lost my wife. I'm kind of on edge."

"I know. I'm trying to comfort you. I understand your loss. But I don't understand why you're being so sarcastic. I love you, Marty. I always have. Can't you see that?"

His only response was a deep sigh, an expression of exasperation.

She said, "I know I haven't always acted like it, but I've always loved you, and I know you've always loved me, too. Yes, you loved Selena, but that doesn't change anything between us."

He stood up and walked over to near where she stood, but not close enough to touch her. He gripped the rail and faced the water. He said, "Look, I know we're both alone and we have a long history together, but —"

She interrupted him. She said, "Was I just a plaything for you? It was OK for us to screw around when we were both married to other people, but now that we're both single and need other people, you're going to turn tail and run? Is that the way it is now?"

He said, "No, it's not like that. It's —" and he stopped dead in the middle of a thought. He realized that he was about to spout some meaningless conciliatory blather just to avoid hurting her feelings, purely out of habit. He held his tongue for a moment, then turned to face her, and he said, "Yes, that's what it's like. We screwed around. It was pretty good, but it was just sex. That's all it ever was."

"Well fu —" She started to say *fuck you*, but even she could see the irony in that. She brushed past him in a huff, marched through the kitchen and to the front door. He shouted behind her, "You better take your dish."

"Keep it," she said. "That can be your reminder of me." She left the door standing open.

#

A year later Marty got a call from a Lieutenant Jasperson with the Seattle Police Department. "We have new evidence and a new suspect in the murder of your wife," he said. "Would it be possible for you to come in and talk to us? We'd also like to talk to the witness, Miss Nagel. We understand she is living with you. Is that correct?"

"Yes, she lives here."

"Would it be possible for the two of you to come in together?"

After Selena was shot, members of a pseudo-Nazi religious group called The Nation broadly hinted on their Web site that they were responsible, but they carefully avoided saying anything that could be used as evidence against them. Their screed seemed to brag about ridding the world of "the Harlot of Sodom" (Selena). They even took credit, again in a careful, non-incriminating way, for the attack on William fifteen years earlier. They thanked the "Super Patriots" who had "beaten the wrath of God into the harlot's sodomite son." The police explained that Super Patriot was code for member of The Nation.

Typing in upper case on the Internet is known as shouting, and The Nation did a lot of shouting about the murder of Selena and the earlier assault on William. They called William "Wilma" and said he and Selena were both leaders of "P-FAG." They wrote: "God bless the SUPER PATRIOTS that gave the SODOMITE Wilma the beating he deserved and the SUPER PATRIOTS that rid the world of that trouble making QUEER LOVER Selena Winters before she turned more innocent boys and girls into homos." They said whoever "beat the crap out of Wilma and knocked off his FAG-HAG mother deserved a medal for service to The Nation."

The Seattle police had arrested a man they believed to be Selena's murderer. He was only eighteen years old, meaning he would have been seventeen at the time of the shooting, a juvenile. "Most of what The Nation calls the ground troops are juveniles," Lieutenant Jasperson explained. "They use juveniles as foot soldiers because they know the worse that can happen if they get prosecuted for a crime is a year or two in juvy. Of course the risk in that is that if the crime is heinous enough the perpetrator can be legally declared an adult."

Jasperson said the suspect was trying to make his mark with The Nation. "The red heart tattoo is a badge of honor. They earn it by making a hit. That means beating up somebody or even killing somebody, usually a gay person. Homosexuals are their main targets nowadays. Their hatred of homosexuals is not just bigotry. For these people it is a religious duty. They are taught that homosexuals are pedophiles and minions of the devil who want to turn all of our children into sex slaves. They have also been known to attack Muslims and former members of their own group who have defected. Once in The Nation, they're never allowed to leave."

"So you're saying this guy shot Selena in order to earn his tattoo?"

"Nah. This one had already earned his mark. We believe he shot your wife just for thrills."

He had not confessed, but had tried to deflect blame to older leaders of the organization, saying he was "following orders."

"He signed his own death warrant when he fingered the leaders. Sooner or later, in prison or not, they're going to kill him. Anyway, we're pretty sure he's the shooter. The leaders of The Nation were nowhere near the park that day. But they were in Olympia when your son was assaulted, and we think we can pin that one on them."

"Wait a minute," Marty said. "Do you mean you've got them both, the men who beat William and the man who shot Selena?"

"We think so. The kid did the shooting, but it was the older guys who attacked William. We've got them all ready for a lineup. We're hoping you can identify them."

It was just like a TV cop show. They took Marty and Chloe to a darkened room from which they could see through a glass into another room where six men were lined up in front of a wall, height markers on the wall behind them. Each was holding a number on a card. Most stood still, looking forward. One shuffled his feet and looked at the floor. A policeman said into a microphone, "Number three, look up."

The man in the third position lifted his head. He looked to be about forty years old. He was short, probably no taller than five-six, and almost a skeleton, but with a bulging little belly hanging over his belt. He was wearing military camouflage pants and an Army T-shirt. A crop of short-cut red hair grew on what Marty remembered as a shaved head. His face was pasty and there were dark circles under his eyes. "That's him, number three," Marty said. "I don't recognize the any of the others, but he's one of the men who beat William up."

"Are you sure?"

"Absolutely."

Chloe said, "Yeah, he's one of them all right. And number six, he's the man I saw in the park. I saw him pull out his gun and shoot it."

"Are you positive?" the policeman asked.

"Oh yes. I'll never forget that face."

On the drive back to Olympia, Marty asked, "How did you recognize the shooter?"

Chloe said, "I didn't. Are you kidding? Those skinheads all look alike to me."

Epilogue

It took a long time, way too long as far as Marty and Chloe were concerned, but eventually two men were charged with the assault on William. They were both older members of the group known as The Nation. The first man they tried was the man Marty and Chloe identified as one of William's assailants. "Yeah, I done it," he confessed on the witness stand. "Gimme half a chance and I'd do it again."

He was found guilty of assault and sentenced to one year in prison. He also ratted on his accomplice. The other man admitted that he had held William while his friend beat him, but he swore he never actually hit him. In a separate trial he was charged with being an accomplice and was given twelve months probation and fined $500.

"That first guy is out now, and the other guy never spent a day in jail," Chloe said to Marty. "Can you believe it? They're both free men, probably cruising downtown for more queers to beat up even as we speak."

"Or just plain out cruising. They're the kind of men who spout anti-gay crap in public and then go and get their kicks picking up young boys in bars."

They both laughed bitterly at that. They lifted their beer glasses and clinked them together in a mock toast to their own cleverness. Three years had gone by since Selena's death. Marty and Chloe now lived alone in the house overlooking Puget Sound. They spent most evenings at home, often, when the weather allowed it, reading on the deck. On this evening Marty was reading, for the third time, Cormac McCarthy's *All the Pretty Horses*. Chloe was working a crossword puzzle. Marty sat his book face up on his lap. He said, "I've pretty much given up on the other guy ever coming to trial."

"Yeah, me too."

The man accused of killing Selena had first been brought before a juvenile court — he was only seventeen — and later was declared an adult, which meant he could possibly be charged with a capital offense. "Yeah, we could ask for the death penalty," the prosecutor said. But he explained that it would be much easier to get a conviction on a lesser charge.

"That's fine," Marty said. "I'm not so sure I'd want to ask for the death penalty anyway."

The prosecutor said his only hope for a conviction was Chloe's testimony. She had said she saw the shooter and could positively identify him. But everybody knew her testimony would be shaky at best due to conditions in the park that day — a large, milling crowd and the glare from a sun that continually played peek-a-boo through the clouds making it almost impossible to identify anyone.

The trial had been postponed twice already. Chloe said, "The longer they keep putting it off, the harder it's going to be to get a conviction."

Marty took the last sip of his beer and stood up with his empty glass in his hand. "You want another?"

"Sure."

"Tell me something true. Do you still plan to say you can positively identify that Nazi creep?"

"Yep. Like the man said, it's my story and I'm sticking to it."

"And do you honestly think they'll convict him?"

"Not a chance in hell."